GW00645006

More Tales I Tell My Mother

MORE TALES
I TELL MY MOTHER

feminist short stories

by

Zoë Fairbairns
Sara Maitland
Valerie Miner
Michele Roberts
Michelene Wandor

JOURNEYMAN

*First published in Great Britain by the Journeyman Press
Limited, 97 Ferme Park Road, Crouch End, London N8 9SA*

Copyright © 1987 by Zoë Fairbairns, Sara Maitland, Valerie
Miner, Michele Roberts, Michelene Wandor

ISBN 0 904526 42 9

British Library Cataloguing in Publication Data

More tales I tell my mother : feminist
  short stories.
  1. Short stories, English — Women
  authors 2. English fiction — 20th century
  I. Fairbairns, Zoë
  823'.01'089287 [FS]   PR 1286.W6

ISBN 0-904526-42-9

First edition 1987

87 88 89 90 91 92 93 10 9 8 7 6 5 4 3 2 1

Photoset by SMC Typesetting, Bristol, and printed in Great
Britain by Robert Hartnoll (1985) Ltd, Bodmin

Contents

True Readings   Michelene Wandor   *1*

'So What Kept You?'   Michelene Wandor   *21*

Une Glossaire/A Glossary   Michele Roberts   *41*

Trespassing   Valerie Miner   *81*

Guest of Honour   Valerie Miner   *97*

Short-Short Stories   Valerie Miner   *112*

The Tale of Mary Fisher   Sara Maitland   *124*

The Curator's Tale   Sara Maitland   *141*

The Wicked Stepmother's Tale   Sara Maitland   *157*

I Was a Teenage Novelist   Zoë Fairbairns   *164*

Mrs Morris Changes Lanes   Zoë Fairbairns   *177*

Lots of Love   Zoë Fairbairns   *188*

Foreword

Just over ten years ago a chance discussion brought Journeyman into contact with a group of writers whose short stories had been offered to no fewer than nineteen publishers, including the newly-formed feminist presses. All failed to see what made *Tales I Tell My Mother* the unique contribution it was to new writing in the mid seventies. The literary establishment then and now accepts the shortcomings of writers isolating themselves from the world, romantically suffering their experience. But when they work collaboratively, discussing their writing, challenging it, learning and unlearning, that is not 'creativity' – the very idea is an anathema, too political, and certainly not worthy of serious consideration.

Journeyman had started in 1974 by publishing socialist reprints and the idea of publishing new fiction – short stories at that – was an exciting challenge. Not only was it a new direction for its list, but there was no money available! As a first step, during those pre-unenlightened-GLC days, approaches were made to the Greater London Arts Association and the Arts Council. Predictably, neither offered any support. The following comment from the Arts Council's Literature Director, Charles Osborne, illustrates the underlying antagonism to the book and its writers:

I have to tell you that applications for Arts Council Writers' Grants for all these ladies [*sic*] were sponsored by Victor Gollancz as recently as last November [*1976*], and came before the Literature Finance Committee in that month. After considerations of the work of all these writers, the Committee found themselves unable to recommend any one of them for grant-aid. To present a further application now to publish their work would, I fear, be a waste of your time and that of the Committee.

Spurred into action by this paralysing lack of awareness, Journeyman, with tremendous help from the writers themselves, set to work producing the book. By late 1978 *Tales* was published and being reviewed:

> 'One by one, each story could be criticised; taken as a whole, the pattern of perception that they lay before the reader is both subtle and simple – and very, very satisfying.' *WRRC Newsletter*

> 'Throughout it, there's a stubborn refusal to participate in the very general view of literature as a kind of cream which rises to the top of experience and is then neatly skimmed off.' *Time Out*

> 'Here we are presented with writing as an active political activity and it poses the question over and over of the relationship between fiction and politics.' *WEA Womens Studies Newsletter*

> *Tales* . . . marks a significant step within the ranks of feminist fiction towards integrating the issues of feminism with the tradition and practice of literature.' *In These Times* (USA)

Since its first publication, *Tales* has been reprinted three times, published in the USA, and translated into Dutch and Swedish. All of the writers have signed with large commercial publishing houses, and successfully launched themselves on serious writing careers. Journeyman, too, gained from the experience of publishing *Tales*, not only by working closely with the writers, but also by reaffirming its *raision d'etre*.

To celebrate their individual success, and by way of marking the development of feminist short story writing over the last ten years, Journeyman suggested that a new collection was brought together. Of course, the authors were working quite separately by now, each extending feminist writing on both sides of the Atlantic. The result has been *More Tales I Tell My Mother*, a collection reflecting a significant cross section of literary talent, unified by a feminist perspective as refreshing and stimulating as the original *Tales*. Journeyman is confident that *More Tales* will be as well received as *Tales I Tell My Mother*, confirming the finally-recognised role of feminist fiction as a thriving and exciting literary form, particularly well-suited to the short story.

Peter Sinclair

True Readings

MICHELENE WANDOR

I got on the tube at Finchley Road as usual. I hadn't been on the Underground for quite some time and as soon as I got on the train I felt as if I was out in the country. Not simply because for the first part of the journey the train runs above ground, but for some reason I couldn't entirely fathom. I got out at the other end, at Charing Cross, went up two silver escalators, gave in my ticket and turned left to the exit to the street that would bring me closest to where I wanted to go. There was a flautist, a young woman wearing tartan jeans which were rather full round her bottom and ended rather tightly just above her ankle. She was wearing a very large bright green sweater, and her hair stuck up in purple and pink punk spikes. She was playing with a clear silvery tone, something which sounded like one of Vivaldi's flute concertos. But since there are only a very small number of classical music pieces which I can identify by name when I hear them, I didn't even try in this case, just allowed the music to follow me in waves as I walked on up the tiled steps. At the top I turned right, walked through Covent Garden, staring at the trendies, and made my way to the small French restaurant in which I was to have lunch.

When I'm at home, my lunch is very predictable. I have vegetable soup, I have a piece of bread and butter, sometimes I have a piece of cheese, and sometimes I have some salad with it as well. Having lunch out is always a great thrill, like playing truant from school, having an extra treat, something one hadn't anticipated. And of course it is always an extra thrill when one is taken out to lunch by one's publisher.

The restaurant was a very small affair, unlike many of the newer places which had opened in Covent Garden recently, which were cavernous, packed with tables and bustle. It was a strange phenomenon, this time of difficulty and recession in the country and even in parts of the city as a whole, accompanied by this wonderful expansion of cosmopolitan European cultural services such as wine bars, restaurants which were a pleasure to be in and to eat in. But then for me it was very much a semi-glamorous excursion into the centre of town anyway.

My publisher – oh, this is ridiculous, of course she was my publisher in the sense in that she was seeing my one book through to its published form, but strictly speaking she wasn't a publisher at all. She was a humble editor, one of ten working in a medium-sized house, producing quite a lot of books, about to be taken over by another publisher, in this case a real other publisher, someone who owned it. My editor was someone whom I had known for a very long time and who had just moved from editing technical books to editing 'real' books, fiction and non-fiction, and she was enjoying her job immensely. We had been friends. Now we were establishing a professional contact. I had submitted an idea for a novel which she had argued through an editorial meeting. Although we had been fairly good friends, I couldn't avoid the feeling that I owed her some kind of obligation because she had in some way put her job or her taste on the line in arguing for my book, in sticking her neck out for my literary abilities. But she had won and I was genuinely grateful, if a little afraid that at some point she would call in the debt.

We greeted each other with kisses on the cheek. I was actually pleased to see her. I think she was pleased to see me. She enjoyed calling the waiter over, calling him by his first name, obviously very familiar, obviously lunched there a lot. Obviously I was not the only writer whom she took out in this fashion. But I allowed her to do this because I enjoyed being entertained. I enjoyed having my drink ordered for me. I enjoyed my editor – well, I should call her by her real name at this stage, I suppose, Jenny – I enjoyed Jenny looking after me solicitously, with concern.

Now the general convention seems to be that if you go out to lunch with your publisher – sorry, editor – you talk about all sorts of jolly things during the course of the meal and you don't usually approach business until you reach the dessert. Had you needed to have a serious editorial session you would, of course, have done it in the office, you would not be doing it in a restaurant. But there is usually some kind of business element to a lunch, and usually it is minor enough to be able to be left until the dessert. I was a bit surprised, then, when even before the soup had arrived (we both ordered cream of watercress soup which Jenny said was delicious, with croutons), even before the soup had arrived, Jenny took the manuscript out of her bag and put it on the table. It was a rather small, round table and I was a little worried that the vase with the single carnation in it would be dislodged by this rather heavy and by now dog-eared manuscript. I joked.

'Are you turning it down?' I said.

'Of course not,' she answered. 'We've signed the contract, you've had your advance.'

'Only a joke,' I replied.

'I want to discuss something with you,' she said.

'There can't be much re-writing to do,' I said, 'if we can discuss it over lunch and on a little table. And you haven't even got your biro out.'

'It's not re-writes I want to talk about,' she said. 'Something more important.'

'Oh?' I said.

The soup arrived at that point and in the business of sorting out bread, butter, salt, pepper, the manuscript sat patiently waiting. As we ate our soup, Jenny went back to the matter in hand.

'It's the ending,' she said. 'Something will have to be done about the ending.'

I continued eating my soup, using the act of ingestion as a cover while I rapidly ran over in my mind what she could possibly mean about the ending. I was rather pleased with the ending. The detail of it doesn't particularly matter, but it was a pretty cataclysmic ending, if a rather moralistic one. The main character, who had managed to live through most of her adult life behaving perfectly amorally and taking lovers from friends and generally managing to be a cuckoo in all sorts of nests, finally got a kind of come-uppance. As a come-uppance it had a touch of the *deus ex machinas* about it, but since the novel in itself had quite a lot of slightly surreal dashes to it, that didn't particularly seem to me to be a problem. In any case, the ending of any story has a certain arbitrariness about it, even when it appears like the neat tying-up of something, such as the end of a detective story or a conventional romance in which the couple live happily ever

after. The reader may feel that they have arrived at a resting
point for the moment, but that is all it is really. An ending is
always a resting point. And sometimes the resting point can leave
you feeling very calm, sometimes the resting point can actually
irritate you because you don't feel it has reached comfort or it
raises more questions than it's prepared to answer. But anyway,
all this didn't run through my mind particularly coherently at that
moment. I was just really playing for time. Finally, as I was tilting
my soup bowl, I couldn't really avoid the question any longer,
and I asked Jenny what she meant about the ending.

'Well,' she said, 'I've thought a lot about how I was going to
broach the subject. But I think in the end the best thing is to be
very frank. I think we should cut the last ten pages.'

'We?' I asked.

'Fair enough,' she said, 'I want you to cut the last ten pages. I
don't want the accident to happen.'

I was silent again. Silence seemed to me suddenly to be very
important indeed.

The first reading:

She was married at the time to a young up-and-coming literary
agent. A man who had joined a very respectable literary firm as a
relatively junior member with an excellent degree in history and
a passionate interest in contemporary writing. An interest, indeed, that was so passionate that he had refused to study the
subject at university, considering literature far too grown-up and
important for such academic trifling. She on the other hand had a
mediocre degree in English literature but a similar passion for
fictional writing. They were invited to his boss's party. It was the
first such party they had gone to together. He was chuffed,
exhilarated. His boss, he suspected, was planning to groom him
as a kind of substitute son for the agency, and he had absolutely
no objections to this at all, his own father having been a man who
never read a book in his life, who only cursorily gazed over the
daily tabloid and then was unable to discuss anything he'd read.

She on the other hand was extremely nervous. She had no
experience whatsoever of the literary London world. She was
thrilled at the prospect of meeting famous names, famous writers,

indeed even a titled famous writer. Although she had her criticisms of the British class system, she was nevertheless fascinated by the elegance, the ease, the sophistication and the extraordinary assurance of all members of the upper classes, the aristocracy whom she encountered in magazines, on television and radio, let alone those members of the aristocracy who had appeared in the many books she had read.

She was very selfconscious about her northern accent, but she knew there was nothing very much she could do about that. However, what she wore was going to be far more important than what she sounded like. She spent a very long time choosing a pattern in a large department store for a very simple, straight dress, and chose a heavy cotton furnishing fabric in a rather dazzling design of reds which mixed a background stripe with a foreground orange zigzag. She worked late into the night finishing the dress to the point where her eyes ached and her back was tense with bending over the material, finishing it off by hand.

On the evening in question they arrived at the party and were shown into the large and sumptuous living room by a butler. As soon as they walked through the door her husband appeared to switch her presence off and she experienced a chill of anxiety that there would be no one to talk to the entire evening, and that she would have to smile and smile and look as if she were enjoying herself. This chill was confirmed when their host came up to them, portly in his dinner suit, pink carnation in his lapel, greeted her husband effusively shaking him by the hand with both his portly hands enclosing the younger man's hand. The boss then turned to her and said to them both with great ease, charm and aplomb,

'Do you two know each other?'

Her husband wasn't sure whether it was a joke or not, but decided to take it straight since it was of course the beginning of the evening, and he said,

'Er, Sir John, this is my wife.'

Sir John batted no eyelid but shook her hand, said he was delighted to meet her, then turned, put an arm around her husband and carried him away across the room, saying, 'you must meet Lady Barbara. She's just finished her book on seventeenth-century embroidery and is absolutely dying to meet her editor.'

She was left, standing in the middle of the room, not quite sure what to do. A lackey came up with a tray of drinks and she took a glass of wine, sipped it and made for the nearest wall of books and a small knot of people who politely opened their ranks as she came towards them. Extraordinarily luckily for her, she felt, there was a woman there with whom she had been at university. For a brief few moments she was able to feel slightly less of a fish out of water, and by then the alcohol was beginning to make her feel a little less anxious.

The time came when Sir John clapped his hands twice and beckoned everyone in to dinner. There were about a dozen people present, and as they all walked in to the dining room she managed to move round so that she was standing next to her husband. As everyone stood still holding their drinks, Sir John seated them, one by one, calling each by name and showing them where they were to sit at the large round table. She was interested and amused at this, but gradually became less amused and her smile more fixed as her husband's name was called and he was seated and gradually everyone else was peeled off until she was the only one left standing there. Sir John could not ignore the fact that she was there. He merely looked a little quizzical for a moment, and then beckoned to the butler quickly to say 'bring an extra chair', and with a grand flourish of his right hand he said, 'and everyone will just have to move up a little bit'.

She was placed between a man and a woman, entirely upsetting the fearful symmetry of the occasion.

The second course was served. The trout with almonds was deliciously light brown with melted butter poured over it. The vegetables, new buttered potatoes, fine green beans and creamed carrots, were tastefully arranged in a tricolour pattern on a small side plate. We had agreed to share a mixed salad. Jenny ordered a steak.

'You don't have to decide straight away about the end,' said Jenny.

'I don't understand why you want the end cut,' I said. 'I mean, it's relatively arbitrary after all.'

'It's a personal thing,' said Jenny.

'Personal?'

'Yes. The same accident happened to someone else in the office some years ago, and I think it would be tactless for us to publish a novel with that kind of ending.'

At first I could not believe my ears. 'Say that again,' I said, digging my fork into a green lettuce leaf.

'The thing is,' said Jenny, 'I know someone to whom exactly the same accident happened. Well, I don't know her any more because of what happened.'

'Yes, yes, I understand,' I said. 'You know someone who was run over on a zebra crossing.'

'That's right,' said Jenny.

'Well, I can't help that,' I said. 'I didn't know the person you're talking about. I didn't write the end with her in mind.'

'I know you didn't,' said Jenny. 'The point I'm making is that the novel will have to go through the production department and this woman's husband works as a copy editor, and I think the experience would be very painful to him.'

'I can't be responsible for the way people respond to what I write,' I said.

'Well,' said Jenny, 'I never thought I would hear you say something like that.'

'What do you mean?' I asked.

'I mean,' she said, 'you have always had very strong views about the relationship between reader and writer, or perhaps I should say between writer and reader.'

'Of course I have very strong views,' I said, 'but that doesn't mean that I can control people's responses. It doesn't mean that I even know what people's response is likely to be.'

'Surely,' said Jenny, 'you must have some sense of your audience.'

'I don't know this man,' I said.

'At the moment I'm not talking about this man,' said Jenny, 'I'm talking about the general point about the audience you have in mind when you write.'

'I don't have an audience in mind when I write,' I said.

Jenny put her cutlery down with what was almost a clatter.

'I don't believe this,' she said, 'I never thought I would hear you say something so apolitical.'

'What's apolitical about it?' I asked.

'To say that you have no idea in mind of your audience when you write.'

'I don't,' I said, 'I have never claimed to have any idea of my audience. I could, if you like, make an educated guess at what sort of people are likely to like my novel and what sort of people are likely to dislike it. But first of all I may be wrong, and secondly it's only an educated guess anyway. There may be all kinds of people who don't fall into either of those two groups who may read my novel and either like or hate it. I have no control over who buys my novel. That, if I may say so, is down to your publicity department, the critics who review the book, the way your reps sell it to the bookshops and the way the bookshops choose to display and try and sell it to the public.'

'Are you giving me a lecture on the trade in which I work?' asked Jenny.

I put my knife and fork down now, but not with a clatter, thinking it would put me in a stronger position if I were calmer.

'Look,' I said, 'I don't quite understand why we seem to be having an argument.'

'We're not having an argument,' said Jenny.

'Aren't we?' I asked. 'This feels very much to me like an argument, and I don't really understand what it's about.'

'Well,' said Jenny, 'why don't we finish our main course and talk about something else and then come back to this later on?'

'Fine,' I said. 'I like trout.'

The second reading:

Some years later she had her first book of poetry published. The publisher arranged for a launch at a rather grand house in Earls Court which was the headquarters of the Poetry Society. The Poetry Society, as they often did, arranged for the reading to be a joint one between her and another woman poet whose work was also being published during the same week, though by a rather more prestigious publisher. She was pleased to have a reading to launch her book anyway, and curious about this other woman poet whose work she didn't really know, although when asked by the woman at the Poetry Society she did claim to know it.

On the appointed evening she arrived a little early, took her glass of wine, her salted peanuts and was introduced to the other woman poet. The other poet was called Greta.

'I thought we should work out a running order,' said Greta.

'Fine,' she said.

'Do you have any particularly strong feelings about when you read?' asked Greta.

'Not particularly,' she said. 'Except,' she added, 'I don't really like starting at the very beginning when everyone's cold. I'm not very good at that. Would you mind starting?'

'Not at all,' said Greta.

'Fine,' she said, 'if you start and read first, then I read for a bit, then we have an interval, then perhaps I could start the second half and would you mind reading at the end of the evening?'

'Not at all,' said Greta. 'In fact I think that's by far the best arrangement. A lot of my poems are very funny, and I'm a very hard act to follow.'

The dessert arrived and there was a lull in the conversation, which we had carefully kept in the area of gossip about mutual friends. I decided I wasn't going to wait for Jenny to start again.

'Look,' I said, 'we can either sort this out now, or we can continue it another time.'

'It's not as simple as that,' said Jenny.

'It seems to me to be very simple,' I said. 'Either I take you seriously and cut the last ten pages, or I decide the text has to stay as it is.'

'Not quite,' said Jenny. 'It's a little more complicated than that.'

'I don't see why it's complicated,' I said. 'You're telling me that somebody I don't know is going to be upset by the book's ending. And I'm telling you that all sorts of people I don't know are going to be interested, pleased or upset by the book's ending. All sorts of people you don't know will have all sorts of reactions to the book.'

'I understand that,' said Jenny. 'But this is something that is personal to my situation and that makes it a different case.'

'Has this person actually read the book yet?' I asked.

'No,' said Jenny. 'I've deliberately delayed passing the manuscript on because I wanted to talk to you first.'

'Well,' I said, 'if we're going to get it sorted out now, my answer is very simple. The end stays as I've written it. I can't take responsibility for your friend's emotional state.'

'Then I'll have to tell you,' said Jenny, 'that we may well not be able to publish the book.'

'What?' I said.

'We may well not be able to publish the book,' repeated Jenny.

'Are you turning my manuscript down?' I asked.

'No,' said Jenny. 'I'm saying you must cut the last ten pages.'

'You're giving me an ultimatum,' I said.

'Possibly,' she answered.

'What if you showed the manuscript to your friend, including the end, and he wasn't upset?'

'I'm not prepared to do that,' said Jenny.

'Right,' I said. 'In that case I will have to go away and think about it. I may ask that you do show him the manuscript before I make my decision.'

'I will consider that,' said Jenny. 'Do you want some coffee?'

'No, thank you,' I said, 'I don't drink coffee at lunchtime.'

The third reading:

Some years after the poetry reading she was rather better known as a writer and in one particular area had made a rather significant mark. She was the editor of a series of books on contemporary writers. This involved matching subject to writer, overseeing the process of writing the manuscript and then working on it editorially with each author. She had no contract as series editor but her name appeared on each volume. There had been seven of the volumes so far, and they had all been fairly successful both in the academic community and in the general literary world. One or two of the writers on this list were well-established – the kind who were regularly reviewed in the Sunday newspapers and the national 'heavies'. But five of the seven writers who had already appeared were either younger or older writers who had not yet made a very major literary mark, and after the third of these she had had a number of skirmishes with the in-house editor who had raised particular objections to one of these writers as trivial, boring and not suitable for the series. Since she had suggested the series in the first place, and since she felt that she could only work with writers with whom she felt some kind of affinity – and, it must be admitted, since she had entire faith in her own literary judgement – she stuck the argument out and told her editor that unless she could go ahead and commission this particular book then there would have to be a very long gap between the appearance of books. The editor gave in. But two books later he got his own back.

She received a letter in the post which was couched in very friendly-seeming terms, expressing concern for her well-being, congratulating her on being so prolific the previous year, and then saying that since she was obviously over-loaded with work the editor had decided to relieve her of the onerous burden of editing this series. Besides, he felt, a series such as this often benefited from having a fresh eye applied to it. And he had therefore decided to ask his former assistant who was now going freelance to edit the next volume for him. He hoped that she would continue to be as productive as ever, etc. etc.

She was very angry. The truth was that she was actually getting rather tired of the series and felt that she had given space to a group of writers who she felt very strongly should be more in the public eye and she was not particularly interested in either grabbing the famous who were already well covered by other publishers, or choosing writers who she felt had not yet made their individual, let alone their public, mark in their writing. But this was really not the point. The point was that there had been no discussion with her as series editor, and also that she felt that the series which had made its reputation upon her judgement should not be taken over by someone whose judgement she felt was very inferior. She wrote back to the editor protesting in the strongest possible terms, received a letter back almost immediately in effect telling her that it was a *fait accompli*. She was a little unsure at this point what to do, but felt very strongly that the matter of principle was the most important one. If the series was to lapse, then it should be by mutual agreement. If she was to cease editing then it should be her decision and not his, or at the very least it should be something they discussed together. He rather magnanimously asserted in his reply to her that of course he didn't rule out the possibility that she might return as editor at a later stage, but she was sure this was just a sop.

She decided this was no way to treat a writer, and contacted half a dozen other writers who were also published by the same publisher, told them what had happened and asked them for their reactions. They were all outraged, they all expressed great sympathy. She sent them copies of the letters, and one of them suggested having a meeting to see whether something could be done They met, and had a long productive discussion about how badly all publishers treated all writers, some of them knowing that they were generalising like mad and that some writers (none of them, of course) were difficult to deal with. But even so, the way the whole thing had been conducted was outrageous. Now one writer, a woman called Rosemary, nodded, listened but very carefully didn't express any opinion of her own, and she noticed this and wasn't quite sure what to make of it. Rosemary left a little early, while the others decided that perhaps they would make representations to the editor and at least ask for some explanation of what had happened. The meeting ended and nothing more really happened. The writers (apart from Rosemary) had written a joint letter to the editor, had had a meeting with the editor, but had made no impact on him. He was very charming and very persuasive, but he reiterated his point that she was overworked and that he thought the series needed a fresh eye. And that of course was that. There'd been some talk of the writers showing their solidarity perhaps by some act of protest, perhaps by delaying delivery of their manuscripts to the publisher, but none of that happened.

She felt both supported and aggrieved. She knew in real terms that each writer had to defend his or her own interest. But Rosemary's silence somehow rankled. She knew that Rosemary had not signed the letter.

Some years after this, Rosemary contacted her. They had both been asked to contribute some poems to an anthology and Rosemary had had a copy of the contract which was horrendous, and appealed for some joint discussion of the terms that were offered. Rosemary made a long speech about how important it was to protect writers' rights, and how outrageously publishers were treating writers these days. She agreed, and proceeded after that to go ahead and negotiate her own contract with the publishers and pursued this despite various discussions witł

Rosemary along the way. She knew from the very first conversation that there was no way that she was going to trust a word that Rosemary said.

She had discovered shortly after the first incident over the editorship of the series that Rosemary had just signed a contract for a new novel with the same editor for a massive amount of money. This poetry book was offering peanuts by comparison, indeed a single peanut might be more accurate. But she felt that whether it was a bushel or a single peanut made no difference. Solidarity was never really offered to her in the first place and she was not going to offer it in the second place. The second incident made her think back to the earlier one and she thought to herself that what she should have done in the first place was put her faith less in the other writers than in a solicitor.

On my way home from lunch with Jenny I went back through Charing Cross tube station and there again was the same young woman with her bright green sweater and her purple and pink spikes of hair. This time she was playing a trumpet, a bright fanfare of sound that splayed out and bounced back from the tiled walls. I was fascinated by her energy, stopped to listen for a while and then dropped fifty pence into the old cloth cap that she had at her feet near the music cases. She grinned at me, removing the trumpet momentarily to do so, then put the trumpet back to her lips and blew another fanfare, bowing in my direction. I grinned back and walked on.

The fourth reading:

It was her first play, a raw spontaneous affair performed in the dingy upstairs room of a pub behind Piccadilly Circus. To it came a variety of people, including a young director fresh out of Oxford running his own pub theatre further away just off Old Compton Street. He came up to her afterwards and congratulated her, said she showed great promise as a writer, would she write him a play?

She was flattered, excited, thought this was the beginning of her career as a playwright. It was at a time when there was more enthusiasm than trade union consciousness in the British theatre, and it didn't occur to her to ask about money. Besides, she was shy of such brutal realities. Carried away on the enthusiasm, she spent every spare moment writing her new play. She sent him the new play six months later, and he wrote back a letter which covered a page and a half, saying he found the jokes repetitive, did not think she had developed any of the characters properly, found the plot difficult to follow, and ended up asking her why she had wanted to write a play of this nature. At first she didn't know what to do. He had been most insistent that she sent him anything, notes, a first draft, anything at all, and here she felt he was responding as if the play was a finished article. She was hurt, she thought honesty was the best policy, she rang up and said she couldn't understand why on earth he had asked her to send him the play if he was going to react to it in this way. Didn't he know that it was a first draft? Hadn't he realised she was hoping for guidance as to how to improve it?

'Come and have lunch and we'll talk about it,' he said.

She turned up at the appointed pub to find him deep in conversation with another man, surrounded by clouds of smoke and a bouquet of empty beer glasses. She joined them at their table and sat vaguely eavesdropping for quite a long time, waiting for the third party to leave the table. The third party did not. They ordered lunch. They ate lunch. She occasionally interjected politely. And as last orders were being shouted, the third party got up and said he must get back to rehearsal now. Whereupon she turned to her friend and said, 'You're not going to do my play, are you?'

'Why do you say that?' he asked.

'It's obvious,' she said, 'you're not going to do my play, are you?'

'I don't understand what you mean,' he said.

'I thought you wanted to talk about my play,' she said.

'I don't understand why you were so hurt,' he answered.

'I don't believe you were ever really interested in my work,' she said. 'You just pretended to be.'

'No, no,' he said. 'I was. I was really interested in your work. I am, still, very interested in you as a writer. I just don't think you've hit the jackpot with this one.'

The lights in the pub were being turned out.

'I'm going home,' she said, getting up from the table. 'You misled me. I wasted six months writing a play that you were never going to read properly anyway. You didn't want to see a first draft, you wanted to see a finished play. You lied to me.'

She was standing up and he was sitting down. She felt momentarily superior.

'I don't understand women,' he said. 'There's no need to be hysterical over a perfectly honest reaction to a piece of writing. After all, it is only my subjective reaction.'

'Yes,' she said, 'it is your subjective reaction. It's also your theatre. It's also your decision. I'm going home.'

And she left, feeling self-righteous and entirely devastated. In her head she had rehearsed all kinds of better things she might have said, things which had gone beyond the truth and which would have made him so see the light that he would suddenly have changed his mind, seen her play for the piece of genius it was, given her the theatre to run, invited her to direct any number of other plays, and submitted some of his own writing humbly for her critical response.

In time, he stopped running the theatre, got a job as a script editor for BBC television for a while, earning a huge amount of money most of which he seemed to put in his bank since he lived on lunch expense accounts according to a mutual friend and then, in some way she never could quite understand, established a reputation for writing plays himself, all of which she thought were shallow and over-written. He was a bridesmaid, never made the first rank either as a director or a playwright, but he managed very nicely, thank you, as a professional bridesmaid.

When I got home after the lunch with Jenny, my head was in a whirl. I wanted the book to be published, I wanted it published by her house since their books got widely reviewed, they had a good distribution system and were respected in the literary world. And I was tired of being seen as some kind of ghetto writer. At the same time I could not ignore her ultimatum. I took out my copy of the manuscript and looked at the end again. It was certainly true that the end could stand without the final ten pages. And yet I was very proud of those ten pages, not just because the writing was effective, evocative and dramatic (unlike this account of events which is deliberately very plain), but also because when I was writing the book this end seemed the right ending. I was in a dilemma. I knew my book would stand to the outside world without the last ten pages and that what readers didn't know they wouldn't miss. But my pride was at stake. I didn't want to be bullied or blackmailed, and yet I knew that I could be both bullied and blackmailed. I could call her bluff and see where that got me. But I thought I had actually tried to do that at the table already. And I knew rather cynically that while it was a very good novel it was very unlikely to make the best seller lists and would not be sold that way by the publishers. So I thought.

In the event, I took the last ten pages and I sent them to another publisher, proposing them as a sample chapter for a novel. I didn't respond to Jenny while this was happening, I thought I would give it a week. Within a week I had an extra-ordinarily enthusiastic reponse from the other publisher, offer-ing me a reasonable advance for a novel, the editor saying he was so impressed with my writing that he would be prepared to take this kind of a gamble. He had read my other work and was sure the gamble would pay off. What he had in mind, he said, was something really quite short, there was a vogue at the moment for rather short books. How quickly could I get it finished? he asked. 'Well,' I said, 'if I write very quickly, and I think I will in this case, since the novel is already there in my head, say two months?'

'Wonderful,' he said.

He and I had our contract sorted out within the following week, and I began writing a novel. I had had no idea when I sent him the last ten pages what the rest would be, but I found that making the end of the previous book the beginning of a new book set off a whole new train of ideas, surreal and exciting. The novel was finished in six weeks, something I have never managed either before or since, and was despatched. Jenny, meanwhile, had rung me a couple of times to ask what I was going to do, and the second time she said I must come to a decision soon because if the book was to be published in their following autumn list it would have to go into production. I promised a response very soon. I suggested we should meet for a drink.

I arranged that on the same day I would deliver the manuscript of the other novel. I took the same journey from home, getting out at Charing Cross underground station, and as I walked out of the station again the same woman musician, wearing this time bright pink tights and a long purple tunic tied in a knot on one side, was busking again. Her hair was green this time, and she was playing an oboe. I stood watching her for a while and the oboe sounded clear and sweet, playing a movement from a Handel Concerto Grosso. She was extraordinary. She played without music. She watched the passers-by with her blackly made-up eyes, and as she reached the end of the movement I came forward to pass her and put some money in her cloth cap. She took the oboe out of her mouth, her lips taut where they had gripped the double reed.

'You've been watching me,' she said.

'How do you know?' I asked. 'You didn't look at me once.'

'I picked you up with my eyes,' she said. 'I didn't have to look at you. Haven't I seen you somewhere before?'

'Yes,' I said, 'I've heard you play. How many instruments do you play?'

'Oh, I can't remember,' she said. 'I never have trouble with instruments. I hate talking, but I don't have any trouble with musical instruments.'

'I think you're terrific,' I said. 'I hope you get lots of work.'

She laughed. 'Musicians don't get lots of work,' she said.

'Nor do writers,' I said.

'Are you a writer?' she asked.

'Yes,' I said. 'I've got a manuscript in my bag.'

'What's your name?' she said.

I told her my name.

'I'll look out for your books,' she said.

'I'd better go now,' I said, 'I'm stopping you earning a living.'

And I went. I delivered the manuscript, and I went to meet Jenny for a drink. Over the drink in a wine bar full of men in grey suits and rather smart young women, I said to Jenny, 'I'm agreeing to cut the last ten pages. But,' I said, 'I will not change anything else in the book on grounds of a similar argument that it might upset someone you know.'

'Fine,' said Jenny. 'We'll go ahead on that basis.'

The fifth reading:

The play was in blank verse. It was adapted from a very long piece of discursive early nineteenth-century verse. It was about a woman who is being pressured to marry rather than to become a writer, at a period when to become a writer for a woman was virtually unheard of in the profession in Britain. It was an extremely good piece of work. She sent it to all the obvious places. She sent it to the BBC, radio and television. She sent it to the big important theatre companies in London and outside. She sent it to a number of drama schools, thinking students might be interested in a play written by a contemporary writer but using a verse form that belonged to another time. She did not circulate it among the many fringe groups who might have been sympathetic to its content but hostile to its form.

She received a number of different responses. It was sent back from the BBC by a woman director who said 'But it isn't a play, really, is it?' She rather lamely replied that she thought it was a play, realising she couldn't convince someone who had decided it wasn't a play. One of the directors at one of the big classical companies sent it back with 'But it isn't Pushkin, is it?', to which she found a ready response which was, 'No, it isn't Pushkin', feeling very proud of herself at such a riposte, but knowing it would make no difference. All the other large companies and the drama schools either didn't reply or replied with a courtesy note, and then she promptly heard no more. None of them returned the script.

Some years later the play was taken up and performed by a fringe theatre group. They worked hard and nobly and impressively. She was not entirely pleased at the result and she conveyed, in a way she hoped was constructive, her mixed feelings at the result to the director, realising the minute she opened her mouth that this was a huge mistake, she should never have said what she thought. She should never have said that a fringe theatre was always going to find it difficult dealing in verse when it had spent so many years working with naturalism and had no experience at all in the use of more formal language. However, she had made the error, she had opened her mouth and said what appeared to be the wrong thing, and it was too late to go back.

She felt marginally uncomfortable about this supposed error because the work of the fringe group gave rise to other events. The radio producer came to see it on the same night she was there, and she leaned over and said to her, 'Oh, it's very much better now that you have re-written it.'

'No,' she said, 'I haven't re-written it. I've cut about four pages, I think. But every word is the same.'

The radio producer nodded sagely, and leaned back in her seat, to prepare for the second half. She did, however, arrange for the play to be bought and broadcast on the radio.

Armed with the information that it was going to be done by the BBC, she sent the play again to one of the classical companies, to a different director, who received the play and its small pedigree with more enthusiasm and arranged for a reading of it.

She took great pleasure in both these 'establishment' performances, since they were the right context for the work, even though the fringe context had also found its enthusiasts. But she felt that the work was far more subversive in the milieu to which it belonged, and also far more effective because it could speak to people who were part of, and committed to, those forms of cultural expression. It was a paradox she was happy to live with and had no objection, but she never forgot the initial responses and she never forgot the way in which the same stone could appear one minute as dull and lifeless and at another bright and shining to the same pair of eyes. She felt protective over the play, which had had to acquire a small cloud of tiny glory before it was allowed to live and breathe in its own space.

My two novels came out within three months of each other. On the day of publication of the first novel Jenny invited me to lunch again at the same place. She was working at home that morning and suggested meeting me at the tube station so that we could walk to the restaurant together. The venue was Charing Cross underground. We met outside the ticket office and began walking out of the tube together. We walked along the Strand and there on the other side just outside the main line station we heard the sound of a flute. I had a vague feeling that there was something familiar about it and I suggested crossing the road to see if I was right. Jenny didn't want to go, so I suggested she just wait there while I just ran across to see.

I went across, and sure enough just outside the station there was my young musician wearing a long floral skirt and a very tight knitted black and silver glitter sweater, playing – it must have been – Vivaldi again. A policeman was approaching her just as I reached the pavement. He grabbed her by the arm roughly, jerking the flute out of her hand until it fell on the pavement. I shouted and ran towards her. I heard a squeal of brakes behind me. I looked round and realised there had been some kind of accident. I wasn't sure which way to go, towards the musician or back to the street. As I stood there paralysed with indecision, the policeman was already taking the musician away. She had managed to pick up her flute. I decided to go back across the road. As I did so, weaving my way through the stopped cars, I suddenly realised that Jenny had been knocked down by a car which had mounted the pavement. I knelt down beside her. She smiled and said, 'Don't worry, I'm all right. I think I've done something to my leg.' There was a traffic warden also kneeling by her, who said, 'I think she's just broken her leg. She'll be all right. An ambulance is on its way.'

The sixth reading:

I don't know whether Jenny ever read the other novel. She never mentioned it, and nor did I.

'So What Kept You?'

MICHELENE WANDOR

EPISODE ONE

'So what kept you?'

'I had business to finish.'

He flopped into a large comfortable armchair, his legs splaying apart, his arms hanging over the sides. She looked at him.

'So I suppose you're tired?' she said.

'Of course I'm tired, what do you expect?'

'I expect you'd like a nice cup of tea.'

She busied herself at the stove, lighting the gas, putting the kettle on the gas. He looked up at her.

'You still haven't got an electric kettle?'

'Why do I need an electric kettle? This does perfectly well.'

'I would think by now you would have an electric kettle.'

'Well, I haven't. Boiling water is boiling water, and boiling water from anywhere makes just as good a cup of tea.'

'I did see something before I came,' he said. 'I saw one of these new water filters, where you pour the water into a red plastic thing and it filters through some sort of white plastic thing and then it comes out pure at the bottom.'

'I don't understand what you're talking about,' she said, getting the teapot and the cups out and laying them on the table. 'How can you have water that goes through red and white plastic and be pure?'

'I'm telling you,' he said, 'that is what it did.'

'Did you bring one with you?' she asked.

'Of course I didn't,' he said. 'I didn't have time. I didn't know I was coming.'

She sat down at the table as they waited for the kettle to boil.

'So what kept you?'

'I told you, I had business to finish off.'

'What kind of business can it be that has to keep you for such a long time? Five years.'

'Over five years,' he said. 'And what kind of business do you expect it would be? It was property. It is always property.'

She got up from the table and went to adjust the kettle. 'I don't want to hear about property,' she said. 'All I used to hear about is property this, property that, land here, land there, houses here, houses there, stones here, stones there. I don't want to hear about property any more.'

'Okay,' he said. 'We won't talk.'

'I didn't say we shouldn't talk. I just said I don't want to hear about property.'

'You asked me what kept me. I told you. Now you don't want to hear.'

They sat in silence, the only sound the soft hissing of the kettle as the water heated.

'Well,' he said, looking round. 'It's a nice place.'

'Sure it's a nice place,' she said. 'What did you expect?'

'I expected a nice place.'

'It's just the same,' she said.

'I can see,' he said. 'Comfortable armchairs, clean.'

'I'll tell you a secret,' she said. 'I washed the kitchen floor.'

'Why is that a secret?'

'Because usually I don't wash the kitchen floor very often. Today I washed the kitchen floor.'

'I'm glad you washed the kitchen floor,' he said. 'I like a nice clean kitchen floor.'

They relapsed into silence again.

'Well,' she said, 'so tell me something. What's the news?'

'News?' he said. 'I don't know what the news is.'

'The girls,' she said. 'Tell me how the girls are.'

'Well, much as usual,' he said. 'They don't change. They haven't changed since they were little.'

'There must be something new,' she said. 'It's been a long time.'

'Well, let me see,' he said. 'The elder one, she's as stuck up as ever. The middle one, she's as bitchy as ever. The youngest one, she's as sweet as ever. Stupid, but very sweet.'

'We shouldn't have given them those names,' she said. 'I never liked their names.'

'We chose their names together,' he said. 'It's too late to complain. They don't mind them, why should we?'

'I think they became like their names,' she said. 'You know how important a name is.'

'Don't remind me,' he said. 'If anybody should know, I should know.'

'So your solution was giving them goyische names,' she said.

'There's something funny about you.' He looked straight at her. 'Something different. I don't quite understand what it is. You're very argumentative all of a sudden. I don't remember you being so argumentative.'

'I've had a lot of time to think.'

'Oh dear.' He looked away.

'I've had a lot of time to think. I've also done a lot of talking. I'm not used to talking a lot. I enjoy talking now, since I've been doing a lot of talking. And I've been thinking about a lot of things.'

'Well, I don't want to hear any of it,' he said.

'Alright,' she said.

They sat in silence for a few moments, drinking their tea. Then she looked at the fingernails of her right hand, the fingernails of her left hand, bit off a corner from her right hand thumb, and looked at him.

'Well,' she said. 'We can't sit here like this.'

'Why not?' he asked.

'Because,' she said, 'it's too much like olden times. Either we talk or you can go back where you came from.'

'You're crazy,' he said. 'I can't go back where I came from. What are you talking about?'

'You will have to find a way,' she said.

He looked round. 'It's very warm in here,' he said.

'Of course it's warm,' she said. 'I've got central heating.'

'You've got central heating?'

'Well, it's underfloor heating. The heat comes up. It's what you would expect.'

They lapsed into another silence. Then she stood up, picked up both cups.

'Here,' he said. 'I haven't finished my tea.'

'You have finished your tea,' she said, 'because I've decided you have finished your tea. This is my house. When you are in my house, you do as I tell you.'

'Well, I never,' he said.

She put the cups into the sink with a clatter, then came back and sat down.

'Look,' she said, 'I don't mind if you want to start. You talk. You tell me what has been happening. And then it is going to be my turn. Okay?'

'I can start?'

'You can start. That's what I just said. Now, tell me what has been happening.'

'It's a long story,' he said. 'Are you ready?'

'I'm ready,' she said.

'You'll listen to me?'

'Of course I'll listen to you. What else will I do?'

'You may go and do something else. You may start reading. You may start looking round the room. You may start knitting. You may start sewing.'

'I could do all those things,' she said. 'I'll tell you one thing. I promise not to do any of those things, but if I get bored I'll interrupt you. Just so you don't go on too long.'

'Fair enough,' he said. 'Right. I'll start at the beginning.'

His story

'When they knew I was going to divide everything up, of course there was a lot of talk. Two of the people who talked most and spread most rumours were Kent and Gloucester. They laid bets as to who was going to get more of the estate. And of course as you'd expect, they wondered which of the husbands was going to get more. Kent always thought I liked Albany best. Gloucester, always a very shrewd man, realised that it didn't really make much difference which one of them I liked the better. And in some ways he was quite right. I have never really had much time for either of them. So my opinion really wasn't going more in the direction of one than the other. Now, I have always thought Gloucester's opinion was a little, shall I say, voyeuristic. After all, a man who can flaunt his illegitimate child with such pride really shouldn't have very much opinion about the way a man of property divides his estate between his legitimate children. Now I know what you're going to say. You're going to say I shouldn't judge another man. Well, quite honestly Gloucester has no shame and has embarrassed me more than once. Just because Edmund's mother was the prettiest thing he had ever seen is no reason to my mind for him to prefer Edmund. Anyway, I think it was probably scarcity value. After all, he had sent Edmund abroad to school so he would never have the nuisance of a child who got on his nerves and argued with him. Like poor old Edgar did. You know what it's like, having two children close together in age. They fight all the time, particularly sons. Well, I'm told particularly sons, I wouldn't know myself, would I? No, alright, I shouldn't have said that. I never blamed you for giving me three daughters. Anyway, where was I?

Let me describe Edmund. He is very tall, he has light brown wavy hair. Looks like his mother, with a very straight nose. Rather rosy cheeks, so that when he has just shaved he has a delicate bloom on his face which makes it look as though he had never grown any hair on it at all. He has got a very straight back. Apparently he was a very sporting child. He played some French form of football when he was abroad. Very strong. An eye for the women, no question, just like his father. And I could tell from the beginning, from the first time I saw him, that he had come back to England to oust his brother. Certainly in his father's affections, if not in terms of any money that might be going. He is charming, a spendthrift, speaks three languages fluently, doesn't know a word of Yiddish. I wouldn't be surprised if he wasn't even circumcised.

Anyway, there we are in Blooms and we've had the chopped liver, and we've had chicken soup with kneidlach. And we've had the chicken and the potato croquettes and the frozen peas. And we've had the dessert, the fruit salad with ice cream, water ice cream of course. And we are moving on to coffee or lemon tea and I decide that it is time. So I take a map out of my pocket. And all the dishes are off the table, so I spread it on the table. And the table goes quiet and people stop playing with the bits of cutlery and people stop heaping up crumbs into little piles on the white tablecloth. And people look in front of them rather than to one side or across at the people sitting opposite them. And nobody looks at me. And gradually when the silence is complete, I put both hands on the map and say, "Well, we all know why we have

come here today." Still nobody looks at me. "We all know," I
say, "that I have made my will, and I want everyone, family and
close friends, to know exactly where they stand. We all know," I
say, "that we have had enough of worry and bother and stomach
ache and anxiety. And I want to hand the benefit and the worry
on to other people. You all know," I say, "that I'm going to leave
my estate to my three daughters, and you all know that I expect
the husbands of two of them, since only two of them have
husbands so far, to look after their money. You all know that our
foreign visitors from France and Burgundy, who today have not
uttered one cross word in their rivalry over the love of my
youngest, are sitting here very quietly at the table waiting to see
what is to be decided for them. Well, we will come to that. Now,"
I say, "I know you are all dying to know who is going to get what
and how much. Well, it isn't going to be quite so simple. And I
think in this age of women's lib that the women should help me
decide." And at this all three girls look up. Different expressions
on their faces. Goneril looks at me, suspicious and puzzled.
Regan looks at me with hate. Cordelia looks worried.

"Look," I say, "I don't want to have control over the estate
any more. I want you to tell me which of you thinks they deserve
the largest part of the estate."

And at this the table goes mad. There's humming and haa-ing
and nudging and noise and everyone speaking at once. Shock.
And the three girls are sitting there saying nothing at all. I am
delighted. I wanted to make as big a fuss as possible. And so far I
seem to be succeeding. So I look at Goneril. She is the eldest,
after all. And I say "You start, kid."

Goneril looks down at the end of her water ice which is in a
muddy pool at the bottom of the glass plate. She stirs it round,
doesn't look at me. She looks down and says, "Dad, I have got no
words for how much I love you. I love you more than everything I
can see. More than every room I have ever been in. More than
every freedom I have ever had. More than everything you have
ever given me. I don't think there is another child who could have
loved as much as I have loved you. And I wish I had the gift of the
gab because then I could use pretty words and I could write you
poems, but I can't do that. You must know how much I love
you."

So I nod, and I notice that Cordelia's got her handkerchief out and is blowing her nose. So then I take a red Pentel from my pocket and I draw a big line round the Willesden estate and I say, "This bit over here and the bit to the north between Hampstead and Highgate just on the edge of the Heath, these will be given to Goneril and to Albany." I can see Cornwall looking at me a little strangely. He has always fancied the Heath. So I ignore him and I turn to Regan. She looks straight at me with her hands clasped on the table in front of her and she leans forward so that she is looking me straight in the eye, and she says, "As usual Goneril's the one who expresses everything perfectly. She speaks for me. There is nothing more that I can say, except that I take no pleasure in anything but the love that you showed me as my dear, revered father." And at this Cordelia sneezes. "Gesundheit" I say to her. She doesn't answer. She doesn't even say thank you. She just blows her nose again. So I turn back to Regan and I say, "Right, for you and for Cornwall and your children, you can have this section over here, going all the way down to Clapham." I know he hates south of the river. And then I turn to Cordelia and I say, "All right, kid. You've got two men fighting over you. What can you say to persuade me that you deserve the best third of my estate. Come on, speak up." She doesn't say a word. "Well?" I say. "Cat got your tongue?" She still doesn't say a word. "Come on," I say. "You've got to say something."

"Well," said Cordelia, "you have made me pretty miserable. I love you, I love you, there's no way I am going to spew it all over the table just to please you." "Well, well," I say, "you better talk a bit more properly to your father, or you're going to be in trouble." "Look," she said, "I didn't ask to be born. I know you have looked after me, provided my food, my clothes, and I've done everything I can. I have done as you tell me, I have been a nice, good obedient daughter, I've stayed at home while the other two went off as quickly as they could and found other men to marry and go and live with. I never did that. I stayed at home. And I must say," she says, "I think there is something a little funny about two women who say they love their father more than anybody else in the world and yet have gone off and lived with other men. If they are going to be that Oedipal," she says, "surely they are kidding themselves either that they love you or that they love their husbands."

"Oh yes," I say. "This is an interesting interpretation on the respectable and busy lives that your sisters lead." "That's as may be," says Cordelia. "That is what I think." "Alright," I say. "If you want to speak the truth in this kind of way, tough on you. See if you can feed off the truth. See if truth provides your clothes. See if truth provides you with a roof over your head. From now on you can forget that I was ever your father, you can forget that we have anything in common and I never want to see you again." And as I say this, young Kent jumps in and starts appealing to me. And I was wild. I yelled at him, I told him to get out, I said when he had a daughter he loved more than any other he would know what it felt like to be talked to like this. And then I made, if I say it myself, a rather good speech to Cordelia. I told her to get out, collect her things, and leave the house. And I decided that what was to be Cordelia's share should be divided between the other two girls. "I am going to sell the home," I said. The two girls looked up at this point, a little bit worried. "Well," I said, "for the time I have left to me, what I am going to do is come and stay with each of you for a month at a time. That means that neither of you will have me to stay for too long, and I won't get bored. I shall hand the office over to the boys to administer the estates. And I have got the keys here, I have two sets cut, and you can have a set each. I will meet tomorrow to sort out who does what."

Now Kent starts rabbiting on again, and tries to convince me that just because Cordelia doesn't say very much, that she loves me just as much, if not more than the other two. He is quite a brave man really, but he really gets my goat at this point. Suddenly got all this phoney nobility and self-sacrifice, telling me he knows my daughter better than I do. I could have hit him. Except that Albany and Cornwall, who also should have known better, stopped me. Kent is actually telling me at this point that I am evil. Me. Someone who is just trying to divide up the estate as he sees fit. Me, evil, disposing of my own. Well, I thought, to hell with him. So I gave him a week's notice. A week to clear out his office and get the hell out of my sight. And I tell you what was typical about him. Here he is trying to pretend he is defending Cordelia, he is only interested in saving his own arse. He doesn't exactly offer to find somewhere for her to live. He just leaves, saying I will be sorry for what I have done, making some pompous little speech to Goneril and Regan about how hypocritical they are. Have you got any more tea? It's thirsty work, all this talking.'

'I've heard all this before,' she said.

'What do you mean, you have heard it all before? You haven't heard it before.'

'It's like when you partitioned Europe,' she said. 'It's the same story all over again.'

'No, it isn't,' he said. 'It's completely different. Anyway, it's about your children. You should be interested in your children.'

'I am interested in my children. But I'm interested in my way.'

She got up and poured some more hot water into the teapot, bringing back fresh cups and saucers to the table with her. As she poured the tea she continued talking. 'Why don't you drink your tea, and I will talk to you for a little while.'

'I can drink and talk,' he said. 'I never had any trouble drinking and talking. Or eating and talking.'

'Well, there's no hurry now,' she said. 'You've got all the time in the world. Just listen to me for a while.'

'You got something you want to say about the girls?' he said. 'I knew you would have something you wanted to say about the girls. I knew you would have strong views about who should have the property. I know you think Cordelia should have it all because she is the youngest, because we loved her the most, because she is the one without a good man to support her.'

'I will talk about Cordelia when I get round to it. I have a lot I want to say about her, and about the other two, come to that. But I want to tell you something about myself.'

'Oh God,' he said, 'who wants to listen to gossip.'

'It isn't gossip. It is something I have been thinking about writing down. I want to know what you think of it. It's just my story. Just an ordinary little story.'

'Before you met me?'

'It starts before I met you. I was born before I met you. That seems like a good place to start.'

'Alright,' he said, 'but no longer than it takes me to drink my tea. Okay?'

'Well,' she said, 'I can always keep pouring you cups. I will stop when I have reached a point where I want to stop. Remember, we've got all the time in the world.'

He smiled for the first time since he had arrived.

'Fine,' he said. 'We've got all the time in the world. We've got long stories to tell, and we must both listen.'

'What?' she said.

'You heard what I said,' he said. 'I will listen.'

'I can't believe my ears,' she said.

'Well,' he said, 'things change.'

Belongings

'I will start where I was born. That was in a little town, but I don't remember anything about it, as the whole family moved when I was very young to a much bigger town called Lvov – at the time Lemburg, being under the Austrian regime. We lived in the centre of the town in a two-bedroomed flat which was in a building. I went to an ordinary elementary school where I was one of the brilliant pupils. I was six. We went to school from eight in the morning. I was the youngest in a family of four. We were two girls and two boys. The eldest was my sister Lola. Within a year and a half was my brother Dolek, whose name was really Adolf, but we called him Dolek. Lola's name was Caroline. We called her Lola. Then came my brother Isadore, who we called Izzec. Then my name was Rosalie, and I was called Rouga. And these were the Polish names. And for eight solid years I was the youngest in the family and spoilt. The only birthday they celebrated in the family was my birthday, being the youngest. And the birthdays were very modest. My mother used to come home in the afternoon and bring bags of sweets and we invited all the children from the building and had a big party of raspberry juice and sweets. That was my birthday party.

After that one of the maids who was from another flat took us all downstairs to the cellars, because under every building there were cellars where people stored vegetables for the whole winter covered in sand, and kept their coal there for the winters' fires. And we sat on sacks on the ground with one candle burning and she told us ghost stories.

When I was eight years old my youngest sister was born. Of course the three elder ones were always jealous of Rouga who was the spoilt brat. So before my sister was born we made a bet. The girls wanted a girl, the boys wanted a boy. Anyway it was a girl, Bronya. And when she was born I was in the centre, and they danced round me, holding hands – "you're not the youngest any more. Bronya is the youngest." Anyway, we loved Bronya very much. She was a sweet baby.

My father was an agent for parquet flooring. Very few people knew about lino, carpets were expensive, so we had parquet flooring and rugs on the floor. My mother was very houseproud. We also had one maid, Hanya. She came to us when my brother Izzec was a baby. She was an unmarried mother. She had to earn money to keep her child. She left it with a relative in the village. She had two or three, I can't exactly remember, and out of the three one survived. Her son, her one and only son.

We had two bedrooms, a living room and a kitchen, and we managed. It's not like in London, and our children, where each child had to have a bedroom. The parents slept in the kitchen on a camp bed which folded up during the day. Before Izzec – Jack – was about a year old my mother expected another baby, so she told Hanya to continue nursing him till the baby was born. And the baby was myself, and Hanya nursed me as well until, I don't know, nine months, a year. So Jack and I were her two children. She loved us more than she did her own son, who she very seldom saw. And she always said, when we'll get married she'll come and live with one of us and look after our children.

My elementary school was quite nice. Under Austria the Jews had every equal right, we were all equal citizens. There was always anti-Semitism but it wasn't out in the open. I was one of the bright ones at school and the teacher, she was an elderly woman. I was good at poetry, and she invited me to her house when she made a party and there was a priest present. And I said a beautiful poem about a poor birdie who was injured and taken care of by a little girl. And I said it full of feeling. And the priest was so taken with it that he took me on his lap and told me that I said the poem beautifully. I was also a very good little actress, so whenever there was a play at school I took part in it.

I wouldn't say my mother was Orthodox, but she kept all the high holidays. My father was not religious at all. In fact he was a very heavy smoker, so Saturday he used to go into the toilet to smoke his cigarettes because Mother wouldn't let him smoke his cigarettes on Saturday. He was a self-educated man. He was a very intelligent man, and very good in business, and we had a comfortable life. In fact we moved into a much nicer flat when I was about ten years old, in a nicer district. It was about 1912.

We had a lovely bathroom. It was a nice building and it had balconies round and better class people lived there. There was one woman lived across from our flat, facing balcony to balcony. She lived on her own and she used to stand on the balcony smoking a cigar, and to us it seemed a terrible thing to do, a woman to stand up there and smoke a cigar.

At the age of eleven I passed my scholarship and I went to grammar school, a Gymnasium. My two brothers already went to one and they were wearing uniforms. Each year they had a new stripe to put on their collar, a high collar. The first year was one silver stripe, the second two silver stripes, then three. The fifth year they had one gold stripe. Jack intended to study medicine, and Dolek went to one they called a Realschule, and they trained them in engineering.

Anyway, 1914 the war broke out, and of course everyone got scared because the Russians were practically on our doorstep and everybody who could escape did so. But where could we go? My mother had a sister who lived in Krakow and her husband was in the Polish army, an officer, and he was stationed in a little town in Mairie Schönberg. That was next to Czechoslovakia, Moravia as it was called. So we packed up, well, we couldn't take much luggage. Bronya was a baby Of course we took Hanya with us. Each child had a little parcel packed up in a sheet, and my father had Bronya in his arms. We got to the station. It was packed with people waiting for the train. It was a terrible situation. I think we got on the last train which left Lvov. We got as far as a little town, Schevorsk, where my aunt lived. She had a public house together with a restaurant. So we stayed there a couple of weeks. Then there was a scare that the Russians are moving on nearer, so we decided the whole family should move on.

We left the flat. We locked it, but we had an iron safe as well. There was nothing in the safe but we locked it as well. The flat, furniture, everything was left behind. We were glad to get away with our lives.

My auntie decided to come too, and she had two daughters, then twins, that's four daughters. My uncle couldn't leave, but he saw us off to the station and his one and only son who was about fourteen wouldn't go without his father – he said in Yiddish "Tata geh, ich geh, Tata bleib, ich bleib." Anyway they persuaded him in the end.

We got as far as a little town, Kshanov, and it was late Friday night, and the Orthodox Jews suddenly decided they're not going any further. "Jews mustn't travel on Shabbas. Off we go." So we all went off in this little town, Kshanov. A few Jewish families lived there, and they put us up and gave us food. Well, we were all put into one room.

Then we travelled on till we came to Schönberg. My uncle and aunt who were there, they couldn't accommodate us because they lived in two rooms. So with great difficulties we found a cellar. You can imagine – mother, father, five children and the maid. Somehow we got together some beds and we were cooking on a primus stove.

There were about thirty Jewish families living in this little town. It was beautiful. A valley surrounded by forests and hills. And somehow a woman who didn't live far away took pity on us, although they hated the Jews in that town. She was a non-Jewess but she took pity on a poor family with all those children, and she gave us a two-roomed flat with a kitchen, and we moved in there and stayed there right through the war.

My mother was a very clean person, kept the place very clean. And they decided we're not so bad, we're quite nice people, and we got friendly with the neighbours. My older brother Dolek had to enlist because he was eighteen, and he went off with the Austrian army. Jack went to the Gymnasium.

My father couldn't go to the bank to get any money because we ran away just as we were, so we were practically penniless. But he had a very good friend who lived in Vienna, so he decided to go to Vienna and see what he could do. He went to see a Mr Tanne – whose daughter I afterwards saved from Hitler – that's how we repaid him his good deed. He lent my father some money to start business on his own.

What sort of business? The only thing he understood was timber, but during the war nobody wanted parquet floors, so he decided to buy up timber for building which was very very difficult to get. But he travelled from village to village and gradually he got a connection. He was a small, quiet-spoken man but he had the gift of the gab and they seemed to take a liking to him, Czechs and Germans, and he did wonderfully well. And they gave him food as well. Food was very very scarce. He brought home potatoes and butter, and all sorts of things which people couldn't really get. We didn't starve. He travelled to Czechoslovakia and he brought home – they were famous for their linens – and he brought home some sort of towels, tablecloths, sheets.

Unfortunately the Austrians were short of soldiers and they decided to take people up to the age of fifty and my father was under fifty and so they took him to the army. Then he was examined and they found out there was something wrong with him. We didn't know what was wrong and he didn't tell us, so he only stayed in the army three months and he was sent home. When my mother asked him, he said "Oh, they thought I'm a bit too old." But actually he was very very ill, and he didn't disclose that he was so ill. I remember my sister and I went to a cinema one evening, and when we came home it was already evening and mother said, "Don't make a noise because your father is not too well." They were both sitting in a restaurant having coffee and he suddenly felt ill so she brought him home. And during the night he got very very bad, and she called the doctor, and two o'clock in the afternoon he died.

Well, it was a terrible thing for me because I loved him very much. I was always his favourite daughter. He was very proud of me. I don't know why. It was a terrible shock.

Jack told me it was his lungs. As I said, he was a chain smoker. Jack said he had lung trouble which affected his heart as well. Anyway, within a few hours he was dead.

To say about these four years, they were good and bad memories. I went to school, I learned German, I spoke German fluently. I had friends, but wherever you went you felt the anti-Jewish feeling. Even when we walked in the streets the young children shouted: "Schweines Jud. Sau Jud." And I felt very miserable about it.

When my father died just before the end of the war, it was the end of the world for me. I was nearly sixteen. Lola took up a course in typewriting and accountancy and correspondence, and she did all his paperwork for my father. When my father died, my mother had to live. She had four children to look after. She didn't know what to do. So all the farmers who were dealing with my father, they wrote to her when he died and said they would carry on supplying us, and Lola could go on running the business. So she did. Anyway, then my uncle, my mother's brother, persuaded us to go back to Lvov.

We escaped the 1914–18 war but we came back into a much worse war which was a civil war between the Ukrainians and the Poles. The Ukrainians occupied Lvov, and the Poles were outside it. And there was street fighting, and the Jewish boys joined the Ukrainians, because they knew as soon as the Poles take over there'll be pogroms. So there were the Jewish Milizia boys helping the Ukrainians. People couldn't get out at all to get food. They lived on whatever they had in the house, potato peelings.

In the end they gave them permission to go out one day and get what they could because people were starving. So there was a one-day armistice for people to go out and get food, and lots of civilians got killed.

I went to the office just the same. People lived a normal life even though bullets were flying round everywhere. On one day, we lived in a ground floor flat in quite a big building, about a four-storey building, and we heard the guns going, and suddenly we heard a big bang. And we rushed out and there was a little old lady living above us and she was standing on the landing covered with flour. She was like a white ghost. I don't know what it was, but it came through the wall. She had a dresser with crockery, so it hit the dresser, all the crockery was smashed on the floor. She was making noodles, rolling out the noodles, and all that flour, it sprayed all over her. She wasn't hurt. We had a narrow escape.

Well, of course the Poles won the war and one nice morning our maid – we lived in the suburb, very few Jews lived there, and we were still afraid to go out in the streets – we sent our Polish maid to buy food. She came back crying bitterly. She said. "You should see the poor Jews running from the Jewish quarter. They're killing all the Jews and they're burning." Anyway, the first thing the Poles did – pogrom on the Jews. They put fire to the synagogue and burnt a few people alive in their houses, and all the Jews ran away. We gave shelter to one family.

The big Polish soldiers came to our house. They were looking for arms. So one of the soldiers says, "Could you give me a drink of water?" I took a glass of water and gave it to him and he said, "You drink it first." I said, "Why?" So he said, "You may want to poison me." So I said, "Okay." And I drank it.

So they went in the cellars and they looked for arms. They didn't find anything in our house. Anyway, at that time the British Mandate took over in Palestine, so all the Jews gave all their jewellery, whatever they possessed for Palestine. I gave my gold earrings. I'd got pierced ears but I gave away my gold earrings.

I couldn't live with the Poles. I just felt I got to get away.'

'So?' he said.

'I'm going to have a cup of tea,' she said. 'I've reached the end of the first bit.'

She poured herself some tea, sat down and drank it.

'You're not telling me anything new,' he said.

'No,' she answered, 'but I'm telling it in different words. You haven't heard me tell it quite like that before, have you?'

'No,' he said, 'but I'm not very interested, quite honestly.'

'Well,' she said, 'quite honestly, I'm not very interested in all the intrigues and the palaver you had trying to decide who deserved Willesden and who deserved Clapham. It's just not something that interests me.'

'You always encouraged me to do well,' he said. 'You always wanted me to get on.'

'Sure I wanted you to get on,' she said. 'But sometimes you can want somebody to get on and then not be particularly interested in where they get on to.'

'You never learned to speak English properly,' he said.

'I speak English as good as I need,' she said. 'I can make myself understood.'

He leaned back. 'I suppose next you're going to say I should never have changed my name.'

'Why?' she said. 'Levy was a perfectly good name. There are lots of people called Levy.'

'But they're not my relatives,' he said.

'Some of them are,' she said. 'Not all of them were given the name Levy by the British Customs officer when they came off the ship because they couldn't spell a foreign name.'

'Now she's preaching history,' he said.

'No, I'm preaching something that's to do with genealogy or something like that, maybe that's not even the right word – something to do with the way people get their names. Heraldry, or something like that.'

He laughed. 'We've got no heralds in our family.'

'We've got no Herods either,' she said.

They both laughed together. He put his hand on hers.

'Well,' he said, 'what are we going to do now? Are you going to tell me about your friends?'

'Well,' she said, 'there are a lot of musicians here. There's a lot of American musicians. A lot of modern rock musicians. A lot of singers.'

'Like who?' he asked.

'Well, like Elvis Presley, Janis Joplin, Jimi Hendrix.'

'Never heard of them,' he said.

'No, I never heard of them,' she said. 'But it's surprising who comes round when they hear you've got chicken soup on the stove. That Janis, I've done a world of good to her with my chicken soup. She was so pale. She smoked like a chimney, she's almost given up. And she's round here every other day for her dose of chicken soup. Elvis is a bigger problem, he spends all his time looking in the mirror. So when he comes round, I just leave the little mirror in the bathroom so that he doesn't spend his time in every room standing in front of the mirror. It's a little bit anti-social. And Jimi –'

'I don't want to hear any more,' he said.

'Alright,' she said.

There was a silence again.

'Shall I carry on?' he said.

'Maybe,' she said. 'Shall I carry on?'

'Maybe,' he said.

Again they sat in silence.

'I'm tired,' he said.

'I'm not surprised,' she said. 'It's a hard journey. Shall we go for a walk?'

'That's a very good idea,' he said.

'Come on,' she said, standing up. 'Get your coat. I'll show you round.'

The reader looked up.

The audience shuffled.

The only sounds to be heard in the room were people shifting on their seats, moving their feet, rustling their arms, moving sideways, taking handkerchiefs out of their pockets, blowing their noses. The reader watched everyone.

'Has anyone got any questions?' she asked.

The shuffling abated a little bit. Then there was a silence.

'I'm happy to answer any questions,' she said.

A woman in the front row looked up at her. 'I didn't quite understand,' she said, 'where were they?'

The reader nodded. There was another silence. Someone further back said, 'Was that King Lear?'

The reader smiled. Silence again. A man right at the back said, 'I was very interested in the oral history.'

The reader smiled again. 'Would you like me to answer those questions?' she said, 'although strictly speaking the last one wasn't a question, it was a comment.' The audience shuffled again, not quite knowing what to say. 'Perhaps I could see what else you want to know,' she said. 'And then answer all the questions together.'

The third speaker began again. 'I find that kind of oral history very interesting, very plain. It doesn't usually have very much description in it, does it, except in a very matter of fact kind of way.'

Someone in front of him turned round. 'Why are you assuming it's oral history? It could be fiction.'

'It seemed very real,' said the man.

And then they continued, one picking up from the other.

'I thought it was a little ludicrous, having the names of King Lear's daughters.'

'Is that really what happens in the first scene of King Lear?'

'Have you ever heard of a Jewish King Lear?'

'I think it's anti-semitic. People always assume that Jews are only interested in money and property.'

'I think they were in heaven.'

'How do you know they were in heaven? Perhaps they'd just gone away on holiday.'

'Perhaps she's gone away on holiday and he's come down later on.'

'Why did she say she liked talking, that she'd found out that she liked talking now?'

'Were they meant to be Jewish?'

'What's the point in having it all broken up like that?'

'Is it autobiographical?'

'Is it based on real people?'

'Is it satirical? Is it political?'

'I found it really boring. There is no sense of tension, of conflict. There wasn't anything driving the narrative along. There wasn't a story.'

'I think fiction should always have a story.'

'It's more like a film moving from one place to another, and one time to another, very quickly.'

'People wouldn't call their daughters Goneril, Regan and Cordelia, surely. Rosalind maybe.'

'Did he say his name was Levy?'

'Is it all a dream?'

'It seems to me based on psychoanalytic theories, particularly those of Lacan.'

'Is that what you call Modernism?'

'It sounded to me like a translation. Why didn't you have the original language?'

'You wouldn't have been able to understand the original language.'

'Then she could have had a dictionary, a translation or a glossary, or some way of explaining the difficult words for those people who didn't speak the language fluently.'

'What language are we talking about?'

'I think it was sexist, because the man told his story first.'

'I think it was really boring. I'm going to ask for my money back.'

'Is it part of something much longer?'

'Would you say it was post-Modernist? And involved a reclamation of narrative from a number of different points of view?'

'Are you very influenced by Borges?'

'What do you think the most important issues facing a fiction writer today are?'

'Has it been published?'

'Where can I buy a copy?'

'Would you come and talk to my writers' group about being a woman and a writer?'

'I don't think you should read workshop work in progress to other people.'

The door to the room opened gently. The hinges had not been oiled, and it creaked slightly. People looked round. A man in a blue uniform looked in, looked at his watch, and nodded to the reader. She gathered her papers together and stood up.

'I'm terribly sorry,' she said. 'We have to leave the room by ten o'clock.'

People began picking up their bags and coats. Raising her voice in order to be heard above the sounds of impending departure, she said, 'Thank you very much for everything you've said.' There was a momentary lowering of the level of preparation. 'It is the first part of a nine-part serial,' she said. 'I shall be here again next week, if anyone would like to listen to Part Two.'

Une Glossaire/A Glossary

MICHELE ROBERTS

ABSENCE

Absence.

My childhood in France is vanishing, a tide going out. Each day, the receding waters stretch further away. Each day, the incoming tide reaches less high up the beach. The absent sea scrawls a memoir behind itself along the tideline, written in seaweed, driftwood, dead starfish, broken glass bottles, fragments of cork. I want to collect up this debris, decipher it, before the sea returns and obliterates it. I need to keep coming back to this seashore at Etretat in Normandy, to walk along the tideline and re-examine these mysterious traces, this line of fluid script, this low water mark dividing the pebbles from the shingle; to re-select and rearrange.

As a child I dream frequently of being erased by the sea. I walk along the beach, the high sea-wall beside me, and watch the violent waves crash over the rocks. The sea advances up the beach, more and more stormy, and I back away until, the wall behind me, there is nowhere left to go. Then the sea flops over my head and swallows me.

My grandmother has already vanished. She died in 1979. For the first few years after her death her absence is marked through her place laid at table for every meal: knife, fork, spoon, plate, glass, silver napkin ring. Then that custom dies, that trace eradicated. The arrangements of the house – furniture, mealtimes – remain the same, and testify to her memory. I find her on the kitchen shelves, upright as the blue and white jars marked *farine* and *épices*. I find her laid away, tidy and fragrant, in the big carved cupboard in her bedroom where her wedding sheets, thick linen with drawn-thread work along the top edge and her monogram in the corner, are folded in boxes between layers of tissue paper.

41

My grandfather has had a heart attack, and two strokes. He lives imprisoned in his chair, his speech thickened and blurred. He's over ninety. How much longer has he got? He clutches the edge of the cliff: the sea lies below, waiting for him.

My aunt, who takes the main responsibility for looking after him in addition to working fulltime, now has breast cancer. She is receiving chemotherapy treatment. Next month (February 1986) she will have a mastectomy. She pits herself against the incoming tide, hands flung out in protest: not yet.

Each day, the debris of memories scattered along the rise of the beach is a little different: new arrangements of shells, torn bits of plastic, broken lobster baskets, lumps of tar. In the past, when I have written about my childhood, one of my sisters or my mother has complained: that's not true; it wasn't like that; you've made it up. Yes, I'm making it up: I'm putting it back together again. I'm walking along the beach, staring at the prospect of the death of the grandfather and aunt I love; of their final absence; of my final separation from my childhood structured in their house. Into the face of this loss I cast my words, pebbles thrown into the sea. I'm going to write a sort of geography. To reclaim the past. The waves race backwards through my fingers, and I can't hold onto them. I lick the salt on my hands, and set myself to remembering.

ARTICHAUTS

Artichokes. Big, fat and green, with closely packed pointed leaves. The inside ones are violet, almost transparent. We eat them, boiled, for supper, pulling off the leaves one by one and dipping them into hot cream before scraping them between our teeth. The heart is the best, mashed up in the cream. Grandpère eats them with *vinaigrette*.

ASSOMPTION

Assumption. The feast-day of the village is the fifteenth of August, the feast of the Assumption of the Virgin Mary into heaven.

At six o'clock in the morning, we are woken by the boom of cannon fired in the playing-field on the Goderville road. My mother brings us an early cup of tea, for we must fast from liquids for three hours before receiving Holy Communion, and from food from midnight.

We dress in our smartest clothes. Cotton dress, navy cropped blazer with brass buttons, white socks, well-polished shoes. At ten o'clock, the bells begin to ring, summoning us to High Mass. We gather in the hall. Waiting for the others, I study the large framed engraving of Theseus bearing off Hyppolita, Queen of the Amazons, to be his bride. She takes it calmly, sitting upright in his chariot, bare massive arms lifted to adjust the transparent veil falling across her face. A stand topped with black marble bears flowering plants, brass candlesticks and dishes, a bronze sculpture of a tiger. I never tire of pulling my fingers along his cold hard upraised tail. White gloves are donned. Missals with gilt clasps are taken up. Grandpère twirls his stick. We are off.

The verger has a red face and black moustaches and wears a braided frockcoat with epaulettes and military medals. He motions us into the church. All through High Mass he knocks his decorated staff fiercely on the ground to tell us to rise, kneel, sit. The vast church is choked with people. Waiting. Then, far off in the distance, we hear the crashing jangly music of the village brass band marching up, up, through the great doors and along the aisle to their special place at the front, a ragged procession of serious men and boys in brown uniforms bearing their great gleaming instruments. They play at special moments all through Mass. At the Consecration and Elevation of the Host, the bells peal out, the organ booms, and the band roars and trumpets. Aged priests weighted down in gold brocade copes, half hidden by clouds of incense, the sweet smoke. Bouquets of white flowers around the altar and side altars at the feet of the saints, suspended from the tall columns. The village widows in black frocks, black bonnets and veils, black misshapen shoes. Everyone in their best clothes. After Mass, the band processes out, playing a sacred cacophany, and we follow them to the cemetery, where we stand in silence to honour the dead of two world wars.

Lunch. The table is extended with extra wooden leaves, to run the full length of the salon, and is draped with thick, gleaming white tablecloths on which shine silver and glass, arrangements of flowers. While the guests are sipping their *apéritifs* in Grandmère's bedroom, transformed into a little *salon*, a gang of women gathers in the kitchen to peel the freshly cooked potatoes. I feel like an adult, received into this bevy of aunts talking and laughing as their deft knives rapidly lift off the hot skins. The kitchen is the sanctuary, the tabernacle of the women, where the superlative feast is prepared by their hands alone, while the men talk to the priest next door.

One dish slowly succeeds another. The noise of conversation washes up and down the long table, eddies upwards from the flat basket of peaches and grapes and plums arranged on scarlet leaves. We're too excited to feel bored. Pale yellow ice cream released from its tall copper mould. Coffee in tiny gold-rimmed cups. Chocolates. Calvados and cognac and Bénédictine.

At three o'clock we go down to the village to watch the procession, finding a good place to stand: high up on a grassy bank at the crossroads. The carts, drawn by tractors, grinning youths perched high up at the wheel, are entirely covered in paper flowers, in pink or white or pale blue, and are decorated to represent different scenes of country life. Little children are animals. Older ones are giggling flower maidens and swains. Lastly comes the Queen of the day: the local village Beauty with her attendants, all got up in satin and flowers, like a bride, a gilt tiara anchored to her beehive hairdo, white satin stilettos on her big feet. We're puzzled as to why she's been chosen: her face is hard and red, her eyes small, her hair crimped and frizzy. Not so is Brigitte Bardot. But she's indisputably female, with her plump bosom and calves, her tossing head, her languishing smile. How can I ever become a woman? This one frightens me. Her sexuality frightens me, though I don't have a word for it.

We go on to the fair, which has been set up in the big field beyond the church. Carnival atmosphere: the normal social relations of the village turn topsy-turvy as the country people swagger arm in arm, in gangs, laughing boisterously, swarming in from their farms to take over the space, enjoy themselves freely, not bother with politeness and decorum. I'm enchanted and scared. We don't matter. Our genteel world shatters. Nobody cares that we are the much-respected Caulle family. We don't know all these people's names, and they don't know ours, and they don't give a damn. We go on the roundabouts, rocking on horses and trains and cars; we throw hoops for goldfish; my brother and father shoot air-rifles. Racks of gaudy dolls dressed in tinsel and taffeta stare down at us. The women running the booths shout in hoarse voices, hands on their silken hips, cigarettes dangling. A neighbouring farmer, Gérard Le Forestier, very handsome with his black hair and ruddy face, very masculine in his severe dark overcoat, whirls me away from my parents and into the dangerous thrills and spins of the bumper-cars, onto the skidding shiny floor where men and youths drive at us, yelling in patois, around the rink decorated with crudely painted panels showing curly-haired peasant boys fondling girls with enormous pointed breasts bursting through their tight bodices. I'm outside my strictly loving and protective family. At the age of eleven, for the first time. Driving, hard and furious, with a man. Wanting to be beautiful and grown-up, to be kissed. With my shiny face and frizzy hair and white ankle socks.

In the evening, after supper, the excitement still pours and tingles. We stand in the darkness, feet planted in puddles and mud, in the field off the Goderville road, waiting for the *feux d'artifice*, the fireworks, to start. This is part of the drama: to stand next to faceless strangers in the night, to see the spurt of a match as a cigarette is lit, to be out in the village so late, to be part of the eager crowd. Then the first rocket goes up, breaking and dissolving high above our heads into gold and silver flowers, and a roaring sigh comes out with one breath from all of us together. Fountains sizzle and leap; catherine wheels jerk and then flare into whirling circles of flaming light; there is the marvellous acrid smell of chemicals, sour burning, in our nostrils. Each of the exploding rockets takes off inside me, each of those staffs of intensity rises up inside me and bursts me into a shower of golden tongues, and I cry out along with the groaning crowd.

The feast of the Assumption celebrates the fact that the Virgin Mary, at her death, rises into the sky, only faintly assisted by angels, and shoots bodily up into heaven where she is crowned Queen. I understand that, watching these fireworks. I doubt it, looking at the simpering plaster statue of Victorian piety and submission in the church. What happened to Grandmère when she died? What will happen to Brigitte? I'll never see that firework display again, yet the fiery virgin rises again and again,

every year, in the muddy field. I'd like to believe she is rising
inside me. I'd like to believe that death does not extinguish those
I love, that they will rise up inside me as bright as rockets and
explode into my mind, these words I write. The smell of cordite,
of burning. The radiance fades against the black sky, and after a
few seconds you wouldn't know that it's ever been there. We
troop home, through the dark village, to bed.

BEURRE

Butter. Butter comes in a kilo block, wrapped in white grease-
proof paper printed with a design, in blue, of cows grazing, and
the name, in swirly blue letters, of the local farm which has
produced it. Butter is very expensive. We are not supposed to
spread it on bread at meals (except at breakfast), though my
father always does and then gets into trouble because he likes his
butter thick. For tea we eat *tartines* of bread and jam. I remember
at a certain point having a craving for salted butter, and my
mother buying it for me in tins.

BONTIÈRE

Bontière. A tall, broad oak cupboard, its upper half set with
glass panes, windows into the interior. Here are displayed the
ancient, fragile porcelain dinner and tea-services which are
hardly ever used, silver boxes and baskets, a massive old fan, an
ivory eggcup and spoon, a gold mesh purse, old velvet-framed
photographs. In the bottom half of the *bontière* are kept the
plates for Sunday and special use. On these days when there are
fourteen or so people to lunch, Brigitte squats in front of the
open doors, lifting out piles of delicate white plates and dishes
and tureens, opening velvet-lined boxes of silver cutlery, shining
black-handled knives, counting, checking. From the top shelves
of the *bontière* she lifts out cider glasses, wine glasses, water
glasses, and sets them on a huge silver tray. Everything is carefully wiped with a clean cloth before being put on the table. We
don't help her, for fear of breaking something. Madame Durécu
who comes to help with the washing-up on days like this, doesn't
touch the best plates and glasses either. She is said to be clumsy.

She does the pots and pans, and the women of the household do the rest.

My mother has brought bits of France with her into England. She has a *bontière* too, and she keeps her treasures in it. We're allowed to touch; to open the door and see what's inside.

BRIGITTE

Brigitte. My aunt's name. Also my middle name: as her god-child, I am named after her. I like this special relationship I have with her. I can lay hands on her, claiming her not just as aunt but as something more. She is my *marraine*. In my missal, at the place where it falls open for the order of Mass, I keep the holy picture she gives me to celebrate my First Communion in June 1957: *le petit Samuel* (Reynolds), looking just like a girl. This is me: a girl-boy, praying, in a white nightie, a bit of a prig. Brigitte also gives me a reproduction of a Virgin and Child by Raphael, in a gilded wooden frame, just like a real oil-painting. I choose it myself, in the shop in Le Havre, and this is a real pleasure: to be allowed to scan all the Botticellis and to reject them, to go for the serene grave Madonna by Raphael. I've been given the image of womanhood. My own mother looks out from the gold frame at me. I'll never be able to become like her. An impossibility. I shan't be a mother. I don't know why. Thirty years later I'm longing for my own child, and I'm discovering all the bits of me not represented in the holy picture. Grandpère says to me: '*depèche-toi de produire ton premier enfant. Je voudrais le voir avant de mourir.*'

Brigitte does not marry and have children. She chooses not to. How much can she choose? How free is she? What are her options? Unmarried, she is certainly not allowed a lover, male or female. Unthinkable. The English word *spinster* gives no clue to her power, her gaiety, her air of eternal youth. Outside the house she is Mademoiselle Caulle, respected in the village both as the daughter of her parents and as herself.

Monique, my mother, is the oldest child. After university she comes abroad, to Dolgelley in Wales, where she works as the French *assistante* in Dr Williams' School for Girls. War breaks out. She meets my father, who is in the army, stationed near the school. They decide to marry. My mother tells me how happy she is to have married an Englishman. She has left home. Broken free. She returns to visit her parents and sister every year, for a long summer holiday, taking us all with her. My father comes for a fortnight, and then has to go back to his job as Sales Manager for the Tan-Sad Chair Company.

Bernard is the second child. My godfather. He marries Anne-Marie Spriet, whose family (the Spriets have fourteen children, of whom seven survive) live just two kilometres away on a big farm, and are old friends of the Caulles. Bernard too leaves home. His job, working for a dairy firm, takes him south, to Rodez. He introduces chocolate yoghurt into France, also a delicious confection called *Campagnard*: cream cheese overlaid with thick fresh cream. Bernard is handsome, youthful: dark eyes, thick dark brown hair, aquiline nose, a smile. His vitality makes him very attractive. He gives me an image of male sexuality (of course I don't call it that then) that means: kindness, having fun, liking women and girls. All the young men of the family he has married into are like that.

Brigitte is the youngest. Secretly we hope that she will marry Charles Spriet, our favourite; the funniest and wildest of the boys; always willing to take us around the farm and play with us. But Charles brings home a bride who is robust, loudly cheerful, *very* sexy; and Brigitte doesn't really approve of her, kind and generous as Monique (same name as my mother) is. Brigitte places great store on behaving *comme il faut* when necessary, and Monique does not even know she is breaking the rules.

One suitor arrives for Brigitte. One day we're told that there's a gentleman coming to tea, and that we're to behave just as though nothing special is happening, just to be polite. He's nervous, correct, *old*. Brigitte spends the following day sitting in the car (the only place where she can find some privacy and not be overheard)outside the house, talking it over with my mother. In the end she rejects him. He only wants a housekeeper, she says: not a real wife.

My earliest memory of Brigitte. We are living in a council house on an estate in Edgware. The railway line runs along the bottom of the garden. The milkman comes round with his horse and cart. We run out to feed sugar-lumps to the horse. I'm perhaps three years old. Then we see Brigitte running along the street towards us, her face smiling, her dark plaits twisted around her head, the skirts of her waisted coat flying out behind her, a pile of books toppling out of her arms.

Brigitte does not grow old. Perhaps that is the secret: to stay with your parents, to remain in the house of your childhood, having survived the planes bombing your back garden and the surrounding fields during the Occupation, to cling to your home and your childhood, your inheritance, and to protect it fiercely. Brigitte becomes, even more than my grandparents, the keeper of the house; the keeper of the old ways. Changes are dangerous.

As Grandmère sickens and grows more fragile and moves towards her dying, Brigitte cares for her. The mother become the child. Arranging Grandmère's cardigan and shawl, prompting her to eat, to drink, to rest, arranging her spectacles and book within reach, taking her breakfast in bed and perching on the end of the bed to talk to her. We peer through the crack in the door and glimpse their intimacy that I sometimes feel shuts my mother out. Brigitte does the same with Grandpère. A loving bossiness. He is her baby now, and she feeds him. The powerful parents under the control of their youngest child. I think there is a certain satisfaction, even a pleasurable revenge, in all this. It's also extremely hard work.

Brigitte is: energy. She's small and dark and determined, her long narrow feet leaping in tennis-shoes around the house and garden, or shod for more formal occasions in elegant leather high heels. She runs, she jumps up and down, she plays tennis, she swims, she walks. Her body in its red swimsuit is firm, ageless. She has good legs. White skin, that browns rapidly in summer, like my mother's.

It's charming, to know my mother has a sister, someone she's known for longer than she's known us, to match the two together and mark their differences, to see my mother as a woman not just as my mother, to wonder how they've each become themselves. Brigitte criticises Mum for her French accent, less pure than formerly, weighted with English sounds. She criticises Mum for abandoning France and the family, despite the fact that Mum returns every year. She's critical of married people, of men. There are no eligible men in the neighbourhood for her to marry.

She's a wonderful aunt. She plays with us, a child herself. She fetches down from the *grenier* her old toys, and shares them with us. The dollshouse made by Grandpère, fully furnished with tiny hand-carved wardrobes, chairs, beds. Brigitte's doll has a trousseau of hand-sewn clothes: a severely-cut winter coat, little blouses with pleats, square shoulders, yokes, dresses with collars and cuffs and tiny buttons. Grandpère has made the doll a pair of fur boots, with wooden soles. The doll has a stove, a real one, on which we cook windfalls in fragile aluminium pans. We don't want our lunch; we want to eat with the doll, who is Brigitte, who has been given the house as her own.

We play with the dollshouse in Brigitte's bedroom, a tidy, spotless sanctum we may only enter when invited to do so. It's an enchantment to penetrate this enclosed world which is all Brigitte's own, shared with no man, to move across the polished floor of golden wood to see the curtain on its brass rod that divides off her washstand, to spot her gold ring lying next to the soap-dish, to see yesterday's silken petticoat and stockings flung across a hanger, to consider the rack of dresses carefully hung inside the built-in cupboard under the eaves. You discover a person by these traces, the way they arrange the brass pots of cacti, the bronze busts and figures on the little antique chest of drawers, the way the pillows on the bed wear day-time covers of fine white cotton decorated with cut embroidered ovals and white ribbon, the way that treasures are carefully placed along the carved brackets above the bed. A grown-up person's things, which we are occasionally allowed to handle. Brigitte's favourite books: *The Wind in the Willows*; encyclopaedias of English and American literature; a glossy illustrated fairytale about gossamer ladies riding in winged carriages drawn by butterflies. No dust. Each prized object in its exact place. Touch cautiously, lest the china mouse drops, and breaks. The panelled wooden walls bear pictures, a couple of green plants trailing down. The low spreading armchair has a fat seat of worn velvet, curled claw feet. The old oblong mirror, set into an ornate gold frame, hangs above the little writing-table with its appurtenances of glass, marble, gilt. Brigitte's missal; her rosary; the crucifix above her bed, threaded with a sprig of palm from the Holy Land. In here we're hushed and tamed. Coming out onto the little landing, we enter a noisier, more ordinary world.

We don't call her aunt. She's Beewee. Or, in other moods, Tante Octavie. Meaning all that she's not: a severe person in a mobcap and spectacles, a stuff gown. (One night we leave an effigy of Tante Octavie in Brigitte's room; she dons the costume and comes to haunt us.) Brigitte wears *salopettes*, sawn-off dungarees in pink and white candy seersucker stripes. She gardens in these, squatting next to her osier basket which she rapidly fills with weeds, or she perches on the kitchen doorstep after Sunday High Mass, having changed out of her elegant dress and jacket, and shows us how to churn the icecream and pack the revolving drum with ice. She picks up a hammer and a thick nail and smashes up the great lump of ice on its bed of coarse grey sacking.

Brigitte has a great friend, Odile, who used to be a Carmelite novice, but who has had to leave the convent because her health is too delicate for the rigorous life. I loved the convent, she tells me: we used to laugh all day long. I blink, unable to imagine this. I want to become a nun too, but I haven't thought the life included laughter. Brigitte and Odile sit in the verandah together, talking and sewing, listening to records, singing songs. They set off in Brigitte's grey *deux-chevaux* for walking holidays. This car is called Cocotte. Her seats are slung on thick rubber bands, and bounce wonderfully as the little car spurts along. The gear-lever has to be waggled, pushed and pulled. The engine starting up makes a coughing whine.

I hang around Brigitte and Odile. Two unmarried women who are close friends. This is something new and fascinating, a way of being that does not fit in to the tidy marital houses of the London suburb where we live. Odile is tall and thin, always laughing and cracking jokes. One Easter her new spring outfit is a suit in coarse navy linen, a navy hat, high heels. She looks wonderful. She wobbles down the rough road to church in her high heels, laughing at their absurdity.

Then Odile gets married and moves away. She and Brigitte remain friends, but it's not the same, I can see that. You have to put your husband and children first. A woman friend takes second place.

Brigitte finds another friend, younger, less fun. Edith. She makes do with what she can get. One summer the three of us go off in Cocotte for a walking holiday in Bourgogne. I'm thrilled that I've entered the category of Brigitte's friends for holidays, even though I'm only thirteen. We walk from monastery to monastery, looping back to the car at night. We eat picnics on the hillsides; cheeses bought from the monks, bread and *saucisson*. Or we make a fire over which we boil tins of *petits pois*, or *macédoine de legumes*, with eggs dropped in and poached along with the vegetables. At night we sleep in cheap small hotels. In Vézelay our ground-floor room opens onto a little walled garden, a pretty wilderness of overgrown flowerbeds and clambering vines. At night, at Brigitte's suggestion, we say our prayers together, aloud. We salute the Virgin. The *patronne* of the hotel does not like us, because at night, rather than eat in the hotel restaurant, which is too expensive, we lock our door and cook ourselves supper over the camping-gas. The patronne bangs on the door, yelling to us: *'c'est défendue! c'est défendue!'* Brigitte yells back to leave us alone, we're getting ready for bed. On the morning of our departure, the *patronne* chases Cocotte all down the narrow little street, screaming that we've stolen a face-flannel. I remember the scoured white spaces of the interior of Vézelay, the capitals of Autun, the *hospice* at Beaune. I remember toiling up the hot hillsides looking for Roman ruins, for flowers, for mushrooms. I remember Edith constantly giggling, constantly brushing her hair. I remember Brigitte leaping over streams, striding along, her long arms swinging.

Brigitte teaches childcare, cookery, household management and nursery nursing, to young women, in the equivalent of our technical colleges. Her subject is a science. She knows all about the exact temperatures for bathing babies, the exact amounts of flour and butter for making puff pastry, the exact proportions of a properly balanced diet. Moderation, she instructions us, frowning at my oblivious father plastering his bread with butter.

One Saturday we visit her school at Le Trait, an old mansion set among terraced gardens high up on a hillside outside Rouen. The top floors are used for the school. We see the kitchen-laboratories, the lecture halls, the demonstration rooms. We play with the doll-babies, heavy and real despite their sacking bodies. Their flopping heads convince us. It's a wild day, winds shaking raindrops from the trees in the jungly gardens we are allowed to explore and to get lost in, enormous orange slugs, their fat bodies swollen and glistening, gliding towards us along the paths. The cellars of the old house yield puzzles and secrets: theatrical props and costumes; the toys of adults. We try on gold paper crowns, purple satin robes, hold wooden sceptres.

Brigitte does all the decorations for the various seasonal festivals of the church. She arranges the flowers every week, graciously allowing the other ladies of the village to help her. She collects pine-cones, dries grasses and the flat silvery discs of honesty that she calls *la monnaire du Pape*. At harvest-time she takes us gleaning. With the permission of the farmers, we cut big armfuls of corn from the edges of the fields and carry them home, where Brigitte plaits and twists them into fantastic pagan shapes and paints them gold. Then she hangs them from the columns in church for the day of the harvest festival. She plants the feminine symbols of fertility and fruitfulness in the church. She makes the church her house.

My mother's birthday is in August. Brigitte makes her a cake in the shape of a bucket, from whose open lid spill out mushrooms made from meringues. The adults are sitting in the verandah, waiting for *le dessert*. Brigitte forms us children into a procession, and we walk in through the house from the kitchen, Jackie carrying the cake and the rest of us bearing great blue hydrangeas and singing Happy Birthday. Another of Brigitte's famous cakes is the great bell, of delicate sponge sandwiched and entirely coated in thick black chocolate, that she makes every year to celebrate Easter. Or she makes *gateau de Savoie*, or a *Savarin*, or a *Diplomate*. She is the scientist in the kitchen. We are allowed to help her, so long as we obey her instructions exactly. Anything less would ruin the finished product. She is ruthless and strict, and we are honoured to be her assistants.

When I go to visit her and Grandpère, she cooks me all my favourite meals, of which I must eat several helpings: *moules marinière*, calves' liver with onions and cognac, *artichauts à la crème*, sausages of pure pork with lentils, salt cod with cream sauce. The present is full of pain and change. We concoct these timeless meals to keep it at bay; we reminisce. Brigitte remem-

bers all the details of our childhood. Remembering, she is young
again. Carefree. The past is the best time, she insists. Young
people today want to tear down all she holds most dear. Feminists are trying to destroy the family, are encouraging women to
murder their unborn children, to go shouting in the streets about
sex. Workers are no longer loyal to their bosses but go on strike.
A socialist government has taken over in France. Married
women are taking the jobs, for more pin-money, that single
women like Brigitte really need in order to earn a living.
Teachers are no longer respected. Modern children are greedy
and lazy and materialistic.

Such a breakdown. Such bitterness in Brigitte's voice. To
enter her house, to love her, I have to leave behind the adult in
me who is feminist and socialist.

'Brigitte has an awful lot to bear' my mother counsels me:
'don't provoke her or argue. It's best not to answer back. Just be
careful what you say.'

Brigitte has grown her hair long. The bulky chignon at the
back of her head, which suits her, is streaked with grey. She sews
at her Normandy costume, every inch of which she makes by
hand: the gathered skirt, the embroidered bodice, the frilled
muslin apron, the wired gauze bonnet with its two long frilled
streamers, the petticoats. Once a week she indulges herself, goes
out dancing with her troupe, performs the ancient dances of the
countryside, summons the order and dignity of the past by moving through complex figures, feet leaping in quick patterns. She
models the costume for me in the garden, moving lightly,
proudly, across the grass. She poses, smiling. She stands for
tradition, for a dangerous dream. No black faces here. The
chickens of imperialism have come home to roost, yet Brigitte's
vision of *la douce Normandie* excludes a knowledge of France's
colonial history, of its injustices, its oppression. Why should
immigrant workers be so angry, so demanding? They shouldn't
expect us to take on their culture. They should take on ours.

I can't love this part of her. I reject it. The god-child in me
embraces the god-mother in her. Our other selves don't touch.

My beloved aunt. Now you have cancer. Perhaps you will live
for another five years. Just before Christmas, all your hair falls
out. My beautiful aunt. You buy a wig. My mother tells me this

over the telephone, for I haven't seen you for six months. I sit in the bathroom, crying. I'm angry with the doctors for invading your body with their harsh chemotherapy and radiotherapy, for making you nauseous and weak, for making all your hair fall out, for preparing to cut your breast off. You, who so respect science, accept this treatment. You say on the telephone: I'm determined not to die yet.

I come to see you. A brief weekend visit in late January, when snow-filled skies press down on the house and icy winds shake it. You say to me: 'the walls are fainting.' You don't like your wig: 'I should have bought a necklace instead, the price it cost me.' You wear a blue wimple to sleep in, and by day a scarlet scarf knotted behind your head. 'This is more comfortable, but it keeps slipping. I have to be careful when I go out. Young people are frightened by a bald woman.' You scratch your skimpy eyebrows, formerly thick and black: 'look, they're falling out too. Soon I'll have none left.'

You look younger than ever. Illness has gentled you, let you accept being looked after, opened you to the realization of how much people love you. The phone rings constantly: your friends calling you. Women friends and neighbours from the village come in and sit with you, bringing you news, pots of home-made blackberry jam. You lie back in your low chair, talking about the cancer, how you feel. You don't care any more about dust in the corners, the washing-up. You call to me from your bedroom, where you lie, exhausted and faint: 'leave cooking the lunch. Come and talk to me.' Your face is soft, smiling. 'On the day they told me I had cancer' you say, stroking the cat: 'I bought a new hat and then I went out dancing.'

You can't make it to evening Mass, so I go for you. The church is freezing, almost empty. My pew has a hook for men's hats, women's gloves. The priest and tiny congregation caterwaul through the limp melodies of the modernized Liturgy, utter a watery poetry full of vague clichés, banalities. The rollcall of glorious virgins – Felicity, Perpetua, Agatha, Lucy, Agnes, Cecily and Anastasia – is no longer sung. I'm glad to be home again with you, helping you search your recipe book for *Tarte Tatin*.

Tomorrow, Monday, when I'll have gone back to England, the

surgeon will give you the date of the operation. Tonight, you're giving a feast. You come into the kitchen to show me how to clean and open the oysters. You instruct me on how to prepare the crab. You teach me the necessity of keeping on creating. You teach me how to accept your death.

C——R

Cancer. The unspeakable word. The word refused by the family. The word whispered in corners but never mentioned on the telephone. Now it's the word that Brigitte utters frequently. A new definition of herself.

CADICHON

Cadichon. The name of the Spriets' donkey. Ancient, amiable, docile, he allows us to mount him and ride him around the farm. He has to be whacked to make him move. Sometimes six of us small brutes sit astride him at once. Sometimes Monsieur Spriet harnesses him to the old two-wheeled trap kept in the coach-house. We arrange ourselves gingerly along the two seats with their worn coverings of leopardskin, distributing our weight evenly so that we won't tip over. Then we're off, wheeling rapidly between the cornfields, rushing through corridors of rustling gold, racing into the unknown, the depths of the farm.

CALVADOS

Calvados. Brandy made from cider apples. Sipped, in tiny glasses, after Sunday lunch. Made on the Spriets' farm, and named after Falstaff, who is supposed to have once stayed there.

CAMEMBERT

Camembert. The round cheese with a rough chalky coat which Brigitte scrapes off before serving it. We eat it for breakfast, often also at lunch and supper. When you buy a camembert, Brigitte instructs us: you must smell it and press it to see if it is really ripe. The inside gushes out, yellow and runny, over the plate. You just eat it. You don't fiddle about with it. None of this Robert Carrier nonsense about deep-frying it in breadcrumbs.

CAUDEBEC

Caudebec. The small town in which my mother is born. The site of the *bac* (ferry) for crossing the Seine en route to Rouen and a picnic lunch in the forest. Also the site of a fine Gothic cathedral, its portals set with tiers of stone saints. We are proud of Caudebec, because it is our mother's birthplace, and beautiful enough to be worthy of her. Mum confers interest and dignity on the town, on the cathedral, on the Seine itself (*Sein*, breast). Every year she gives us the great treat of boarding the ferry, going across the wide river to the other side.

CAULLE

Caulle. My mother's family name. My mother is now called Roberts: the name of my father's family.

CAUX

Le pays de Caux. The Caux region. The part of Normandy in which the family lives, inland from the coast stretching between Etretat and Le Havre. Flat landscape of wide high skies; farms surrounded by high screens of beech trees; long straight roads flanked by tall elms; cows grazing in the pastures; fields of oats, barley and wheat. The Seine loops between Le Havre and Rouen, edged by orchards of fruit trees, stone houses with pointed slate roofs, small chateaux, old half-timbered cottages with irises growing along the ridge of the thatch, the abbeys of Jumièges and St Wandrille. The fine August drizzle comes down, and our bare feet slither on the soles of our leather sandals. The banks on either side of the gravelled roads are thick with purple and yellow flowers, raindrops hanging in the long grasses and spilling against our knees. We clamber up to pick nosegays, eye to eye with the cows munching steadily behind the barbed wire fence.

CINEMA

Cinema. Home movies. Grandpère has brought back from
Canada a ciné-camera, which is used by him and Brigitte to
record and invent the doings of the family. Every summer, the
night arrives when we ask to see some films after supper. The
silver screen is pulled up and hung in front of the window, and the
rounded massive projector placed on Grandpère's desk. Darkness. Brigitte clatters film cans. A whine, a purr. White beam of
light slicing past our heads.

I learn about our history by seeing it on film. My memories are
given to me by the screen. We have two main favourites: the film
of Bernard and Anne-Marie's wedding; and the film of our early
childhood. Brigitte, film-editor, constructs wonderful narra-
tives: a wedding; darkness; a bouquet of flowers; darkness; a
newborn baby; darkness; candles on an invisible birthday cake
being blown out one by one; more flowers. There are Margi and
me, pushing dolls in prams round and round and then stopping to
kiss each other passionately. There's Andy, fat and smiling,
crawling across the parquet floor with a hearthbrush. There's
Jackie in a fur Eskimo suit. There's Mum, glamorous in a short
fur coat, her dark hair pinned up in swoops and rolls, and Dad, in
shirt-sleeves and fair-isle pullover, leaning grinning on his spade
outside our half-built house. There's Brigitte, in Hawaii, wearing
a grass skirt and swaying her hips.

Brigitte, camera-woman and director, doesn't show murder
directly on screen. Yet I know I've attempted it. There's my
three-year-old brother Andy at Bernard's wedding, strutting
with a thick bandage on his hand and arm. Every year, as we
watch this film, the grown-ups coo: 'poor Andy, however did it
happen?' I tremble in the darkness, waiting for Andy to
denounce me. Every year, all through my childhood and
adolescence. I know I tried to kill Andy. I pushed him over in
the cellar, wanting him to die, and he slashed his hand on
broken glass. Why doesn't he speak? What's he waiting for?
Finally, aged twenty-seven, I ask him: 'didn't I try to kill you
when you were three?' Surprised, he replies: 'you weren't anywhere near me, I fell over all by myself.'

After the age of ten, after the the onset of menstruation,
breasts, frizzy hair and spots, I appear less on film; I flee the

camera. Sometimes it catches me, scuttling rapidly across the lawn, squinting into the sun at the back of a family group. Who is this hideously embarrassed girl with plump knees under her unflattering brown shift dress with a gilt belt, frowning, ugly? I remember how much she hated herself, her rounded body and shiny childish face. I remember how desperately she yearned to be pretty and confident. She leaves fleeting traces: an elbow, a snub nose. She hides. Smiling bravely. Pleading: please don't look at me. I look at myself aged five, aged fifteen, aged twenty, and feel so protective of that clumsy surface I put up to shield myself from the gaze of others. All through my childhood and adolescence I draw obsessively: pictures of lovely naked women. I still do; but now they are allowed to have big swinging breasts, curving thighs, genitals, furry triangles of hair.

CREME

Cream. A staple in our diet. The cream here is very thick, slightly yellowish, slightly salty. Fresh. You can't find cream like this anywhere in England. We eat it poured over beans, over cod, over artichokes, over potatoes. It is unbelievably delicious.

The milk, which we fetch from the farm down the road every morning, has to be boiled before it is fit for drinking. Grandmère skims off the cream, which rises to the surface as a thick skin, and keeps it in a glass bowl in the fridge. After a week or so, there is enough cream for her to make her special cake *gateau à la peau de lait*, a sort of rough rich sponge with a golden crust. We eat it for supper, with home-made pear conserve.

CRIQUETOT L'ESNEVAL

Criquetot L'Esneval. The name of the village where the family lives. Not just a geographical place: a place in the heart, in the psyche. My mother's home. The past. A way of life. A system of values. A group of people we refer to with respect and love.

The village straddles main roads that led to Fécamp, to Goderville, to Le Havre, to Etretat. Around its outskirts lie the farms, straggles of old cottages. Its centre is simple, and small. The main street contains a few shops, the post-office, the blacksmiths where the horses are shod, a bar we never go into, and the imposing neo-classical front of the *Mairie* with its double stone staircase which we dare each other to run up and down. The *place* behind has the back of the *Mairie* on one side, shops on the others. The haberdasher's, run by an ancient mademoiselle in velvet neckbands. The ironmonger's, full of radiant silver buckets, tools, pottery. Madame Le Fevre's dim, cool grocery smelling of ripe melons to which we come with our stoppered glass jar to have it filled with fresh cream from the great vat in her cupboard. On Tuesdays the fish-woman sets her baskets outside, and we have mussels for lunch.

The church is just beyond the *place*, with a smelly men's lavatory, screened by corrugated iron, attached to its backside. A huge church, dark, with cold stone floors, smelling of incense, set with statutes of saints and stained-glass windows whose images I know off by heart. After High Mass has ended, every-one collects outside in groups, talking, exchanging news. Certain families we shake hands with. Others we don't. Everybody knows who everybody else is: the 'good' families, the farmers of 'good' family, the farmworkers and farmers lower down the social scale. A red face and hands, a raw best blue suit, mark a man off from a lady in pleated silk. Then we go to the *patisserie* to buy *galette* for a late breakfast, cakes for lunch. Grandpère likes *babas au rhum*. When I choose *réligieuse*, a double round *eclair* with brown icing decorated with little tongues of cream, Grand-père says solemnly: 'you see the nun? Those flames on her mean she is burning in hell.' He stands up all through Mass; he doesn't kneel. I understand this: the boss of the household doesn't need to kneel in church. Tall and severe in his grey suit, he's more formidable than M. le Doyen, the parish priest. When I faint at Holy Communion, weakened by the obligatory fasting from midnight, by the long hours of kneeling and standing in the stuffy church, Grandpère picks me up and carries me out. I'm so ashamed of myself, so humiliated (my sister tells me: your knickers were showing), and Grandpère teases me to cheer me up. '*Tu es tombée dans les pommes*' he explains: 'you have fallen in the apples.'

The village is not beautiful, does not feature in tourist brochures. This is of supreme unimportance, because it's the place where Grandpère and Grandmère and Brigitte live, the place we live in during the long summer holidays. We don't look for beauty in such a place. It is familiar, familial, ordinary, interesting. It is France, *tout court*. Not abroad. Home. The village is the people who live and work in it, whom we know, whose houses we visit.

Our house is a little way out of the village, on the Fécamp road, standing on a high grassy bank that Brigitte has tamed and sown with flowers. Blue and pink hydrangeas rear in front, redcurrant bushes along the wall at the side. The shutters are dark green. Geraniums are everywhere: spilling out of the window-boxes and out of the old wooden sabots hung on either side of the front door. The kitchen leans at one side. Three small windows in the roof.

The village changes, ancient cottages come down, replaced by concrete villas. An old people's home is built. The roads are widened, the verges lopped. Some of the ancient walled kitchen-gardens, with their rows of lettuces and sweet peas and gladioli and cabbages, are replaced by little plantations of hideous orna-mental cypresses, stifling open displays of gravel, regimented beds of scarlet begonias, fences of looped chains. The village looks more like a suburb now. Tidier. Cleaner. Of course this means a higher standard of living, but, sentimentally, I miss the old ramshackle charm, the miraculous shrine on one of the back roads heaped with babies' shoes, the women sitting outside their little houses at sunset shelling peas together, the village pump from which we fetched water when our well ran dry, the ancient half-timbered tenement leaning against the church in which a dirty old woman lived. This proves how much of a tourist I've become, how I seek for the picturesque, how I don't live there any more.

'*Nous n'irons plus au bois,*
Les lauriers sont coupés –'
When Grandpère and Brigitte die, when the house is sold, as I suppose it will have to be, Criquetot will be a different place. We shall be totally absent from it, and its life will flow on without us. I know few of the village families now. I used to say hello to everyone I met. Now I'm a stranger there, met not with welcome but with indifference. My mother, who visits her father and sister

several times a year, as often as she can afford on her earnings as a part-time teacher of evening classes (she's over sixty, can't teach in schools any more), still knows quite a few of the village people. She urges them, when she meets them in the butcher's or the baker's, to come and visit Grandpère, who is so lonely. But few of them do.

FRANCAIS

French. The French language. My mother's tongue. My mother-tongue, that I take in along with her milk. The language of my childhood in France (the language of my childhood in England is another matter). My tongue lapping at pleasure. Hearing French spoken suddenly, in the street in London, or on top of a bus, makes me tingle with that pleasure all over again. The French I speak today is a ragbag of influences: the correct politenesses of the rituals of daily family life; the phrasing and archaisms of the novels by Gide and Mauriac I read as an adolescent; the utterances of relatives; the slang words taught me by my young cousins.

Bits of French buzz out of books of poems, and stick on me. *Douce mélancolie et harmonie du soir. Mais priez Dieu que tous nous veuille absoudre. Homme libre, toujours tu chériras la mer. De la musique avant toute chose. Poète, prends ton luth. Rappelle-toi, Barbara.*

We pray in French at Mass. *Je vous salue, Marie, pleine de grace.* Religion feels different in French, a light elegant flavour like a soufflé in our mouths. *Le matin dans la clarté/Le Christ est ressucité.*

We sing French songs as we tramp along the roads on our walks. *Au clair de la lune, mon ami Pierrot, prête-moi ta plume pour ecrire un mot.* We sing rounds, too, the four children, my aunt keeping time. *Mordis sois-tu, carilloneur, que Dieu créa pour mon malheur.*

Ma petite poison, croons a neighbour to her baby: *ma petite poison.*

GLOSSAIRE

Glossary. According to the Shorter Oxford English Dictionary:

'a list with explanations of abstruse, antiquated, dialectal, or technical terms; a partial dictionary.'

To gloss: to explain away; to read a different sense into; to veil in specious language; to render bright and glossy.

GRANDMÈRE

Grandmother. Grandmère's name is Michelene. Mum and Brigitte and Grandpère call her Maman. Dad calls her Mère.

I do not know her well. Her thoughts and feelings remain remote to me when I'm a child. She's busy running the house, living her social life as one of the ladies of the village. Her power is gently expressed, but you feel it: the house is her domain. She's not cuddly and affectionate like my English grandmother. I can see that her husband and daughters love her tenderly, but I don't get close enough to her to do so. She belongs to Brigitte, anyway. Brigitte is the one who goes into her room to talk to her, when she's having breakfast, or resting. We see her mainly at meals, which are a formal and collective affair. She's gently humorous in the face of Brigitte's possessiveness. She's sweet. She dresses in soft colours, soft fabrics. She's fragile.

She's often not well. Perhaps that sets her a little apart from the noisy children. One summer, she goes into hospital for a nameless operation. We're not told what's wrong with her. We're taken to visit her, told we must be utterly quiet. We tiptoe along the empty hushed corridors of the clinic, hover in the doorway of her room. Brigitte sits on her bed, holding her hand, love and anger and tears mixed up in her face. We're talking to Mum. Brigitte hushes us crossly: can't we hear that Grandmère is trying to sing *Ma Normandie* for us? We have made too much noise trooping into the hospital; going out, we must be even more like mice. That summer is particularly full of trouble and tension, centred on Grandmère's illness. Brigitte is very upset, and takes it out on Mum and Dad. Nana, our English grandmother, has also come to stay, and to help look after us. Brigitte is jealous of her, and shows it. Nana takes us out blackberrying. The relief, to be out of the house. There are too many of us. We take up too much space.

When she's well, Grandmère enjoys her rituals. She puts on

her hat, takes her purse and her parasol, and goes into the village to shop, stopping to chat to all the people she knows and to enquire after their families. Or she goes to visit two poor widows: Madame La Flandre and Madame Avisse. She does a lot of good works: visiting, giving money to charity. Sometimes other ladies from the village come to tea, wearing hats, ladies of a certain class. Not the butcher's wife, for example. They sit in the salon, sipping their tea, nibbling little home-made biscuits and cakes. They address each other formally: Madame Caulle; Madame Le Forestier; Madame Spriet. To me these visitors are frightful women, so mincing and polite, a female mafia discussing diseases and marriages. I'm a tomboy. I'll never be one of them. I don't know how to attain their heights of femininity. Don't want to. It frightens me.

My mother is not one of them, either, though she sits there with them. Here in this house, I can see Mum as a girl again, sitting talking to her mother, a beautiful sturdy girl with brown shoulders above her cotton sunfrock. Mum lives in a wider world, goes out to work for her living, has travelled, dyes her blowing hair golden blonde, has been to university. Sitting here among these village matrons in their expensive ugly dresses and jackets, she simply doesn't fit. I'm suddenly glad we're half English, though I spend half my time in England defending the fact we're half French.

When we come down in the mornings, we kiss Grandmère, once she's up, and she remarks, in what's meant to be a kindly fashion, on how we are looking today. *'Mimi a bonne mine au jour d'hui'* she will say, or: *'Mimi n'est pas bien coiffée.'* I wriggle; labelled, pinned down. One day she remarks how white and ill Margi looks, and my mother whispers: *'ce sont de mauvais jours pour elle.'* This means having a period. Margi also hates having her appearance commented on. We're both of us awkward in our teen-age, and we don't know what we can do about it.

Grandmère suffers increasingly from heart-disease, though this is never discussed in front of us. At mealtimes she takes different coloured pills, swallowed down with a glass of water, and the contents of glass *ampoules* sawn in half by Brigitte with a razor blade. She eats special, different food. She mustn't eat salt. This plump, capable, white-haired person suddenly becomes a chronic invalid, her head poking forward and down, her belly swelling, her whole body thickening. She speaks little.

I leave home in 1967, to go to university. Over the next ten years I visit Criquetot irregularly, infrequently. I don't get to know Grandmère. I still don't know who she is. I don't remember her dying, her death. Grandpère tells us he doesn't want us to come to the funeral, so we stay away.

I think that my grandmother is the house. The storehouse of food and plenty. The cupboards stocked with sheets and table-cloths, tea and dinner services, boxes of silver cutlery and black-handled knives brought out for best occasions. She is still there.

Brigitte says to me in her jealous mourning: 'I think your mother grieved more for Nana's death than for Grandmère's. I think she was closer to Nana.' My mother loved them both. She has a big heart. Plenty of room for both her mothers.

GRANDPÈRE

Grandfather. The maker. The creator, whose capable hands invent surprises for children: a tree-house, a slide, a cart, a giant papier-maché whale, a wigwam. God is a grandfather, a carpenter, who delights in making, from his storehouse of bits and pieces, whatever's needed by the women in the household, by the children.

Grandpère is very tall, and spare, with fierce blue eyes under tufted brows, thick silky white hair, long arms, beautiful hands with long fingers. He is usually busy: carving, sawing, planing, nailing, glueing.

After lunch he sits in his red armchair by the table at the window and packs his pipe with tobacco, pressing it down in the bowl, applying a lighted match from the big Gitanes box, drawing, sucking. We bring him Three Nuns from England. He keeps his tobacco in a wooden box with a roll top, like a desk, and his instruments for cleaning his pipe, one silvery and spike-tipped, one like a thin spoon laid out on a big square ashtray. The table is covered with his copies of the *Journal de Criquetot*, and the copy of *Le Figaro* that the pharmacist leaves for him every morning on the windowsill. (The pharmacist's wife, by the ʹay, is so thrifty that she sews little patches onto the borders of the sheets to save them being worn away by her husband's bristly chin overnight.)

Upstairs is Grandpère's study, hung with old maps and charts of the port of Le Havre where he has spent most of his working life as an engineer. Here he writes his articles on local history, archaeology, topography, folklore. Also his short autobiography, which he entitles *Souvenirs d'enfance*. At one time we try to get it published. Without success. So it circulates just among the members of the family.

Grandpère eats his breakfast in the kitchen; usually before the rest of us are up. Big cup of *café au lait* into which he dunks his bread; crumbs swept neatly off the oilcloth patterned with wreaths of flowers. The tiles on the floor, designed in the 1930s, are scrolled with blue and yellow. The cat, Chouchou the Fourth, sits here, waiting for a snack.

After my breakfast I go to the lavatory upstairs. The windows, with their attached muslin-frilled curtains, have been flung wide to the view of sky and trees and fields, and the whole room smells deliciously of Grandpère: *eau de cologne* and pipe tobacco and shit. Any one of these smells, anywhere in the world, brings him back to me immediately. Now that he's had the heart attack and strokes, he can't climb the stairs any more. His little dressing-room, opening off his bedroom on the ground floor, has been turned into a bathroom for him. This is the place to which we come with our cut and bleeding knees to have iodine put on by Grandmère. We are proud of the red stain on our skin: a decoration to be flaunted, bizarre as a tattoo. Grandmère's bed is still here, under the window. Piled with cushions, it acts as sofa. How chilly, how chastely tidy, how spotless this room is, with its grey marble fireplace, its gold-framed oil paintings, its little buttoned and frilled armchair, its carved cupboard, its *jardinière* of ferns and aspidistra. Grandmère's no longer in it, but it's still her room.

Grandpère is a patriarch. The absolute head of the family. The law-maker. The judge. Lunch must be on the table at one o'clock sharp. The tall clock in the corner chimes out the time, and one of us beats the gong in the hall. During these summer holidays we eat in the glass verandah, floored with speckled yellow tiles, at the back of the house. Children must eat neatly, speak only when addressed, never fidget or giggle. We three girls, trading good behaviour for love and approval, help serve and clear away the meal, trained by my aunt how to take away the dirty plates from the left and offer the clean one from the right. We while away the interminable interval before we can run out into the garden by moulding our bread into greyish pellets and figurines, day-dreaming, whispering. My brother lacks these sensible tactics, draws attention to himself by talking too loudly, complaining of boredom, answering back. Once he is shut in the coal cellar for three hours.

Nor does my father fare much better. The conversation at table is only in French, rapid and collective talk which Dad can't follow, though we can. The others have little patience with his slowness, and don't hide this. Nor do they approve of his eager gulping of soup (it's all right for Grandpère to make a noise drinking his), his liking for butter on bread, his quick swallowing of wine, his laying the table with the spoons facing the wrong way round. Dad does the washing-up after meals while we dry and put away. My aunt comes round afterwards to check he's done it properly, inspecting the porcelain sink for drip marks, the interiors of saucepans for traces of grease. Pouncing with a triumphant cry when she discovers a smear.

Dad's an Englishman. An outsider. Not one of the Caulle family. He tries so hard, making laborious French conversation with Grandpère about all the things he knows will interest him, being kind and polite to Grandmère, teasing and complimenting Brigitte on her looks, her clothes, her cooking. He can't realise how we ache in sympathy for him, that we feel his hurt; for we can't let him know that we have witnessed his humiliation, that we squirm for him, how much we pray that this lunch-time everything will go well, that there will be no trouble, no *sotto voce* remarks in French by my aunt on his awkwardness, on his manners, that he won't challenge Grandpère too openly on the latter's opinions of the trade unions, the youth of today, the English.

Grandpère praises me for the drawings I do. He scolds me harshly for daring to appear at the lunch table with mascara on my eyelashes, and I run out of the room crying. When my first novel comes out, he reads it. Part of it is set in Normandy, and he's delighted to be able to point out the details I've got wrong. *'Eh bien, ma fille,* he growls: 'the labourers did it *this* way, the hay-making.' And he gives me a proper explanation. The heroine of the novel is a lesbian. In Grandpère's eyes I am now a woman of experience, and so, anti-clerical, he treats me to some of his scandalous stories about priests preaching in the pulpit with piss-pots hidden under their robes. He pours me wine, no longer mixing it with water: *'tu es une fille sérieuse.'*

Arthritis strikes. Grandpère can't move much. He hauls himself about on sticks.

Brigitte and I decide to take him for an outing in the car. I suggest visiting André Gide's grave, which is just up the road at Cuverville. All the way there, Grandpère, dresed in his navy beret, tweed jacket, blue jersey and blue and white striped shirt, grips his stick in one hand and waves the other in the air.

'André Gide! Mais c'était un salaud! Un salaud!'

'Pourquoi, Grandpère?'

'Il était responsable, lui, ce salaud, pour des millions de jeunes suicidés, je te le dis –'

On the way back, we go to lay a fresh bouquet on Grandmère's grave in the village cemetery, the square walled place thick with crosses which we can see from the bathroom window. Brigitte and I fill a plastic watering can from the tap in the corner, top up the vases on the grave, arrange the flowers we have brought. Grandpère waits for us in the car.

When I leave, to go back to London, Grandpère presses a hundred and fifty francs into my hand.

He bursts into tears.

'Ça peut être la dernière fois. Je ne sais pas si je te verrai encore.'

The steamroller stroke flattens and thins him, and the strong heart he rides on kicks and bucks, throwing him. Now he is the king of a small country: the red armchair. Beyond it, the household clicks and revolves, and he frets, not knowing what is going on.

His blue eyes are still fierce. His white hair is still silky and thick. Now it falls in long waves around his face, giving him the look of a beautiful old child.

He has learned to talk again. Sometimes his mouth stops and

works, and the sound won't come, and he clenches his hands on the arms of his chair. I place my chair close to his, so that I can lip-read as well as listen.

Above his blue jersey his face is the same, and yet not the same. Is that because of age, and illness? Or because I am not frightened of him anymore?

He looks back, with tears.

'J'ai fait si peu de ma vie.'

He weeps, his brown mottled hand placed trembling over his eyes.

'Tout est fini.'

He presses his handkerchief to his eyes. When he removes it there is still water shining in the brown creases of his skin.

'Je n'ai pas le courage de viellir.'

I take his hand in mine.

He gestures at the green glass beer bottle on the table beside his chair.

'Une chose qui a été faite doit pas etre jetée.'

Now we're both crying. Brigitte's sharp ears are on the alert: she bustles in from the kitchen, angry at me for letting Grand-père get upset.

'What's going on here? What's going on?'

The only way she can cope with looking after Grandpère singlehanded as well as working at her job in Le Havre is to be busy, practical, efficient. Grandpère needs to talk and to be listened to, and she hasn't got time. He has quarrelled with most of the people in the village over the last few years, and so he has practically no visitors.

'You can't imagine how terrible it is' she tells me: 'sitting here at night, when Grandpère's depressed and irritable. I'm so alone. I'm so lonely.'

Lunchtime. Brigitte hauls Grandpère from his chair. His tall stooped body totters. His long legs look as though they will collapse. She supports him. He leans on her, and holds onto a small wooden chair. He creeps across the carpet to the dining table, lowers himself slowly and heavily into his chair, in Grand-mère's old place.

'Don't watch him eat' Brigitte has warned me: 'he can't bear people knowing that he needs help with his food.'

His spoon wobbles its way to his lips. Brigitte cuts up his bread for him. He spills his soup. He insists on his big white napkin being fastened to the front of his blue jersey by two large wooden clothes-pegs, waving away the two tiny plastic ones Brigitte offers him as an alternative. He spreads the other end on the tablecloth, and watches his soup-plate being set down on it again.

'*Tu vois*' he tells me: '*je ne peux rien faire pour moi-même.*'

Tears of anger spill down his face. He is distraught by his weeping, and cries more. I start to tease him and to crack jokes, and he cheers up a little.

At the end of the meal he instructs Brigitte to fetch a bottle of champagne. He watches her critically as she opens the door of the *bontière*, sets tall crystal *flutes* on a silver tray, brings them back to the table, uncorks the bottle, pours foaming champagne into each glass. The ritual must be performed, as it always has been, in exactly the right way, with dignity, with delicacy and grace.

He holds his glass in his trembling hand. He toasts me. He welcomes me to his house.

Brigitte joins me in the kitchen after she has settled him back in his chair, and we do the washing-up. I remember where everything goes: the enamelled yellow saucepans onto their rack over the humming fridge, the bread into the bottom drawer, the plates onto their shelves in the cupboard on the wall by the window. I put my arms around Brigitte and hug her, and she hugs me back. Except when we visit, she's got nobody to hug. The other teachers at school are all married, busy with their families, and don't visit her.

Going back into the sitting-room, I see that Grandpère's flies are undone, and that the covered basket I noticed earlier behind his chair is now on a stool in front of him, a wide-necked plastic bottle poking out from it. I tiptoe through the room so that Grandpère won't know I've seen him.

Grandpère's asleep. Two girls from the village, shrill and cheerful, have arrived to help Brigitte with some sewing. Later the priest will come, bringing Communion, and will stay just five minutes. These are the afternoons I remember so well: the absolute order of the house, the regular breathing, the women sewing and talking, the ticking of the grandfather clock.

On my latest visit, he's tired, subdued. The presence of a full-time nurse, now that Brigitte is no longer strong enough to look after him, seems to have helped him accept his ageing. He doesn't cry. He doesn't rage. He whispers: *'tout est fini.'* He points out the baked salt and flour sculptures that he and the nurse have made together. He teases the nurse at supper for taking only two helpings of pudding. He smiles at me with great sweetness, his blue eyes shining, when I go into his bedroom to wish him goodbye. His skin is very soft. I kiss him gently on both cheeks. He's had his early morning tea. Now, helpless, dignified, propped on white pillows, he's waiting for breakfast. It's still dark outside the closed shutters. He whispers: *'merci d'etre venue. C'était un grand plaisir.'* All night long, the cat's been dancing about the room, worrying a mouse. Grandpère laughs.

GRENIER

Granary. The store-house. The place where things are made. The place where Grandpère works. Where treasures are piled up: home-made shallow boxes of paper, string, nails, pine-cones; jars of brushes, tins of paint; racks of carpentry tools; trays of electrical spare parts; reels of straw and raffia for re-caning the seats of chairs; bottles of varnish and turpentine. The boxes sit on shelves, stacked one above the other, unnamed, closed, mysterious; masked with dust. From the outside, the *grenier* looks quite small. Inside, it is enormous, its far end impenetrable, swallowed in darkness; endless. In my dreams I fumble my way to the end of the *grenier*, to where the oldest memories of the family, the earliest relics, are stored, to where the floor dissolves and I am falling, falling, into a new country that is neither France nor England. Always I wake up too soon. Before I land.

Grandpère's kingdom is high up in the sky, reached by a ladder-like staircase, open slats of wood, a shaky rail. Its outer wall, plastered a creamy yellow, is faced with criss-crosses of timber. Through the open door, as I sit on the top step, I can see Grandpère seated at his wooden work table, mending a broken china cup, amber glue oozing between his fingers onto the blue and white glaze. Looking the other way, I see white clouds and blue sky, wind in the cracks. Below me, the high garden hedge.

cows noisily swallowing grass with a slapping of jaws. White cows for milk, Grandpère explains: brown for tea, and black for coffee. The church bells, swinging in the steeple half a kilometre away across the fields, give the quarter hour in long rolling chimes. Summer can mean lying facedown on my bed sobbing with rage; it can also mean this high windy solitude, the bells dividing the blessedly long and lonely morning, a book in my lap.

Behind the *grenier*, at right angles, is the high bank, set with a close row of towering beeches, that shelters the farm next door. The trunks of the trees are grey-brown, glossy. They turn away the active August wind, shine in the drizzle.

Underneath the *grenier* staircase, between the field hedge and the hedge bounding my grandparents' garden, is a long narrow gap filled up with weeds and rubble: a wilderness where only we children go; one of our secret places. We crouch here, draw the greenery over our heads, confident of being unseen by the adults, and become archaeologists, turning up shards of pottery, bones, bits of painted tile. Or we scoop at the damp earth with our hands and make clay pots and dishes which we decorate with violets stuck about the clumsy rims. A favourite aunt, invited to enter our hiding-place and inspect our art-works gives them a cursory glance and suggests smashing them as it is teatime.

Below the *grenier* is the coal cellar, and, next door, the wine cellar, cool dim apartment with an earth floor, no windows, and a wooden door locked with a great iron key. Sent from the kitchen to fetch two bottles of cider for Sunday lunch, I come down the narrow path skirting the lawn, stepping past the curly fronds of fern that reach from the flowerbeds, loaded with dew, to pick at my red cotton dress, parting the bushes that lean together at the entrance to the tiny courtyard. To my left the *grenier* steps; ahead of me the two cellar doors: to my right the door of the shed in which Grandpère stores lumber, his old bicycle, the slide and the papier-maché whale he has made for us; and the door of the disused lavatory. We are not supposed to go in here but we do: another hiding-place. We lift up the wooden lid from the plank-like seat, and peer into the black hole smelling of ancient shit. Now I enter the dark wine-cellar, propping open the door to let in a shaft of light; scent of earth, mustiness, dust. I pick out two unlabelled green glass bottles from the iron rack on the side wall, bear them back to the house where I wipe off their film of cobwebs with a cloth and set them, uncorked, in the big fireplace in the *salon*.

The *salon* bears witness to Grandpère's ingenuity, to his use of carpentry tools kept in the *grenier*. It used to be two separate rooms. During the Occupation, the *sales Boches* inform the family that since they have two downstairs rooms, they will have to have a German officer billeted on them. Overnight, with the help of friends, Grandpère knocks the two rooms into one, buiding a wooden arch between them. When the Germans arrive in the morning, they see that they have made a mistake. The officer lodges in one of the upstairs rooms. That's not quite so bad.

A mossy old statue, with the blurred features of a dancing goddess or nymph, used to lean against the cellar wall underneath the *grenier*. It vanished long ago. I don't know what happened to it.

LINGERIE

Linen-room. The first floor of the house, originally attics, is converted by Grandpère into bedrooms, bathroom, study, when he moves the family there from the little house in the middle of the docks at Le Havre. The staircase, narrow and steep, twists up abruptly from the little hall into a tiny landing. Back across the top of the stairs, over a little bridge, is my aunt's room, with the one my parents occupy next to it. Opposite are Grandpère's study, in which my brother Andy sleeps during the summer holidays, and the bathroom. The corridor bends away from here, just wide enough to let a body through, and turns a corner. At the end of this passage is what used to be the maid's tiny room, where my elder sister Jackie sleeps, and then finally the *lingerie*.

In summer, two little beds are set up here for my twin sister Margi and me. The rest of the year, this is the place where the ironing is done. The ironing table is covered with a thick grey blanket, a white sheet laid on top. The bulky iron sits in a steel cradle. Scorch marks, like rings of damp, on the white cloth. The smell of cotton and linen, dried outside in the sun and air, and the hot smell of ironing. White shirts sway on hangers. Sheets drop from a line suspended from the ceiling, white wings.

The magic room under the roof, that changes into our bedroom. Twin cotton bedspreads in faded paisley, pleasing worn red and yellow, a faint design. The roof slopes sharply down under the eaves, a window set in it, screened against mosquitoes. Between Margi's bed and the wall run cupboards built by Grandpère that house boxes of sewing material and old magazines. The wall alongside my bed, panelled in plywood, bears shelves of books: Mum's old schoolbooks, old exercise books. Grey or red cloth covers; strange typefaces cramped on the yellowing glossy pages. We find her adolescence here, her pencilled notes, her underlined words. Texts we cannot understand: Latin, Greek, chemistry, maths. My mother aged sixteen, seventeen. Long before we came into existence she had a life of her own. We finger the books.

The light-switch for the landing and corridor is just outside our room. The inevitable terror of coming upstairs in the dark draws nearer all day long. Up the black well of the stairs, feet finding the way across the landing, then down the blind inkiness of the passage to our bedroom. Something lurks there, waiting for me. Press down on the china switch. Next terror to be negotiated: the large furry moths, with fat barrel bodies and clattering whirring wings, that beat from wall to wall and bang against the lightbulb. In those days I have no pity for trapped moths: I shout for my father to kill them. One night, just as we're falling asleep, there is a sudden whining, buzzing, metallic thumping. A moth we thought dead has resurrected itself and is screaming with pain in moth-language. Going to the lavatory in the middle of the night: I put it off as long as possible. The stairs are dark and invisible, and a white headless ghost runs up and down them, waiting for me. Back in bed, I stare at the huge wardrobe. Moonlight glimmers in the mirror on its door in strange shapes. The elaborate carved knot decorating its top changes into a hideous face that grimaces at me, teeth bared.

The mornings deliver me, with light and sun. In the afternoons I come up here, in the interval between the end of lunch and the time for going to the beach, when the women are sewing in the verandah and Grandpère and Dad are dozing, and I read and read. Reading means privacy, solitude, a room of my own, a world away from the family. I re-connect with my mother, aged sixteen, studying her chemistry textbook. Free time, time of my own. The need for this takes root here, in the *lingerie*.

MAISON DANS L'ARBRE

Tree-house. Grandpère builds us the tree-house, in the branches of the old apple tree at the foot of the garden in front of the *grenier*. A ladder leads up to our high fenced platform. We lounge here, all summer through. Our hideaway, which the grown-ups are not allowed to enter unless we invite them. Rows of dolls. Books. Dreams. Picnic lunches.

The apple tree grows diseased, and eventually has to be cut down. From its wood, Grandpère makes each of us four children a three-legged milking-stool as a souvenir.

MOISSON

Harvest. *La fête de la moisson*, the harvest festival, is held in late August. For many years I don't realise that it's not an official Catholic feast like Christmas and Easter. It follows so logically upon them. It is their culmination.

The church is decorated with great swags and bouquets of braided golden corn, cornucopias of fruit and vegetables. The farmers are praised, their produce blessed. We all give thanks.

One year our celebration supper is held in the glass conservatory at the back of the Spriets' house, a great table, covered in white, stretching from end to end, and the talking and feasting going on underneath the great vine growing along the ceiling dangling bunches of purple grapes. Afterwards, there are fireworks in the courtyard outside, and dancing. Coloured Japanese lanterns sway in the trees, piercing the thick darkness. The young men treat us girls as adults, taking us in their arms and waltzing us away, giddy, drunk on pleasure.

NOCES

Wedding. Bernard, Mum's brother, is marrying Anne-Marie Spriet. One of the great events of these years. Better than the

Coronation of Queen Elizabeth, because it's local and we can join in.

Ten bridesmaids follow the bride in pairs, graded from tiny to quite big. Our hand-sewn dresses stick out like lampshades, white frilled tiers, and have small neat collars and puffed sleeves. We wear white net gloves and clutch our partners' hands. We've been told we mustn't let go. We carry little hooped baskets of white straw, which we use for taking the collection during Mass. One girls spills hers right across the floor. Also we wear narrow silver bracelets, the gift of the bridegroom. Anne-Marie's dress is white too, long and plain with a little collar and buttons down the front. Her long veil, streaming away from her small round flat head-dress perched on her chestnut hair like a nurse's cap, is spread out between the ten bridesmaids and carried by us. Margi and I are five. We concentrate. Jackie is seven, more capable. Anne-Marie leans on her father's arm; he is wearing tails, a black bow-tie, a stiff shirt, a pointed collar. Madame Spriet, although it is only morning, is in full evening dress and furs. Bernard wears a double-breasted suit, and has gone into the church ahead of us. We stumble after Anne-Marie, gripping her long gauze tail. The black mouth of the church swallows her up, and then us.

My brother Andy, aged three, is an onlooker, like Dad. But he too, like the bride, is an object of interest, for his arm is bound up in a great bandage after he has fallen over and cut his hand open. The doctor has mended it with a metal clip.

All the guests stand talking and laughing on the great lawn, with low spreading cedars at its far end, in front of the Spriets' house. This lawn is where we play croquet, fielding the wooden balls from the long flowerbeds filled with white flowers and silver leaves. Now it's thronged with strangers. Lunch has been laid in the old coach-house. The major-domo, in full evening dress, stands in the doorway, calling out names, in pairs, and the men come forwards with crooked arms, to take the ladies in.

Gaiety. Dancing. The adults transformed from parents and relatives into relaxed playful young men and women. Mum looks beautiful in a swirly white nylon dress covered in large black spots, black high-heels. Brigitte wears red, sleeveless and figure-hugging. Dad's a boy, throwing Andy up and down in his arms, smiling. Grandmère is elegant and gracious, a fine lady. Grandpère is very tall, very handsome, in his dress-suit, his figure tall and erect, his white head towering. We bridesmaids, released from standing still and being good, tuck up our stiff skirts and race about, shrieking. Bernard and Anne-Marie, our former playmates and companions, have walked a little away from us, into a different place. They're more like the grown-ups now. We are celebrating this change. Very soon after, it seems to me, they are showing us their first baby, smothered in lace and wool wrappings in the height of summer, squalling and cross. To me it's as though they've been given a doll as a present. As a reward.

NOCES DE DIAMANT

Diamond wedding. My grandparents have been married for sixty years. There is a special Mass in the village church, attended by all the family (children, grandchildren, great-grandchildren, plus many other relatives) and friends, and many of the village families. My grandparents have special red velvet armchairs and *prie-dieux* set for them in the aisle. M. le Doyen praises them, their example, in his sermon. He speaks of their lives here in Criquetot, and the lives of their children. He praises Brigitte for giving up so much in order to care for them.

Back at the house, the immediate family attends the *vin d'honneur*. Grandmère is very frail now, and can't cope with too many people. We toast her and Grandpère in champagne. Kisses and laughter and tears.

Lunch is at Charles and Monique Spriet's house. Charles' two unmarried sisters, Lou and Geneviève, live in the big house now. The Spriet parents are dead. Charles and Monique have restored an old half-timbered farmhouse in the grounds, and live there with their four children. There are thirty or so of us sitting around the table: family, old friends, the priest. At each place is a little gold sabot filled with gold flowers: symbol of my grandparents' house, which is called *La Sabotière*. We have printed menus. Two waitresses, in black frocks and tiny white aprons, serve us with salmon and roast lamb. Starched white tablecloth. Four different wine-glasses at each place. Terrific noise of laughter and talking. This lunch is the real Mass: the celebration of this community of relatives, of the bond between us. I'm part of this huge, enduring, passionate family; yet my life in London also makes me an outsider. I'm so glad to be back amongst them all, yet I'll take flight as soon as this festival is over. I sit down at the end of the table, my back to the enormous rustic fireplace, and watch them all.

Lunch goes on for most of the afternoon. Bernard, as the son of the house, makes a long speech, and we all drink a toast in champagne. Mum, I'm pleased to see, also makes a speech. Flown on wine and Calvados, I stand on my chair and recite a poem by Baudelaire: *'Mon enfant, ma soeur, songe a la douceur/ d'aller là-bas vivre ensemble/ . . . Là, tout n'est qu'ordre et beauté/luxe, calme, et volupté.'* Grandmère, stricken by her last illness, has made an enormous effort to gather the strength necessary to be present at this day. She sings to us, in a tiny quavering voice. It is her farewell to us. This diamond wedding feast is our farewell to her. She dies soon afterwards.

PAIN BENIE DES HOMMES

The men's blessed bread: a sort of *brioche*, yeast dough made with butter and eggs. The feast of the *pain bénie des hommes* falls in the summer, between the Assumption and *la fête de la moisson*. The men of the village go up to the altar rails during Mass and receive this special bread, which they bring away in their hands. I wonder why the women don't receive it too. We're allowed to eat Grandpère's share, when he brings it home. Yellow, spongy, salty. A big piece we tear apart and share. It's all right for us to eat it, because it's not the body of Christ. It's a pagan communion, and we are the priests.

PLAGE

Beach. Almost every afternoon, after the washing-up has been done and the coffee drunk and the women have had their chatting and sewing while the men snooze, we go to the beach, leaving Grandpère and Grandmère behind. We pile into the car, Brigitte in the front passenger seat because she gets car-sick, Mum and the four kids squashed into the back. Usually we go to Etretat, eight kilometres away down the little valley of small rolling golden fields. The road gets narrower; the cliffs start to rise up, and we're there. Etretat is an old-fashioned Edwardian watering-place, with ancient tea-shops and hotels, a covered market, tall red-brick houses faced with fancy designs in white stone, a long wide promenade overlooking the bay with its three dramatic arches of cliff, its old oyster beds, its pebbled beach and wooden beach-huts painted in worn pastel colours. The flag flying from the flagstaff is green, which means it's safe to bathe. We pick our way along the steep hill of round stones, and spread out our things.

We undress under towels, complicated wiggles. We children wear bubbly nylon suits laced at the back with long strings, and rope-soled canvas *espadrilles* to protect our feet. When we come out of the water, the knots in the laces of the *espadrilles* are difficult to untie. Back at home, we put them on the top of the well to dry, and they go hard as cardboard. The water is always icy. We race straight in; it's the only way. First the shriek at the cold shock; then frantic swimming in order to warm up. Usually the waves slap high and lively, and we dart up and down them. Or we hire a *périssoir*, a two-seater canoe, or paddle around in old inner tyres, black and enormous. Sometimes Mum and Brigitte don't swim, but stay on the beach knitting, and I don't understand their carefully coded explanations why. Tea on the beach tastes so good: gritty bright yellow lemonade, lengths of *baguette* with a piece of bitter dark chocolate stuffed down the middle. We lie back on Dad's old army blanket, heads propped on damp towels, feeling the sun's warmth enter our bodies. Or we look for pebbles with holes in, or ones shot through with glittering quartz, or pieces of green glass worn into emeralds. Treasures to bring back in our pockets.

Sometimes we climb up onto the cliffs and go for walks through the dry gorse in the keen salty wind, past the red summerhouses scalloped and fretted with white, the golf-course in the distance. We stand on top of the highest cliff arch, named the *Chambre des Demoiselles*, whence a wicked baron once rolled his brides, one by one, in spiked barrels, down into the sea. Or we explore the far end of the beach where the fishing boats are drawn up and where the fishermen sit mending their nets amid piles of lobster-pots. Some of the old boats have been turned into tiny cafés, with thatched roofs, where you can sit and eat seafood at night and listen to the waves pounding the beach just below while the juice of *moules* runs down your chin. Sometimes, at low tide, we scrabble around on the rocks covered in slippery green weed, poking for crabs, trying to prise off limpets, feet springing on sopping mess. Tunnels lead up from the base of the cliffs here, link up with the gun emplacements higher up. The floor of the cave is ribbed sand, white, damp and hard. We're forbidden to go far in. We might get lost, and never come out.

The beach means freedom from clothes, from most restrictions, from polite behaviour. Freedom to run, climb, swim, roll and yell. Freedom to dance in the water, to glide and float, to lie on the shingle at the water's edge looking up at the steep shelf of the beach while the waves break over me, half-submerged. Freedom to be languid, to dream.

I walk along the beach at low tide, inspecting the debris scattered along the tide-line. A white lace glove. A pipe. A chipped blue enamel serving-dish. An apple core. A yellow novel. An old franc piece. A pleated white terylene skirt. A packet of rough brown lavatory paper. An amethyst and silver rosary.

I must put them into some sort of order. Make a list. The tide's turned, is coming in fast. My aunt's voice on the telephone: 'yes, come and see us again soon. We'll have a good time. Just like in the old days.'

Come back.

Viens.

TRESPASSING

Valerie Miner

Exhausted from four hours of traffic, Monica and Josie almost missed seeing the two doe and their fawn drinking at the pond. The women waited in the car, cautious lest the noise of opening doors disturb the animals. The deer lingered another five minutes and then stepped off gracefully into the wings of sequoias. Last sun settled on the golden hills. Night noises pulsed: Frogs tested their basses. Crickets whittled industriously. Mallards argued. Wind whispered across dry grass. Jays barked from the top of the hill. As the sky grew roses, Monica and Josie watched Jupiter blaze over the Eastern mountains.

They unloaded the Chevy quickly and sloppily, eager for the comfort of the compact wooden cabin they had built with their friends over five summers. Josie opened the gas line outside the house. Monica lit a fire, reflecting on the joys of collective ownership when the rest of the collective was absent. She could hardly believe it – two whole days of privacy and peace.

Suddenly starving, they decided to eat right away. Afterward they would sit in front of the fire and read to each other. Monica chopped salad while Josie made pasta and whistled. The sky got redder and then, abruptly, the cabin was dark. With heavy reluctance, Monica walked around and lit the lanterns.

'Oh,' Monica said.

Josie turned and caught a flick of brown before her, like an insect crashing on a windshield.

'Damn bats,' Monica shook her head and picked up a broom.

'Bats!' Josie screamed. 'I thought Iris got rid of those gruesome things last month.'

'Must still be some holes in the sun porch,' Monica shook her head.

A dark object dropped beside Josie, like a small turd falling, from the eaves. It disappeared. She worried the wooden spoon through the pasta, watching another tiny brown mass cut its fall in mid-air and swoop across the room. It was too much.

'Bats!' Josie ran outside. She felt safer in the dark.

Monica stayed in the house, sweeping bats out the windows and back door.

Staring up at the stars, so benign in their distance, Josie considered vast differences between Monica and herself. Rational, taciturn Monica was probably calculating the increasing velocity of wing movement as the bats ignited to wakefulness. Josie, herself, still cringed at Grandma's tales about bats nesting in little girls' hair. And, raised as she was in a Catholic tradition where intentionality was more important than action, where danger didn't exist if one closed one's imagination to it, Josie was given to the substitution of 'good thoughts'. Like how she and Monica met. It was a miracle if you thought about it; *who* would have expected romance at the faculty xerox machine? But there was Monica copying quark diagrams for her Physics 100 students while Josie waited to xerox a new translation of 'La Cigale et La Fourmi'. If Monica hadn't run out of toner, they might never have started talking.

'All clear,' Monica called. There was no disdain in her voice for she had always envied Josie's ability to show fear. She should tell Josie this.

Josie craned her neck and stared at the sky. 'Glorious night,' she called back. 'Wanna see?'

Monica ducked out the front door and ran through the pungent pennyroyal to her friend. Josie took her hand. Together they stood quietly until they could hear the frogs and the crickets once more.

*   *   *

They slept late and spent the next morning eating eggs and fried potatoes and rye toast. Josie noticed some wasps dancing around the table, so they cleaned up and went outside to lie on the warm deck.

Later they spent an hour putting moulding around the edges of the glass door to the sun porch, sealing the house seams against nocturnal trespassers.

At noon the women drove five miles to town for forgotten

country necessities – ice, water and an extra flashlight. Josie secretively checked the shelves for bat killer, but she didn't find any and she knew Monica wouldn't approve.

Monica, now completely restored by the country air, bounded into the house with a bag of groceries.

Josie moved the Chevy into the shade of an oak tree which was being gradually occupied by Spanish moss. As she locked up the car, she saw a fat man with a rifle, waddling out of the forest. He wore a yellow cap, a striped t-shirt and bluejeans.

He looked like a bumblebee, she thought. Then she warned herself to get serious. A shiver ran along her collarbone. The land was clearly posted, 'No Trespassing. No Hunting'. She wondered if he were, perhaps, a dyke hunter. They were half-a-mile from the road here. It could be weeks before anyone investigated.

Josie decided to be friendly and waved.

'Hello there,' he was winded, hustling to meet her.

Josie closed her eyes and hoped Monica would stay in the house until it was all over.

'I got lost,' he said, nodding his whole body, 'how do you get back to the road?'

'That way,' Josie tried to calm herself. If she didn't watch out, she'd start speaking French as she did in tense moments and then no telling what he would do. 'Up the road there.'

He looked her over. 'You got any water? A glass of water? I been walking for hours.'

Biblical tales filled her head. The Woman at the Well. The Wedding at Cana. The Good Samaritan. 'Sure,' she said as noncommittally as possible. 'I'll be right back.'

'Who's that?' Monica greeted her.

Josie tried to be calm. 'Water man. I mean, a lost man who needs water.' She watched Monica's jaw stiffen. 'Now let me handle it. He just wants a glass of water and then he'll be on his way.' Josie poured water from a plastic jug into an old jam jar they used as a glass.

'Water, my foot, what is he doing on the land? It's posted "No Trespassing", for godsake.'

'Listen, Monica, he was hunting and . . .'

Monica took the glass and poured half the water back into the jug. 'Don't *spoil* him. He'll only return.'

She stalked out to the man, who was leaning on their car, his gun on the ground. Josie stood at the door and watched.

'Thanks, Mam,' he reached for the water.

'No shooting on this land,' Monica said and released the glass.

'Sorry, mam. I was hunting up there on the North Ridge and I hit a buck. But he got away. I followed, to make sure I got him good. Then I got lost and I guess I wound up here.'

'Guess so,' Monica said. She held her hand against her leg to stop it from shaking.

'I'll be off your land soon's I finish the water,' he promised.

'That's right,' she kept her voice even.

'But I'll need to be coming back to get the buck. See, I finally did get him. But since I was lost, I couldn't drag him all over tarnation.'

'We don't want a dead buck on the land,' Monica conceded. 'When're you coming?'

'Tomorrow morning?' he asked. 'About 8:00?'

'Fine, and no guns,' she said.

'No mam, no guns.'

'Right then,' she held her hand out for the jam jar. 'Road's that way.'

'Yes, mam.'

Monica watched him climb the hill and walked back to the house shaking her head. Josie reached to hug her, but Monica pulled away. 'God damned hunter.' She was on the edge of tears.

'How about some coffee or lunch?'

'Naw, are you nuts, after all we ate this morning? No, I think I'll just go for a walk. See if I can find the buck. If there *is* a buck.'

Josie nodded. 'Want company?' She wasn't keen on viewing a dead deer, but she didn't care to admit being afraid to stay in the house alone, not after her melodramatic performance with the bats last night.

'Sure,' Monica was grateful. 'Let's go.'

Josie locked the ice chest and dropped the jam jar in the brown paper garbage bag on the way out.

It was hotter now, about 85°. The pennyroyal smelled mintier than last night. The day was dry and still – yellow grass, golden hills scumbled against teal sky. A turkey vulture glided above the oak grove. As they walked around the pond, they could hear frogs scholop into the water. Monica stopped to inspect the eucalyptus trees they had planted in the spring. Four out of five still alive, not bad. Further along, a salamander skittered across their path. Josie felt cool even before she entered the woods. In a way, she hoped they wouldn't find the buck. But if there was no buck, who knows what the bumblebee man really wanted?

The woods were thick with madrone and manzanita and poison oak. It was always that way on the land, Monica thought, pleasure and danger.

Josie wished she had worn sneakers instead of sandals. But Monica didn't seem to be bothered about her feet as she marched ahead. Right, Josie reminded herself, this wasn't a ramble. They continued in silence for half-an-hour.

'Round here, I guess,' called Monica, who was now several yards ahead. 'See the way branches have been broken. Yes, here. Oh, my god, it's still alive. Stupid, damn hunter.'

They stared at the huge animal, its left front leg broken in a fall, panting and sweating, blind fear in its wide eyes.

'I told Myla we should keep a gun at the big house,' Monica cried. 'What are we going to do?'

Josie didn't think about it. She probably wouldn't have been able to lift the boulder if she had thought about it. But she heard herself shouting to Monica, 'Stand back,' and watched herself drop the big rock on the buck's head. They heard a gurgling and saw a muscle ripple along the animal's belly. Then nothing. There was nothing alive under the boulder.

Josie stared at the four bullet wounds scattered up the right side of the buck. The animal's blood was a dark, cinnamon colour. She noticed sweat along the hip joints.

Monica walked over to her quietly and took her hand. 'Good, brave,' she stuttered awkwardly. 'That was good, Josie.'

'Yeah, it seemed the right thing. But I must admit I didn't think about it.'

Monica hugged Josie and gently drew her away from the dead buck and broken bush.

They walked straight out to the trail. Neither one seemed to want to stay in the woods for their customary ramble. Monica watched her friend closely, waiting for the explosion. This silence was so unlike Josie. Soon, soon, she would erupt with anger and aggravation and guilt and a long examination of what she had done in the woods. For her own part, Monica could only think of one word. Brave.

'Let's go swimming,' Josie said, trying to focus on the trail. 'It'll cool us off.'

The two women stripped on the makeshift dock and lay in the sun beside each other. Monica was slim, her legs long and shapely. She had never bothered much about her body. It had always served her well. She never seemed to be too thin or too plump. Josie, in contrast, fretted about her zoftig breasts and hips. Her skin was pinker than Monica's, a faint pink. Monica curled up beside Josie, her legs across Josie's legs, her head on Josie's shoulder.

Josie closed her eyes and told herself it was over. They were all right. She had never killed anything before and she felt terribly sad. Of course, the animal was dying. It was a humane act. Still, her chest ached with a funny hollowness.

'What's that?' Monica sat up.

They listened, Josie flat and Monica at right angles to herself.

The noise came again.

A loud whirrrrr.

Like an engine.

whirrr.

'Quail,' Monica relaxed back on her elbow. 'Come on, let's wash off the feeling of that creepy guy.'

She lowered herself into the water from the wooden ladder. Splash, she was surprised as Josie jumped in beside her.

'Freezing,' Josie said, swimming around her friend and noticing how Monica's blonde curls sprang back the minute she lifted her head from the water. 'Freezing,' she complained.

'You'll warm up,' Monica said, herself breathless in the cold water.

'You're always telling me to stop daydreaming, to stay in the present. The present is freezing.' Josie laughed and splashed her friend.

Monica giggled. She ducked under the water, swimming low enough to catch Josie's feet, which were treading earnestly.

'Hey watch it,' but Josie called too late. Now she was below the surface, tangled in Monica's legs and the long roots of silky grass. It was green down there and very cold.

They dried out on the sunny dock and dressed before starting toward the house. Often they walked naked across the land, especially after swimming when they didn't want to wear sweaty clothes. Today that didn't feel safe.

Back at the cabin, the afternoon grew long and restless. Both women felt fidgety. Monica put aside her equations and washed all the windows in the house. Josie couldn't concentrate on her translation, so she worked on lesson plans for the following week.

About five o'clock, she looked up at Monica on the ladder. She was stretching recklessly to the skylight.

'Careful up there.'

'Sure, hon.'

'What did we bring for dinner?' Josie picked through her blank mind.

'That beef chili you made this week. And rye bread.'

'Hey, why don't we go out?' Josie paced in front of the fireplace. God, she wished Monica would be careful on that ladder.

'Out. But the whole point of being up here, oops,' she tipped precariously and then straightened. 'Hey, just let me get one more lick in here and we can talk. There.' She started down the steps. 'But the whole point of being in the country is to rest together in solitary bliss. And what's wrong with your chili? I thought this batch was perfect?'

Josie shrugged and looked out the big bay window across the grass. She told herself to watch the horses ambling along the ridge or the hawk hovering over the pond. Instead she was caught by a line of lint Monica had left in the middle of the frame. 'I don't know. Not in the mood. Guess I'd like vegetarian tonight.' Her eyes stung.

Monica stood behind her; still Josie could sense her nodding.

'Why not,' Monica said. 'Be nice to take a ride this time of evening.'

* * *

Edna's Cafe was practically empty. But then – Monica checked her watch – it *was* only 5:30. Edna waved menus from behind the counter. Josie and Monica said yes.

'Coffee girls?' Edna carried the menus under her arm, the pot of coffee in one hand and the mugs in the other.

'Thanks,' Josie said.

'Not just yet,' Monica smiled. Edna reminded her of Aunt Bella who worked in a coffee shop in the city.

While Monica looked over the menu, Josie went to the restroom and then to the phone.

Monica felt easier when Josie returned to the table looking relaxed. She felt a great surge of affection as the other woman studiously appraised the menu.

'I think I'll have the chef's salad with cheese only,' Josie decided.

'Sounds good,' Monica nodded. She was so relieved to see Josie looking happy. 'Two chef salads, with cheese,' she called over to Edna.

They talked about plans for the following summer when they could spend four straight weeks on the land.

'You two girls sisters?' Edna set the salads before them.

'No,' laughed Monica. 'Why?'

'Don't know. You kinda look alike. 'Course when I stare straight at you like this, there's not much resemblance. I don't know. And you always order the same thing.'

'In that case, I'll have tea,' Monica laughed again. 'With lemon.'

They ate silently, perhaps embarrassed at being the only ones in the restaurant. Monica could hardly get down the lettuce. She'd feel better after she made the phone call. She wouldn't tell Josie who would get nervous. But it was responsible to report the intruder to the sheriff. 'Excuse me. Now I've got to use the bathroom,' she said to Josie. 'Don't let Edna take my salad.'

'I'll guard it with my life,' Josie grinned.

The sheriff's number was posted beneath the fire station number. She dialled and heard a funny moist sound, as if the man were eating. She concentrated on the sturdy black plastic of the phone. 'Hello,' he said finally. She began to report the incident.

'Listen, you're the second lady to call me about this in half-an-hour. Like I told the other one, there's nothing I can do unless the man is actually trespassing on your land. Since you've invited him back tomorrow, he ain't exactly trespassing.'

'We didn't exactly invite him."

'OK, if it makes you feel easier, I said I'll swing by about 8 a.m. That's when the other lady said he'd be coming.'

'Thank you sir.'

Sir, she shook her head as she walked back to the table. She hadn't said sir in fifteen years.

Josie had finished her salad and was doodling on her paper napkin. Definitely signs of good mood. Monica sat down and stared at her until she looked up. 'So I hear you have a date with the sheriff tomorrow morning.'

Josie grinned. 'Hope you don't think I'm stepping out on you.'

By the time Monica finished her salad, the cafe was filling up.

'Refills?' Edna approached with a pot of coffee and a pot of hot water.

'No, thanks, just the check,' Josie said.

'Guess you girls didn't mind my asking if you was sisters?'

'No, no, not at all,' they spoke in unison.

* * *

It was a warm, richly scented evening and they drove home with the top down. Jupiter came out early again. Josie thought how much she preferred Jupiter to the cold stars.

They were both worn out as they collapsed on the couch together. Their feet on the fruit crate coffee table, they watched pink gain the horizon. It was almost pitch dark when Josie reached up to light the lanterns.

She hesitated a moment, remembering last night, and then proceeded. Light, *voilà*, the room was filled with sharp corners and shiny surfaces. Monica picked up her book, but Josie drew it away and cuddled closer.

'Here?' Monica was surprised at her own resistance. After all, they were alone, five miles from town.

'Where then?' Josie tried to sound like Lauren Bacall. If she couldn't look like Lauren Bacall, she could at least sound like her.

Monica sighed with a breath that moved her whole body, a body, she noticed, which was becoming increasingly sensitive to the body next to her. 'Mmmmm,' she kissed Josie on her neck, sweet with summer sweat.

When Josie opened her eyes, she thought she saw something.

No, they had sealed off the sun porch this morning. She kissed Monica on the lips and was startled by a whissssh over her friend's head. 'Bats,' she said calmly, pulling Monica lower on the couch.

'Don't worry,' Monica said. 'I'll get rid of him.'

Worry, Josie cringed. She wasn't worried; she was hysterical. Calm down, she told herself. Think about the invasion of Poland. This is what her mother always said. Think about people who had *real* problems. It's all in your imagination.

Monica opened the windows and doors and set forth with the broom again, but the bat wouldn't leave. Eventually it spiralled upstairs into the large sleeping loft. Monica shook her head and closed up the house against further intrusion. She shrugged and returned to the couch, where Josie was sitting up, considerably more collected than the previous night.

'It'll be OK,' Monica said. 'It'll just go to sleep. You know they're not really Transylvannian leeches. They're harmless little herbivores. And rather inept.'

Herbivores, Josie thought about eating salad for absolution after she murdered the buck. She and the bat were in this together.

Monica reached over and brushed her breast, but Josie pulled away. 'Not now, sweetie. I can't just now.'

Monica nodded and picked up her copy of *Science in Context*. Josie tried to read *Correspondance* by Madame de Sévigné, but found the women even more insufferable than usual, so she worked on a crossword puzzle. About 10 o'clock, Monica yawned, 'Bed?'

'OK,' Josie was determined to be brave. 'I'll go up first.'

'Sure,' Monica regarded her closely. 'You light the candle up there and I'll get the lantern down here.'

They settled comfortably in the double nylon sleeping bag. Monica blew out the light. She reached over to rub Josie's back in hopes something more might develop. When suddenly, whisssh, whisssh, whisssh.

'Looks like our friend is back.' Monica tried to keep her voice light.

'Just a harmless little herbivore,' Josie rolled to her side of the bed and put a pillow over her head.

*   *   *

That night Josie dreamt that she had become Mayor of Lincoln, Nebraska.

Monica slept fitfully, hardly dreaming, and waking with the first sun.

She lay and watched Josie breathing evenly, blowing the edges of her black hair, her body ripe and luscious in the soft light. If she woke up early enough, they could make love before Mr. Creepo arrived. And the sheriff. Had they made a mistake in phoning the sheriff?

The loft grew lighter. Monica lay on her back with her head on her palms, wondering about where the bat had nested, about the reliability of her research assistant, about whether she would have to go home for Christmas this year. Then she heard the noise.

Her whole body stiffened to attention. No mistaking the sound of a car crawling down the gravel road toward the house. She looked at her watch. 7 a.m. Shit. The sheriff wouldn't arrive until their bodies were cold. Maybe Josie would be safer if she just stayed in the house; maybe she wouldn't wake her. Yes, Monica pulled out of the sleeping bag. Suddenly she was grabbed by the nightgown.

'Not so quick, brown fox,' Josie said sleepily. 'How about a cuddle?'

She was adorable in the morning, thought Monica, completely 'dérangé' as Josie, herself, would admit, before two cups of coffee.

The noise outside grew closer and Monica stiffened.

'Don't you even want to hear how I got elected Mayor of Lincoln . . .'

'Not now,' Monica couldn't stem the panic in her own voice.

Josie sat up. 'What is it, honey, what is it?' Then she heard the truck's motor dying.

'I'll just go check in with him,' Monica said nonchalantly. 'You wait here and I'll come right back to snuggle.' She pulled on her clothes.

'No you don't, Joan of Arc.' Josie stood up and tucked her nightshirt into a pair of jeans.

The two walked downstairs together.

The fat man was approaching the house empty-handed. His

friend stayed behind, leaning against the red pick-up truck.

Monica called out to him when he was three yards from the house. 'Back again.'

'Sorry to bother you, mam. As you can see we didn't bring no guns. We'll just get that deer and then git offa yer propert'y as soon's we can.'

His friend shuffled and looked at his feet.

'OK,' Monica said gruffly. 'We don't want dead animals on the land. By the way, we finished him off for you yesterday.'

The man opened his mouth in surprise. His friend moved forward and tugged him back. They closed up the truck and headed into the woods.

Josie watched until they were out of sight. Monica went to the stove and made coffee.

Half-an-hour later, as they sat down to breakfast, another vehicle crunched down the hill. Josie looked out. 'Our hero, the sheriff.'

They walked over to greet the sheriff, a solid man, who looked them over carefully.

'You the girls who called me yesterday?'

'Yes, we did,' Josie smiled.

'Yes,' Monica nodded, the 'sir' gone as quickly as it had come. She didn't like his expression.

'Only ladies listed on the deed to this land, I see. Looked it up last night. Some kind of commune? Something religious?'

'Just friends.' Monica stepped back.

'Edna says she thought you were sisters.' He squinted against the bright sun. 'One sort or another.'

'Just friends.' Monica's voice was more distant.

'Sooooo,' the sheriff held his ground. 'You want to run through the nature of that problem again?'

As Monica talked with the sheriff, Josie inspected the pick-up truck. The bumper sticker read, 'I live in a cave and one good fuck is all I crave.' Inside, dice hung from the rearview mirror. On the seat were a parka and two empty cans of Dr. Pepper. The dashboard was plastered with several irridescent signs. The sun glared so that she could read only one. 'Gass, Ass or Grass, No One Rides for Free.'

The sheriff noticed her and explained, 'Leon's truck. Just as I figured. Leon Bates, a local man. He's, well, he's strayed off the hunting trail before.'

'Isn't there something you can do about it?' Josie felt the heat rising to her face. 'He might have killed one of us. On our property. With a gun.'

'Today,' the sheriff's voice was cool, 'today, your friend tells me, that he has no gun. That in fact, you said he could come back here to get his buck. That right?'

Josie closed her eyes, feeling stupid for imagining this man might protect them. Now official talk seemed the only way out. 'Right. But can't we make some kind of complaint about what he did yesterday?'

'Sure can,' the sheriff nodded. 'If that's what you want.'

'What do you mean?' Monica's back tightened.

'You're weekend folks, right?' He lit a cigarette.

'We work in the city, if that's what you mean,' Monica spoke carefully, 'and don't live here year around.'

'None of my business what you all have going on here. Not Leon's business either, for that matter. But if you file a complaint and we take it to court, well, he's bound to do some investigating and . . .'

'There's nothing illegal about our land group,' Josie snapped.

'Miss, Miss, I never said anything about legal, illegal, but you know there are natural pests the law can't control. And it's better maybe not to get them roused.'

Monica and Josie exchanged glances. 'Well, perhaps we'll check with Loretta; she's the lawyer in the group. We'll get back to you.'

'Yes, mam,' he grew more serious. 'That about all for today, mam? I mean you said they didn't bring no guns with them. You feel safe enough on your own?'

'Yes,' Josie said. 'Safe enough on our own.'

'Then if you'll excuse me, it's almost 8:00 and services start early around here,' he stamped out his cigarette and softened. 'Church is always open to outsiders and weekend people, by the way. Just three miles down, on the road by the gas station.'

'I know where it is,' Josie said. 'Good-bye, Sheriff.'

Josie and Monica watched him roll up the hill and returned to the house for breakfast. They were both too furious to talk.

Monica hardly touched her food, watching out the window for the trespassers.

About 10 o'clock, she saw two pregnant-looking men pulling a buck through the dust by its antlers. Her first thought was how powerful those antlers must be. She tightened and Josie looked up from her book. 'At last.'

It took the man ten minutes to reach the truck. They were huffing and sweating and Josie had to resist the urge to bring them a pitcher of water. She followed Monica out on the front porch.

Leon Bates glowered at them, as if weighing the value of wasting breath for talk. He and his friend heaved the buck into the truck. On the second try, they made it.

Leon's friend wiped his hand on his jeans, waiting with an expression of excruciating embarrassment.

Leon straightened up, drew a breath and shouted. 'That'll do it.'

'Good,' called Monica.

'Gotta ask one question,' Leon leaned forward on his right leg. 'What'd you have to go and bust in his head for? Ruined a perfect trophy. Just look at the antlers. Would of been perfect.'

'Come on, Leon,' his friend called.

Monica stood firmly, hands on her hips. Josie tried to hold back the tears, but she couldn't and pivoted towards the house.

'The road's that way,' Monica pointed. 'Only goes in one direction.'

*   *   *

Monica stamped into the house. 'Damn them. Damn them!' she screamed.

'Hey, now,' Josie reached up to her shoulders and pulled Monica toward her. 'Hey, now, relax, love.'

'Don't tell me to relax. This man comes on our land, shoots living things, threatens us. And you tell me to relax.' She banged her hand on the table.

Josie inhaled heavily and pulled Monica a little closer. 'They've gone now.' She looked over Monica's shoulder out the back window, which gleamed in the mid-morning sun. 'See, they're over the hill.'

'Out of sight, that's what you think, you fool,' Monica drew apart.

Josie held tight, hoping to melt the contortions from her friend's face.

Monica pushed her off. Josie lost balance, falling and hitting her head against a pane of glass in the sun porch door.

The glass cracked, sending a high pitched rip through the room.

Josie ducked forward, her eyes tightly shut, just in time to avoid a shower of glass.

Drenched in sweat, Monica shook her and shouted, 'Josie, Josie, are you all right? Are you all right? Oh, my god, Josie, are you all right?'

'We'll never keep out the bats this way,' Josie laughed nervously, on the verge.

'Josie, I didn't mean it.' Tears welled in Monica's eyes. 'I love you, Josie, are you all right?'

Josie nodded. They held each other, shivering.

Josie stepped forward. 'OK, yes, but I feel a little like Tinkerbell. Scattering all this glitter.'

'Tinkerbell!' Monica laughed and cried and choked. The room seemed to be closing in on them. Hot, tight, airless. She could feel herself listing.

'But you, hey,' Josie frowned. 'Let's go upstairs and have *you* lie down.'

* * *

They sat on the bed, holding hands and staring out at the land. The day was hot, even dryer than yesterday and the golden grass shimmered against the shadowy backdrop of the woods.

'We really should go down and clean up the glass, put a board over the shattered pane.' Monica whispered.

'Yeah, if we don't head home soon, traffic's gonna be impossible.'

Monica rested her head on Josie's breast. She smelled the musk from the black feathers beneath her arms. Her hand went to the soft nest at the bottom of Josie's generous belly. Josie slipped off her clothes. Monica followed. They sank down on the bed, swimming together again, sucked into the cool sleeping bags.

'Home,' Josie murmured.

'Hmmmm?' Monica inhaled the scents of Josie's sweat and sex. Suddenly she pulled back. Was her friend delirious? What was going on?'

'Home,' Josie kissed her with a passion so conscious as to take away both Monica's concern and her breath.

'Yes,' Monica moved her fingers lower, separating the labia, swirling the honey thicker. 'Yes.'

Josie crawled on top of Monica, licking her shoulders, then her breasts, burying her nose in her navel, kissing her legs. Then she was distracted by a slow fizzzzz, as if their airmattress were deflating.

*　　*　　*

Josie looked up. Two wasps hovered over them, bobbing and weaving and then lifting themselves abruptly out of vision. Maybe if she just continued Monica wouldn't notice. But it was too late.

'They always come out in the middle of the day,' Monica said drearily. 'For food. For their nests.'

Josie shook her head and stared at the unsteady, fragile creatures.

'What the hell,' Monica shrugged, inching away from Josie.

'What the hell,' Josie murmured and returned to the pleasures between them. The continued to make love for another hour.

When they had finished, Josie curled around Monica. She explained how she had been elected Mayor of Lincoln, Nebraska.

*　　*　　*

The wasps wove over and around the two women. Even as they fell asleep.

Guest of Honour

VALERIE MINER

The parking lot at Leo's Prime Ribs was packed. They couldn't all have come to hear her, Anna reminded herself. This was a popular spot on the weekend with a number of banquet halls. 'The Pavillion Room,' Mr. Swenson had instructed. Anna had promised the man with the charming Swedish accent that she would read her poetry at The Seattle Writers' Gathering tonight. She was feeling shy and tired, but had had agreed six or seven months ago to be their Guest of Honour. And her editor Marilyn said these speaking engagements were good for one's reputation. She took out her box of books and locked the car.

Making her way through Leo's noisy corridors, Anna sniffed succulent odours of dinner to come, realising that she had skipped lunch. Maybe they would have hors d'oeuvres at the cocktail hour. The Pavillion Room was four doors up on the right, according to a harried waiter, whose badge identified him as, 'Hi, I'm Goodwin'. He pointed and gave her a quizzical look.

Inside the Pavillion Room, she found dozens of men in parkas and heavy flannel jackets. The room was smokey and reeked of beer.

'I'm Anna Lanthier,' Anna tried not to imagine the source of this group's curiosity with women's poetry.

A ruddy faced young man looked her over sympathetically, 'You want the Western Decoy Association?'

'No, of course not, I mean, I was told the Pavillion Room, this is it, isn't it?'

'Yeah, lady, the Awards for the Western Decoy Association.'

Anna inhaled sharply. It *was* the fifteenth of November. It *was* Leo's Prime Ribs. 'Do you know where the writers are?'

'In the newspaper, I expect,' he laughed and then took pity on her again. 'Hey, Walt, you know where a writers' group is meeting tonight?'

'Tell her to go back to the lounge and ask for Marv.'

'Thank you,' she managed, hiking her box of books higher on her hip.

The bar was dark and empty. She knew it would be busy soon enough because Leo's Lounge had a reputation around town.

'Marv?' she asked the women bartender, whose nametag said, 'Hi, I'm Beatrice'.

'Oh, he's sick tonight, honey.' Beatrice inspected Anna. 'Do youself a favour. You look a little delicate for this line of work. Try typing or something. I typed for years myself and it's not so bad.'

Abashed, Anna decided to move on. She considered her red silk dress and high heels. Surely Beatrice hadn't pegged her because of the cliché clothes. Well, maybe all the other young women who 'asked for Marv' as she did, had a particular objective. Calmly, she walked to the front dining room. Damn heels; her feet ached already.

She found the maitre d' and inquired confidently. 'I'm looking for the Writers' Gathering. What room have they been moved to?'

'Oh, that group, let's see, they called to say it would be a small crowd tonight, so they've moved to the Cosy Corner. Five doors down on your right.'

6:10, still, it was hardly her fault that they had moved without informing her. Small crowd, she tried not to take it personally. Maybe people couldn't handle this cold weather. The Cosy Corner was a brightly lit, pleasant little *empty* room.

The harried waiter – Goodwin again – hustled across the floor and did a double take. 'Somehow I didn't think you was with them decoy folks.'

'Do you know where the writers are?' Anna tried to curb her desperation.

'Let's see,' Goodwin observed her more closely. 'Yeah, you look more like a writer.' Then he pulled a schedule from his back pocket. 'Writers' Gathering: Cosy Corner; minimum table settings.'

He watched her face rise and fall. 'Are you Anna Lanter?'

'Lanthier,' she felt pitifully grateful.

'Guest of Honour,' he tried to sound impressed. 'Says right here, next to your name.'

'Yes,' she blushed. 'Thank you. I think I'll just wait here.

'Right then. They're scheduled to arrive at 6:30. Should be any time now.'

'Thanks,' she said.

'Can I get you something?' he frowned. 'Coffee? Cocktail?'

'No thanks,' she smiled.

Bored after five minutes of sitting on a distinctly uncosy folding chair, Anna stood and arranged her books on the front table. Stepping back, she admired the display. Two volumes by Anna Lanthier. Two books published. Six years ago she wouldn't have believed it. She was lucky. She should be honoured that they invited her. Half-an-hour off – she was sure he had said 6:00 sharp, that he would meet her here and help her set up the books – what did it matter?

Two women walked down the hall. 'I know it's here somewhere,' said the younger woman. She tugged on a curl. 'The Pavillion Room is where we met last time, isn't it?'

Anna wanted to call out to them. 'It's the Cosy Corner this month.' But she felt too foolish – being the guest of honour standing in the smaller capacity room all by herself admiring her own books. Maybe she could go to the toilet and return after they had discovered the corner, but she would have to pack up the books again. While she was deciding the two women walked back.

'Here it is, Loretta, the Cosy Corner.'

'Yes,' the older, heavier woman sighed. 'And none too soon.' She set down a cashbox and a red folder.

The younger woman noticed Anna first. She hesitated for a second and then offered her hand. 'Are you here for the Writers' Gathering, dear?'

'Yes,' Anna stood. 'I'm Anna Lanthier.'

'Ohhh, the guest of honour, Loretta said. 'Welcome. Welcome. A poet, I understand. A feminist poet, Darlene.'

Anna smiled and nodded.

Darlene smiled too, 'If you're anything like me, you always get to a place an hour ahead of time.'

'Half-an-hour,' Anna said in spite of herself. 'Mr Swede, rather, Swenson, asked me to come, to set up the books, to meet the officers . . .'

'Lars, oh, Lars can't make it tonight. Or maybe he changed his mind, if he told her, what do you think, Loretta?'

'You know Lars,' she shrugged. 'Well, this will be very nice indeed, cosy, as they say, good for an *intimate* group.'

Anna leaned against the wall, seething at lackadaisical Lars and trying not to vent her frustration on Darlene or Loretta.

'So Darlene, want me to handle the cashbox?' The big woman plopped behind the front table.

'Yeah, and the tickets for roast beef or chicken, all set,' she turned to Anna. 'Of course we pay for *your* dinner. That's our way of thanking you for coming.'

'Thank you,' Anna nodded, almost blind with her accumulation of anger.

'I only wish we had done more publicity. You never know. Last month with Leonard Flicker, we had an overflow crowd. I don't know which is more embarrassing, that or this . . .'

'Oh, here's Ernie and Keith. And Clyde with his girlfiend Gloria. We may get a little group here after all.'

Anna sat down at the far end of a table and counted her breaths. She would have to calm down before she appeared as guest of honour. The writers stood around the front table greeting each other and gossiping. When she felt she had settled enough, she walked over towards Loretta and Darlene, now her old friends. No one who fit the image of Mr Swede. She stood waiting until Loretta looked up, 'Oh, Ernie, let me introduce you to our guest of honour.'

A thin, blonde, fiftyish woman considered her curiously. 'The feminist poet? Anna Lanter. Pleased to make your acquaintance. I'm Mrs Ernie MacDonald, Chairman of the Writers' Gathering.'

'Happy to meet you,' Anna said. 'Actually, it's "Lanthier".' After an awkward sag of silence, she asked, 'What kind of writing do you do?'

'Oh,' Ernie sighed and looked around. 'I haven't written a speck in five years. But history. Natural history. I've published a bird guide and a number of articles.'

A portly man approached and Ernie relaxed, 'Keith, dear.' She took his arm.

'Anna, let me introduce Keith MacDonald, my husband. Keith, this is our guest of honour, Anna Lanthier.'

'Believe that's pronounced "Lanth-e-ay", isn't it, Miss?'

'Actually, I don't know if she is a Miss or a Mrs.'

'"Lanth-e-ay', is the French pronunciation, all right, but my family gave up on that years ago. I answer to anything which sounds vaguely like the name.'

'Sense of humour, always nice on a pretty lady. You wouldn't care to go a roamin' in the gloamin' with me?'

'Pardon?'

'A Scottish song, you know, "A roamin' in the gloamin' with his lassie by his side . . .".'

'Can't say I know that one,' Anna smiled and turned to Ernie, 'So members of your group write about various things?'

'Yes,' Ernie perked up, 'Clyde writes computer software and articles for *Disc World*. Evelyn does children's books. Arthur, Arthur's not here yet, but he'll come, he's the life of the party, does freelance travel pieces now that he's retired. Yes, quite a variety we have here. The Gathering has been convening for sixty years now; it's a very established group.'

'I see,' Anna smiled and felt as if someone had stripped plastic tape across her mouth.

'Get you a drink, Annie?' offered Keith.

'Thank you. Mineral water would be great.'

'Hitting the hard stuff early, eh?' He looked disappointed.

'Well, maybe I'll have something stronger after my talk.' She wanted to kick herself for answering him.

'That will be a little while now,' Ernile apologised. 'We don't eat until 8 pm and then there are some little ceremonies before we open it to you – as the treat of the evening.'

Keith turned away and Anna whispered to Ernie, 'Do you think I could borrow your comb? I forgot mine. I did just wash my hair this afternoon,' she noticed the panic in her voice. 'And I'd kind of like to freshen up.'

'Of course dear,' she pulled a small white comb from her evening bag. 'I think the Ladies is just around the corner.'

The rest-room was cramped, with someone smoking in the stall. Anna hated smoke, but she didn't want to stand out in the hall and make herself vulnerable to members of The Gathering. Relax, she told herself. Gather your wits. So they're not fancy writers with important names. Some of them are quite serious.

They're decent people and they are honouring your work. The evening will be over soon. You can leave after your talk, slip out the back door. Tell them you have a date with a villanell tomorrow morning. It will be fine. She ran Ernie's comb through her hair and watched her shoulders relax. Ernie had been sweet about the comb, understanding her need to escape. It will be fine. Suddenly the stall opened and out walked Beatrice, the bartender, too preoccupied with her cigarette, at first, to notice Anna.

'Oh, it's you,' Beatrice said. 'I told you Marv's not going to be here tonight.'

'I found what I was looking for, thanks,' said Anna as she walked into the stall.

'Well, be careful honey. Your line of work is precarious enough. But we have a banquet of police detectives down the hall.'

Beatrice slammed the bathroom door behind her before Anna realised what she was talking about and burst out laughing. She couldn't control herself and didn't realise that anyone else had walked into the bathroom until she heard Ernie's voice, 'You OK in there? Just thought I'd check that you didn't have nerves or something.'

'No, no,' Anna cleared her throat. 'I'm fine, just fine.'

'Nice to see you smoke too,' Ernie sniffed and lit up a cigarette. 'It's so unfashionable, one feels like a pariah doing it in public, if you know what I mean.'

'Pariah, yes.' Anna finished peeing and warned herself to calm down. Reputation. Remember what Marilyn had said about reputation.

Anna emerged from the stall and handed Ernie the comb. 'Thanks. I'll see you back in there.'

Ernie winked and ducked into the stall. Anna could hear the slow fizzzzz of Ernie's cigarette dying in the toilet bowl.

Keith handed her the mineral water. Mercifully Darlene walked up at the same time. 'Now, maybe we can visit. I looked at both your books and they're beautiful. I especially like the cover on *Faces of Sun*.'

'Thank you,' Anna nodded. 'Yes, I like that illustration a lot. And how about you, what do you write?'

'Oh I've been working on the same project for years. History.'

'Like Ernie? Natural history?

'No, human history. Actually, it's a history of The Writers Gathering.'

'Oh,' Anna took a long drink of the mineral water. 'I understand the group is sixty years old.'

'Yes,' Darlene was pleased. 'I guess we have quite a reputation in this area. That's what makes the book challenging. I'm writing about the forties now.'

'I was at Midway, myself,' said Keith. 'Wounded there, so I had to sit out most of the war in Tacoma . . .'

'I should like to introduce myself,' a large, elegant woman approached.

Anna stepped back and then realised she was being addressed directly.

'I am so happy to meet you, Ms Lanthier. I believe we have several friends in common, Ralph Wharton and Antonia Brownell.'

'Yes,' Anna smiled, feeling the plastic again. What a waste of time this was, all this socialising. Why had she agreed to come?

'And we have our books side by side on the display table today,' she pointed to her thick novel with a colourful cover. 'I am Vittoria Puci, author of *Passion's Heritage*, about women in the royal families of Tuscany.'

'Delighted to meet you,' Anna was pleased at the spirit of her reply. Patience, she reminded herself; they're all sincere people.

'So you have heard of *Passion's Heritage*?'

'No, not yet, but I look forward to reading it.' Anna regretted this immediately. The book must cost at least $18.95.

'I am going on a national tour next week. Ten cities. And I wanted to ask your advice about this, about clothes and such.'

'Well,' shrugged Anna, 'I wouldn't know. My publisher hasn't sent me as far as Spokane.' Reputation, she reminded herself, no this was definitely the wrong thing to say.

'Yes, well with poetry it's different,' Vittoria said graciously. 'I know that. Very hard to publish too. I look forward to reading your new book because I admired the first one so much.'

'Thank you,' said Anna.

'Yes, it's a shame there aren't more people here,' said Darlene. 'Poetry is a special taste.'

'Yes,' Anna said, staring into her glass and wondering if she shouldn't change her mind and have something more potent.

Vittoria and Keith were comparing European trains.

'Darlene,' Loretta called from the cashbox, 'Did you say twenty roast beefs and ten chickens?'

'Excuse me a minute,' Darlene hurried over to her friend.

Anna leaned against the wall and looked at her watch. Only 7:15. Another forty-five minutes of conviviality before dinner. Yes, maybe she would have a beer and a package of peanuts.

'Ms Lanthier?'

She looked up to find a tall red-haired woman and a shorter woman with grey hair. Names, they had names, but Anna couldn't remember any more names just now. They had travelled down from Port Angeles to hear her. No, neither of them wrote. The grey-haired woman called herself a reader and the other woman was a painter. Anna could barely control her urge to hug the reader. They had bought her new book weeks ago and had some particular questions. They could even quote entire lines. Anna was interested in their lives, since she had thought about moving to Port Angeles herself. The painter worked mostly in oils.

She didn't notice her watch again until the red-haired woman said. 'Looks like it's time to eat,' and pointed to the people seating themselves at vertical tables extending from the head horizontal table.

Anna nodded and wistfully watched them walk off. She waited to be told where to sit. For some reason, the places at the head table were the last to fill. She waited and waited until the waiting seemed ridiculous. There were those lovely salads. People were already digging into the bread. Why couldn't she just sit with her friends from Port Angeles? She wasn't meant to speak until after the meal anyway. So she walked over to the women. Vittoria floated forward. 'Do you mind if I join you?'

'No, not at all,' Anna patted the seat next to her own. There was something appealing about Vittoria. Something grand. For instance, she had written all those pages.

Several minutes later, the grey-haired woman nodded to Anna. 'Someone looking for you.'

Ernie broke into their conversation, 'No, no, this won't do at all,' she put her hands on the back of Anna's chair. 'You must sit at the head table, as guest of honour.'

'But,' Anna could not stop the force of her own reason. 'I'm *happy* here. I'd rather sit here.'

'No, it won't do,' Ernie smiled with her conspiratorial smoking smile. 'People want to *see* you. Now, come and bring your salad with you.'

Vittoria protested. The two women from Port Angeles looked disappointed. And Anna obeyed, embarrassed to be carrying her salad across the dining room.

'Oh, the salad!' Ernie said once they were seated. 'it was a joke; you didn't have to bring your salad.'

'Guess I just need practice in being guest of honour,' Anna shrugged.

'Let me introduce myself,' said man on her left. 'I am William Larkin, this year's Talespinner.'

'Yes,' Ernie leaned over. 'William has won our story contest. You'll be hearing him read later. Before the guest of honour, of course, *you* have the prime spot on the program.'

'Oh, yes, nice to meet you.' Anna managed. She dug into her salad. Prime spot; prime ribs, Anna sipped the water and tried to clear her head.

'And this is my wife, Anna,' said William, 'now isn't that funny. I'm surrounded by Annas. But then there's something to the name Anna that does surround itself, if you know what I mean.'

Anna thought this was very clever until she looked at his wife's face and realised it was a tired joke between them.

'So you're a poet, Anna?'

'Yes,' she noticed too late that Goodwin the waiter had cleared away her salad for the next course.

'What's your line, sonnets?'

Her eyes widened, 'Free verse.'

'Free verse,' he laughed, 'I like that. What most writing is nowadays, I guess. Free. Ha!'

'Now William, don't forget that money you made off the *Reader's Digest*. $500, wasn't it?'

'Yeah, $500 for a personal adventure story. They run some poems. Short ones. I imagine they pay for the poems. You write short ones?'

'No, unfortunately not,' she said. 'Hopelessly long ones.'

'William and his wife met at Swingletarians,' Ernie offered.

'Pardon?' Anna asked.

'Swingletarians,' William said. 'When I retired from the Navy at forty-five, I decided it was time to find a wife. And Anna here had just been widowed. So we dated for a while and, actually, tomorrow is our fifth anniversary.'

'Congratulations.'

'My fork, William, did you take my fork?' the other Anna asked.

'No, hon, I don't think so.' He inspected the Anna on his right. 'She only has one fork too.'

'Well, someone took my fork. How can I eat roast beef without a fork, I should have ordered chicken.'

'Hang on, Annabelle, we'll get you another fork. Hey, waiter . . .'

'Is that your name,' Anna felt ridiculously relieved, 'Annabelle?'

'Yes, Mama loved Poe.' She scrutinised Anna as if divining her purloined fork. 'I guess we both liked good storytellers, Mama and me.' She glanced affectionately at William.

'Yes,' nodded Anna, looking with nostalgia at the table with Vittoria and the two women from Port Angeles.

The waiter returned to fill their glasses.

Anna thought she was going to explode. The bathroom was her only escape. But could you leave in the middle of a meal like this? Why not? She was the guest of honour; she was bound to be nervous. They would understand. A little neurosis went a long way for the old reputation. 'Excuse me,' she moved behind William and Annabelle to the aisle. 'I'll be right back.'

'Of course, dear,' they looked at her with concern.

What if the bartender was in the toilet again? Well, she didn't say she would report her. She was just warning her. Besides, Anna reminded herself as she tentatively pushed open the lavatory door, she wasn't what the bartender thought. She was the guest of honour. Wasn't she?

Blissfully empty. Anna entered the stall and sat down with her clothes on. It was going to be fine. They were nice people. She only had to read for an hour. This was good for her reputation. She couldn't wait to talk to Marilyn.

Out at the sink, she ran each wrist under the cold stream and splashed water on her flushed face. It was going to be fine. As she walked back into the room, Vittoria nodded encouragingly. She liked Vittoria more and more.

As she squeezed behind Annabelle's chair, she stepped on something which flew in the air, hitting her knee. A fork. No point in mentioning it now. Annabelle had finished her ribs.

'Feeling better?' William looked worried.

'Oh, yes, thank you.'

'Butterflies, I've got a few myself,' he patted her shoulder.

'Excuse me,' Ernie interrupted, 'but I need to check some facts with the guest before I introduce her.'

Anna turned.

'Cigarette?' Ernie winked.

'No, thank you.' How could she tell Ernie that she was allergic to tobacco, when it was the source of their friendship? 'I, I never smoke before I speak. Bad for the throat.'

'Oh,' Ernie was disappointed, but politely returned the pack to her evening bag.

'Now the details. I'm afraid I didn't have time to get them organised before this. Let's see, you've written two books, which are?'

Anna slowly and politely offered her credits, fighting off rancid memories of job hunting.

'Splendid, now, about your personal life – married, children . . .'

The waiter appeared with sherbert and ice cream.

'Sherbert, please,' Anna said.

'Me too,' Ernie said resolutely. 'Good for the throat.' Then she looked at her watch with alarm. 'Oh, dear, I better get going. They close up at 10, you know.'

Anna checked the wall clock. 9 o'clock. She had prepared to read for an hour, but if William was going to spin tales, she'd have to cut it to half-an-hour. Well, that was probably better anyway.

'Ladies and Gentlemen, I am honored tonight to chair our meeting and to introduce our guest of honour – which I'll do momentarily. First, as always, we'll go around the room and say what we've been writing this past month. Now don't be shy. Share the success.'

'Well, I'm Arthur Whitney and I sold a camping article to *Northwest Life* this month.'

A round of applause.

'I'm George Wilkins and I haven't had anything published this month, but I bought a word processor, so just wait until next month. . .'

More applause.

'Norma Clarendon. Poetry, two poems in our church magazine.'

'Evelyn Pope . . . Milton Wright . . . Darlene Burnaby . . . Loretta Milhous . . .'

'Gloria Sage. I'm not really a writer. I'm here with my good friend, Clyde. But I aspire to write. I've worked at the post office for ten years and I've always wanted to write about that. So much to say about the various people you meet. And the colourful stamps. Sometimes about the two of them together because of the way that people would fight over their favourite stamps if you were running out as we often did because we were a pokey little substation. Which isn't to say we didn't have events. Once we got a package from Tasmania, addressed to a gentleman who was never home and would never pick it up. Finally, one day, I'd say months after he received the notice and we really should have returned the parcel, but you figure something comes all the way from Australia – that's where Tasmania is – and you don't want to return it right away. Anyhow, he comes in as casual as you please and says, "I hear you're holding my mother." "Pardon," I say and he explains that it's his mother's ashes in the box. We've been sharing that dinky little office with a dead woman,' Gloria took a sip of red wine. 'I know that Clyde will say I'm talking too long, but this is an interesting story, don't you think, anyways the parcel didn't do any harm sitting on the back shelf like that. And you know the man was very nice, brought in flowers for me and the other girl who works at the substation, to commemorate his mother's passing, so to speak. Well, those are the things I'd like to write about. Someday . . .'

She was interrupted by Raoul Arnaud who described his two recent articles about acid rain. Next Myrna Houston said she was just about to submit her first play.

Ernie looked at her watch and the others spoke more quickly.

Finally she stood and led a round of general applause. 'And now,' she cleared her throat, 'our Talespinner of the Year, Mr. William Larkin.'

William approached the podium enthusiastically. Anna's mind was still reeling from Gloria's story, which she thought had possibilities. Was she losing her mind, or just loosening up?

'I brought my whole repertoire of tales tonight,' he began.

Anna's heart sank enough to make her want a cigarette.

'But time is getting short and I'm sure you're all as eager as I am to hear our guest of honour,' he nodded hospitably.

Anna found herself blushing. What was going on with her? Why didn't she blow up? First they 'invite' her to the wrong room thirty minutes early. Then no one greets her. Then they treat her like a gatecrasher. This evening would probably induce a five year writer's block. She thought about Annabelle's fork flying in the air and tried to suppress her hysteria.

'So I'll just read a short ditty that appeared in the *Reader's Digest* . . .'

Anna was engrossed in the story and disappointed when he shrugged at the end, 'That's it.' William nodded shyly at the applause. And sat down.

'Now,' Ernie checked her watch with concern. 'Last but certainly not least is our Guest of Honour, Ta Ta, Anna Lanthier. Ms Lanthier, because I never did find out if she was married or single, is a local poet of some reknown. She has published two lovely books of poetry with exquisite covers, which are for sale on the back table. I'm sorry that we don't have a bigger crowd for her – like the crowd we had last month for Leonard Flicker – but I'm sure we will be a receptive, *intimate* audience. I'm looking forward to hearing her work because I've never read it. On the back of her book it says, "She represents the best in new women's writing." Because time is short tonight, Ms Lanthier will read for twenty minutes. Now, without further ado, I give you, Anna Lanthier, new woman.'

The applause was warm and loud. Anna noticed that it was more than William Larkin received and was appalled at her petty ego. She imagined Annabelle glowering.

'I am honored to be here,' she began. 'I've enjoyed talking to a number of you individually.' She was surprised to detect a particular fondness for Ernie. She smiled to Vittoria, who was sitting forward intently, and to the women from Port Angeles. 'And I would like to start with selections from my new book.'

She timed herself carefully.

Ernie looked relieved as well as grateful when she said, 'For my last poem . . .'

The applause was long and wild. Afterward, Anna was amazed how many people bought books and how kind they were in their detailed responses to her poems.

She noticed Vittoria waiting on the sidelines and tried not to let the woman's intensity curtail her conversations with other people.

The pair from Port Angeles said they would like to organise a reading for her there.

Gloria said that she had never really thought about poetry for herself, but she could see ways that it might be more suitable to her purposes. She bought three books.

Goodwin winked at her as he wheeled out the centrepiece, 'Good going, much better than the *yawn* they had here last month.'

Finally Vittoria stepped forward, carrying *Passion's Heritage*. 'I wondered if you would agree to a trade – your books for mine. Mine is more expensive, of course, but I would be happy to trade, myself.'

'Yes,' Anna said, noticed that her breath was not taken away as it would have been at the beginning of the evening. 'Thank you.'

'Thank you,' Vittoria shook her head. *'I savoured every word.'*

When the crowd cleared, Ernie escorted her to the door, where she collected her empty box.

'Thank you so much Anna. Why I think this is the best reading we've ever had. I also wanted to say you've been most gracious all evening. Some famous writers find us a little down home for their tastes. But you fit right in.'

Anna nodded thanks, disarmed and a little guilty about her irritability.

'And you know I never did find out if you were married or single.'

Anna nodded again and said good-bye. She turned right.

Ernie called out, 'Wrong way, the exit is in that direction.'

'I know,' Anna said. 'I need to visit the Ladies first.'

'Of course, of course,' Ernie agreed, looking around for Keith. 'Nerves. Well, thank you again dear. And good luck.'

Over. It was *all* over, she thought as she pushed open the bathroom door. The stall was occupied, so she leaned against the sink, her eyes closed, holding her empty box.

The stall opened and Anna looked up at Beatrice, who seemed more interested in her box.

'Grapefruits, eh? Hmmm, I've seen some covers in my time, but this is u-nique. Well, you don't have to worry about the cops no more. Gone home. And frankly when they're off duty they're no different than any men. Although I did see several women there tonight. Lady cops. What's next?' She soaped up vigorously under the warning, 'State law requires that all employees wash their hands before returning to work.'

Anna set down the box and pushed into the stall.

'Say,' the bartender spoke above the hot air dryer. 'You sure this line of work is for you?'

'Some jobs are harder,' Anna volleyed.

'Yeah, well, it's been a long night for both of us. Good luck.' The bartender pushed open the door to the corridor.

Beatrice paused and called in a friendly voice, 'I'll tell Marv you was looking for him.'

'Thanks,' Anna answered automatically, then was caught in a fit of giggles. She heard the door swing closed. And she felt horribly alone.

Anna walked out to the car and put the empty box in the trunk. As she turned on the ignition, she wondered what it would be like to live up in Port Angeles.

Short-Short Stories

VALERIE MINER

Here are five short-short stories of varying styles which seem to be unconnected. I like to write and to read short-shorts. I appreciate the economy of language, perhaps because of my thrifty Scottish mother. I guess I write them because I don't write poems. I enjoy them in the same way I enjoy playing with intricate glass paperweights which contain snow and sculptured scenes. Like the paperweights, these stories can be experienced at odd, quick moments and they are always different – depending on the sunlight, the observer's mood, the pace at which they are considered. Short-shorts, unlike much longer fiction, are designed to be played with again and again.

Worms and Women have Spun Magic

Silk threads stream like sunlight against the hard-clanking metal machine. She perches on a moving chair, delicately capturing strands onto wooden spools. Her fingers are as graceful as those of a Beijing Opera star.

Outside, beneath high blue sky, they are building another factory wing. Outside, past a gold sign declaring monthly quotas one sister carries bricks; another slaps mortar. They prepare for more rooms of colour and clank and silk.

A white cotton baker's cap covers her short black hair. Tucked near the rim are seven strands of silver. This hair is silver, not grey, and shinier than anything spun in Suzhou. She first found the silver

112

in her photograph, one of twelve, on the model worker poster.

Outside her daughter sings in the nursery. There she boards for five days at a time with other workers' children. Down the slide she streams, sleek as satin. Clapping her hands, she squeals high. It is hard for a mother to hear so far away. It is hard to hear at all after a week of screeching spools.

Inside from the outside, come tourist women to flash cameras and take notes in little books. a dozen foreigners talk quick as thread as if she could not understand – or hear. They point and stare at her white hat, ricksack apron, flowered blouse and black shoes. She trains her attention on the silk and soon they disappear.

Outside they return, burdened by bags of clothing from the factory shop. Worms and women have spun magic in Suzhou since the Tang Dynasty. Marco Polo, himself, made several trips here from the outside.

Pressing the foot lever, she zips to the end of the turquoise row. She supervises blue quivering into green into scarves, drapes, dresses, robes. For Marco Polo's followers. For flashing ladies to wear outside to the Beijing Opera.

Or inside-out, like so many reversible robes bound for Paris. Four thousand years on the Silk Route, Suzhou now boasts sturdy new wings. Meanwhile, she imagines her daughter's sleek laughter. Stealthily, she tucks the silver threads beneath her white cotton cap.

Japanese Vase

'You look good,' he says. 'Slim. Well.'

The first words to his daughter in four years. As he collapses in the overstuffed chair, she notices that he is not well. Nor slim. Two-hundred-fifty pounds on five-foot-ten. All these years his weight has trailed her like Claudius. She is sad, repulsed, confused that she could ever be so fearful of her father.

He plops a packet of snapshots on the coffee table and surveys her apartment. She takes in Indian wall hangings, small Persian rug, gladioli in the Japanese vase. Does he recognise that vase, she wonders. Does he remember when he brought it back for her in high school? Or was it college? She does not remember. He regards the vase, puzzling, himself. When he notices her noticing him, he shifts his glance.

'An electric typewriter,' he says, considering her neat desk from a distance. He will not go closer. He has never intruded. 'But I guess you need it for your work.'

Can he imagine the months it took to convince herself that she did need an electric typewriter to be a good union organiser? For surely she could organise on the falling-apart model from college with the semicolon missing. Easy enough to insert that extra dot over the comma. How many semicolons does a good union organiser need?

'Yes,' she says, 'it's useful.' She sweeps her blondeness back in the hairpin. Strawberry blonde like his hair before baldness invaded. 'Would you like an omelette or scrambled?' she asks, knowing already the omelette will be too effete and trying to recall how much milk to put in scrambled.

He follows her into the kitchen, with a cup of black coffee in his hands. He tells her how he is canning tomatoes. And cactus pickles. She cannot believe the soldier has retired to a farm. Now he lives in the desert with his dogs. Retrievers.

Glad he is talking because she could never cook and talk at the same time – how had Mama done it with five kids underfoot and always hot soup on the stove – she listens hopefully in between his words.

As she butters the muffins he watches, fascinated, like a caveman. Finally he says, 'You use *real* butter.'

She wants to explain that she bought it at the Co-op where it's almost as cheap as margarine. But a suspicious smell invades from behind and she makes a mad rescue of the scrambled eggs. Not enough milk after all.

'Good grub,' he flatters from behind his loosely fitting false teeth that make her think, oddly, of a hen clucking. 'Just like Mama's.'

He is lying. For eggs like Mama's he should visit Carolyn or

Ann Marie or Ellen. Even George cooks better eggs. But visiting George would expose him to more than electric typewriters and he could never admit that his own son was a faggot. Why was she the one he always chose to visit?

'English muffins,' he says brightly.

She is touched by how hard he is trying to be pleasant, trying to make conversation.

'Remember when we used to get raisin muffins at the day-old bakery?'

She nods, thinking about the brioches and croissants to which Kent has introduced her. She has made a special trip to the A & P for these muffins and she doesn't want to feel guilty that they are not day-old. She sips her coffee and tries not to cry.

Sensing her silence as boredom, he pulls out the snapshots. Two golden retrievers on the front lawn of his desert home. Frisky and Miranda. Both females. The photo of the back garden overflows with peppers and melons and – ah, yes, the cactus. How can he live in the desert? He is eating another muffin. His fifth. 'Better to have too much,' Mama would say. He carefully wipes the jam off his thumb before handing her a picture of the desert in winter.

She digs out photos of recent Christmases with Carolyn, Ann Marie, Ellen, their husbands and children. Brother George is off to the sidelines, a silver bow around his neck, clowning under the tree. Or pouring himself a drink in the corner. She notices that George is always alone. And she, being the family photographer, isn't in any of the pictures.

The family – so much family talk – perhaps this makes him miss Mama.

'My work,' she offers, 'is going well. We've organised three companies of office clerks this year.'

He tells her how the union is screwing him out of a pension.

'I've more or less settled down,' she says, glancing inadvertently at the Japanese vase. 'After all those years of organising around the country, I got tired of Motel Sixes.'

'Yes, you can get dysentery from the water in those places,' he says. 'You know I had another bladder operation?'

Why does she want to smash that damn vase against the wall? Who cares why? She'll do it when he leaves.

No, perhaps she won't. For she doesn't own anything in which flowers fit so well.

He pulls out another snapshot. Frisky and Miranda by the flagpole. '19.95', he says proudly, 'at Sears.'

Sears. One of her earliest memories is set at Sears, searching for her father lost among the long male legs at Sears in Hackensack.

He looks at his watch. 'Gotta go,' he says, suddenly. Does her face betray disappointment?

'You remember Bo Bo,' he says unsurely, 'stationed in Nam with me. Lives in Baldwin now. Old soldiers shooting bull this afternoon.'

She nods to knock back the tears.

'Nice neighbourhood,' he says on the way down the stairs. He is much more talkative going down than coming up. 'You get many coloured around here?'

At that moment Juana emerges from the downstairs flat. He blushes and looks at his shoes, which, she notices, are the same old kind with perforations on the top. Very forties. He has always worn such shoes – from Sears.

'Will you take our picture, Juana?' she asks, handing her neighbour a small instamatic. 'Will you shoot us together?'

The Nicest Smile

You've got to understand that I wasn't destitute, ugly and bow-legged, but I wasn't Corina Sherman either. And at sixteen, that's who I wanted to be – Corina Sherman with the camel cashmere sweaters and the boyfriends who was Miss February, March and April in the Queenstown High School Yearbook. She had straight teeth, 'nicest smile', everything. Smart too. Always going to plays in the city and galleries. Cultured family. Not that my family was stupid, they just didn't have time for books. I mean I'm not complaining. Mom let me take violin as long as I could keep up with my homework and the after-school job. I've been playing violin ever since.

So when I had this concert in a fancy hall on the Upper East Side I felt like I had come a long way from Queenstown. Solo performance of my own compositions. Pretty heady treatment. The dressing room had those little lights around the mirror. My friend Sally sent coral roses.

The hall wasn't exactly packed, but there were enough people to keep it warm. The first sonata went well.

Intermission was 20 minutes. Twenty minutes too long for my jutters. I tried sitting it out in that little room with the snazzy mirror, but the roses reminded me of Mom in the hospital. So I went to the lobby and ordered a Coke. No sooner was I disappointed to taste this warm, weak excuse for a Coke (they rip you off everywhere in New York City) but someone with chartreuse punk hair came up and said, 'You don't remember me.'

'Corina Sherman,' I said. 'Of course I remember you. But how did you wind up here?'

'Well, I read about your performance in *The Voice* and I said to myself, 'There can only be *one* Connie Winston . . .'

I wasn't listening because I can't listen and look at the same time. Yes, I checked out the nice smile, the beautiful eyes. The camel cashmere had melted into fucshia silk. Terrific with green hair.

'I can't believe it,' I heard myself. 'I mean if you could have guessed my idea of success when I was sixteen, it would be that Corina Sherman would read about me in *The Voice* and come hear me play.'

'Well, here we are.' She smiled and clicked her brandy to my Coke, 'Success.'

By this time the lights were flashing and I knew my agent would have fits if she didn't find me back in the little room with the lighted mirror. I tried to say good-bye, but we wound up with a date for drinks after the performance.

I floated through the second half. I couldn't see beyond those damn stage lights, but I imagined the hall filled with Corina Shermans. Corina the Head Cheerleader. Corina, Miss February. Corina, the Homecoming Queen. Corina, Corina, Corina, Corina.

'It must be hard to teach high school as well as your music,' she said over the bartender's clatter. 'Why don't you give up teaching?'

'Can't afford it,' I said, unwilling to consider just how much I'd like to quit. 'And what are you doing now?'

'Trying to write,' she said. 'I have a novel in mind.'

I nodded, remembering that over the years friends had told me Corina was going to be a dancer and then a sculptor. Something in her voice stopped me from asking more about the writing. Nervous, I took a long drink from my Perrier water. Even in New York they don't water down the Perrier water.

'May I ask you a personal question?' she inquired tentatively.

'Sure,' I said, not feeling at all sure.

'What did you think of me when I was in high school?'

I remembered clearly. 'I thought you were very popular and I felt jealous. But you weren't a snob like Tally Bankman. Just out of reach.'

'Can you imagine what it was like going from Head Cheerleader into the real world?' she asked, licking salt off a potato chip.

I remembered a doe I saw in Yosemite last summer and felt the same kind of protective sadness.

'Tough,' I imagined.

'Don't you want to know what I thought about you?' she asked intently.

'To tell you the truth,' I said, 'I didn't think you noticed me.'

'Oh, I always wanted to be your best friend,' she said. 'I thought you were so, I don't know, so *deep* with your music. I knew you would grow up into something splendid, an artist.'

'Well, I wish you had told me. It would have saved a lot of anguish.' I noticed how my fatigue was making me snide. 'Listen,' I said, 'I've really got to hit the sack. Got to work tomorrow.'

'Of course,' she said, pulling away the bill. 'Let me give you my card. Next time you're in New York for a concert, let's spend some real time together talking about the old days. And there are some people I'd like you to meet. People in the music world.'

Interval

It wasn't the cigarette in the cut glass ashtray that bothered me, even though you know I hate the smell of stale tobacco.

I could have forgotten it because I immediately get lost whenever I sit in your – womb – I want to say womb instead of room. The very first thing I noticed about that room was the African animal photographs. It was as though you had hung them in my honour. Although I've never been to Africa, you know I've always been planning to go.

It wasn't the lipstick on the Spode cup that bothered me. I did notice that she drank coffee with sugar and cream, whoever *she* was. A certain contrast to my Spartan tea with lemon, don't you think? You always had the tea ready for me, always with a fresh linen napkin before. This seemed thoroughly elegant, your basement Chelsea flat with the potted plants and the exotic prints, the ancient china and Jackson's Darjeeling tea.

It was almost ready; I do understand. It would have been ready if the train hadn't been five minutes early. I saw the sliced lemon on the counter and I heard the kettle rumbling to a boil as I walked in today.

I'll tell you what really bothered me. It was that the footstool was in a strange position and the seat of the chair was still warm. Clearly someone had preceded me and had not quite left. Rive Gauche lingered. As you puttered in the kitchenette behind the charming Javanese screen, I wondered if you ever took time for notes after sessions.

At the price you charge, Dearie, you might consider fifteen minute intervals.

Toasting the Cold North Star

Mariele sits on the steps of the Molivos Hotel, on the bottom plank, close to the beach, cupping a brandy in her hands. She doesn't usually drink alone, but the darkness – an hour before moonrise – brings a chill even to this Aegean coast. Waves lap inland and then ripple south toward the Equator. In the distance, off the Turkish shore, eight fishing boats tip and rock, their own lights brighter than the stars. Boats. 'Ship not boat,' Father would remind her that he was a skipper, master of a ship, not a boat. Mariele, herself, has seen more boats than ships on the seas.

*   *   *

'Telegram,' the word had spiralled from behind a morning breeze as Mariele took her customary walk from Molivos to Eftalou. 'Telegram,' came the voice, heavy with information (the postmaster knew her movements, knew her daily walks although she had told no one about them. He cared enough about her to chase two kilometres on a hot morning. Something terrible must have happened to one of the few people in her past who knew where she was), too much information on a sweltering morning.

For a moment on that road dusty with purple sage, Mariele considered not turning around. Perhaps she could ignore the summons. She knew people who had cheated death, whose will, or stupidity, had been so strong that they struggled against all odds. 'Telegram,' the voice pierced her meditation. Determined, his voice was, yet edged with confusion. Surely Mariele must hear him. In English, too. Did he think she was aphasiac? If he knew about the walks, he might also know that she often 'spaced out', as the California woman called it. Perhaps they all knew: Maria and Elene and Strados. Did they type her as one of those peculiar expatriates who nest their loneliness among friendly strangers? What did they think of her? After six months was there a consensus, a label, a reputation? Not whore. They had tried, of course. ('Last summer I had sixteen beauties,' confided Nicko. Yet just as she knew she wasn't a beauty, he knew she wasn't countable.) 'Telegram,' the voice persisted. And forgetting her fear, remembering that one answered when one was called, Mariele turned around to face the breathless postmaster under the unrelenting sun.

*   *   *

Venus is brilliant tonight. And Mars just a shade to the left of yesterday. Mariele remembers that her father navigated by the stars and she used to think he was Copernicus. At age six, she stood at the Boston pier with Mother, waiting for the *Jefferson City Victory* to dock. They had watched the ship for over an hour, so much waiting before he could walk down the gangplank and back into her life for another week. Would he stay as long as a month this time? (At school she learned how the Greeks studied constellations. Someday she would go to Greece.) Grasping Mother's hand, she asked for the North Star. 'Shhh,' Mother had said, 'I think I can see him now.'

This evening the North Star holds a cool region on Molivos. Almost cold. Stern enough to quell disco music rising from the far end of the beach. Strong, perserverant, this star is an anchor for her life. From the direction of Petra, graceful village with a church set high on a rock, automobile headlamps swirl light into the sea. Light is power here in Greece, louder than any noise. She peers out at the waves, as far as light would take her. One crest follows another, as far as those fishing boats. Sea always farther than she could see. She knows this. As far as the coast of Asia Minor. Alone here in Molivos. Always alone, it seems, though she has known lovers on all the beaches of her life. So many under the cool North Star.

*   *   *

'Telegram,' he repeated louder, after she had turned to him on the hot road, back in the direction of town. Louder. Why did people shout when you didn't understand them? Volume destroyed delicate translations. 'Yes, nai,' she assured the con-

scientious old man. 'Nai, Kosta,' she nodded and extended her hand. Pulling back the telegram to shade her eyes, she imagined touching the smooth barrel of a rifle to her forehead. It was a white envelope, with airmail efficiency stripes on the side. As Kosta handed her the telegram, she noticed a smudge, from where his thumb had tightly gripped it, sweating all the way from Molivos. Two kilometres on the road to Eftalou. 'Efaristo, Kosta,' she said, 'Thank you,' unable to break her gaze from the postmaster's worry.

*   *   *

The fruity sweetness of this Metaxa recalls cognac Father brought for Christmas. So sometimes he *had* come home. How could she forget? Yes, there were five, no six Christmases. And several birthdays. Then he would sail off again. Yokohama for the final ten years. Container ships carrying tinned fruit and soups to the West-hungry Japanese. Mariele sniffs the brandy, but the stars have diluted its pungency. She can still feel the warmth soothing down her throat and settling in the roundness of her belly. No. She stops the thought before it fully forms. She is too old now – at forty, for godsake – to have children. Adoption would be more useful. She remembers all the homeless urchins in Tetuan. Sea urchins. Street urchins, rather.

Fog horns in the distance. She held Mother's hand, waiting for the fog horns in Boston and New York and Philadelphia and Mobile and New Orleans. She thought the waiting would never end. Then, when Mariele was almost grown, Mother received a telegram – in a blue envelope. 'Sick,' Mother had read, shaking with relief that he was not dead, sighing with gratitude for the illness which brought him back to her, to the marriage he had promised for twenty-five years. Mother took the telegram to church the next time Father Cyril was blessing rosaries. Later, she stowed it beneath her Javanese scarves in the top drawer.

*   *   *

'Telegram,' Mariele repeated slowly, as if she were teaching Kosta English or telecommunications. Actually, she was count-ing the years between Mother's blue telegram and now. Twenty years since he retired and Mariele, herself, had left home and

pursued ghosts at sea. Kosta watched carefully, holding her with ancient eyes. 'Oki, oki, no,' she shook her head and smiled. How could she smile at a telegram, she imagined him wondering, at all that importance in the white envelope. 'Efaristo,' she said again and turned back toward Eftalou. Kosta was a kind soul, but she could not share this with anyone. The ripped envelope. The clear words. She had been awaiting this sentence for twenty years, waiting with a patience that only comes of movement, since he left the sea.

* * *

Mariele remembers now that he had always promised her the sextant. She finishes the brandy, raising the bulb of her glass toward the stars, gazing through the coated crystal with the precision of an astronomer.

The Tale of Mary Fisher

SARA MAITLAND

She woke up again too soon, cold and slightly shaky; the sky was paling and in the greyness the distant stars were extinguished one by one. The distance had form but no colour. She stretched wearily and climbed out from under her rock – like a woodlouse she thought and smiled at so homely an image. Below her was the sea, as pale as the sky, milky, expectant, enormous. She waited, patient and pale as the stones at her feet.

When the sun rose out of the sea abrupt and bright, the world was flooded with colour like a miracle. On an instant as though out of its own substance, in response to the sun but not caused by it, the dry earth was golden brown, the sea and the sky together blue and gold and pink and warm. She took a slow breath in, wriggled her shoulders, shifting the stiffness and as suddenly as the colour had come so did happiness; she felt happy and free. She drew a handful of dried fruits from her bag and stuffed it into her mouth, she chewed into its roughness with great and simple pleasure, pushing her tongue against its hidden sweetness. Then she straightened her dress and hair as best she could, turned her right shoulder to the sea and the sun and started walking to Adrianople again.

So many mornings in ten years she had awakened in strange places. The best of them were outside like this morning. Mornings had come to her in many ways and many colours and still who not rejoice, who could not feel the surge of hope, even when the dawn caught one deep in a prison cell. In Boston the windows had been boarded over to protect the pious citizens from the contamination of her presence, but even there, shady and nervous the morning had come sneaking in, making its arrival known, creeping round every barrier, dispersing the horror of the night. She pushed Boston away quickly, concentrating on the hard

124

cracked ground beneath her feet. In the Barbadoes the heat had come with the dawn, damp, strong-smelling, potent, but here although it would be hot later the morning was cool; golden but cool.

As she walked she listened and waited, But the inner voice was silent so that she could hear the first birds, the early song of insects, the inaudible murmur of the sun warming rocks and dust and shrubby plants.

Later though she was vouchsafed a word:

If God is for us, who is against us? What shall separate us from the love of God? Shall tribulation or distress or persecution or famine or nakedness or peril or sword? No, in all these things we are more than conquerors. For I am sure that neither death, nor life, nor angels, nor principalities, nor things present, nor things to come, nor powers, nor height, nor depth, nor anything else in all creation can separate us from the love of God.

She chewed on the words with the same relish as she had chewed on the dried fruit in the dawn of the day, probing them too for their hidden sweetness. She pushed aside Boston, Boston and also the clawed dampness and the mean winds of Cambridge, as though they were husks, hard seeds to be spat out; she savoured the sweetness of the Barbadoes, and of Pontefract where she had been shaped in the image of Christ, a prophet like him despised in her own town. In Selby too, and in Virginia, she had been more than conqueror, empowered in a moment of her own choosing. She smiled, digesting the well known words comfortably, grateful for the gift of them, and still walking on with the vibrantly blue Aegean rocking its islands tenderly below her right side and the great mountains of Macedonia and Thrace curving downwards on her left.

She had not expected to find the country itself so abundantly pleasing; the rockiness, the desert of it. Was it so also in the Holy Land, had the Christ walked in his desert even as she did now? Did he rejoice to see the lizards dart away, nervous, swift and silent? The dry golden brightness seemed even lovelier than the hot brilliance of the Carib Islands. She was walking now where no free born English woman had ever walked before. The thought amused her. And she walked here alone. That thought delighted her.

She walked all day and saw no one, just like the day before. Three nights ago she had rested in a small village among noisy goats and curious children. The folk there had been baffled but kindly; they had not spoken because they had no common language, but they too had their spark of inner light, sufficient for them if they did but know it, and her straight-eyed respect had calmed their doubts. They had been kind to her. Nonetheless by the middle of that afternoon she knew she would sleep alone again. And with the knowing came the shadow. She rebuked herself. She had chosen to be here and to be here alone.

'I am led,' she had told the York meeting, 'I am led to cross the seas again. When I was in the Islands of the New World I heard a clear call to go and preach the truth in the places of the East, to speak to him whom the world calls the Sultan, the Emperor of the Pagans.'

They had not been unduly surprised, and why should they have been? They did not question her call, nor she theirs to stay at home; they made such preparations as they could and prayed her on her journey. Somewhere far away northward and westward they would be praying for her still, if they were moved to do so, and she knew they would be so moved. But it was very far away and she could find little comfort in it.

The shadow was much nearer. It was very near now, she could feel it waiting, ready to pounce, greedy and strong. It was not fear of the dark, of the night. It was another shadow, a fear not yet named. It had been prowling after her ever since she had arrived in this new, ancient land. Leaving the ship she had left the company of others, and for the first time she was truly alone. The shadow attached itself to her and followed her.

She would not succumb to sickly imaginings. *She would not.* She was a free born woman, empowered in the Spirit, and nothing could prevail against her.

So as the golden day faded she found a safe place to sleep and checked that there were no snakes lurking there. She was a hardened and experienced traveller now, who only six years ago would have screamed at the thought of a snake. She spread her cloak and burrowed into the protecting rock; and at the same time she burrowed into her own silence, listening for the voice of her own inner truth, hushing breath and waiting for comfort.

There was no comfort.

She had been vouchsafed a Word. A Word was never given to no purpose.

The heart of the shadow was inside her now; she did not want to have listen to it, but she must. She had to know. The key to the shadow was in the Word she had been vouchsafed and she did not want to know.

The night had come now, fully black, the stars above humbling her in their indifference and their distance. There was no wind, no sound except the whisper of the waves lapping. There was nothing – no haste, no urgency, no meeting house, no contest nor battle. There was no need for her; no one needed her consolation, her courage, her witness, the clear bell of her calling. No one needed those things here, except herself.

In the enormity of silence she turned back to the Word she had been given because there was nothing else to turn to. She chewed over the words again: tribulation, distress, persecution, famine, nakedness, peril, sword. She had tried them all, like Paul; and like Paul she had boasted of it. The great night mocked her. Well, then, not the sword perhaps, but imprisonment and persecution and famine. In Boston they had stripped her naked and searched her in public, probing and poking, seeking for the witch-marks while she had been eyed, greedy-eyed, by the Puritans of that city, men who could not laugh let alone lust. Nakedness. She pushed aside the humiliation and returned to her text. She was not afraid of death nor life, nor the powers and principalities of this world. The thought almost made her smile. Usually it was they who were afraid of her.

'Things present and things to come.' The night, the meeting with the pagan prince, final judgement. There was no shadow in these things, only curiosity and determination. She listened to the silence, bearing down on the words, forcing them to come to life in her. But under and through her her own silence there was a greater silence; something was missing, there was a hollowness in the text, and out of that hollow crawled the shadow that destroyed her own light. There was a deep hole, a chasm, at the very centre. But a word was not given to no purpose. Never. She had to find the purpose. Slowly, aloud, she repeated the whole text, focussing all her power on it, holding it steady before her and refusing to be distracted by her fear.

And then she knew. She knew what was missing and therefore what the shadow was. She was not glad to know. 'Things past.' Paul had overlooked the 'things past'; perhaps that had been right for him; but for her the things from the past could separate her from the Love of God. They had done so.

And she was alone and tempted in the wilderness. Satan did not offer her miracles nor bread nor the Kingdoms of the world, because he knew those things held no charm for her. Instead he offered her forgetting and forgetting and not having to remember. All her own power Satan had used to deceive her. For ten years he had tempted her with authority and words, with preaching and fame, with business and exhortation. She was a woman admired and loved, serviceable to the Lord. And it had been vanity, vanity. Satan's way to tempt her from the true silence, where she would have to turn again and confront the past if she wanted the serenity of the Love of God. It was to her past that she had to turn, if she ever wanted to be free, if she ever wished to hear her own inner truth again.

It was hard, so far from home and alone. It was very hard. But she was a strong woman; sturdy and trained, practised in seeking the truth and proclaiming it, even in the heart of desolation. She rebuked her fears. She called upon Daniel who had walked all night in the lions den, and she lay all night huddled against the ancient earth, within the singing sound of the great inner sea which had carried Paul to preach the word of life. And there, under the shelter of the rock she went travelling back into the past, holding her courage to that last point, as she had held it to so many things before.

She had been born in Pontefract in Yorkshire, a weaver's daughter, in the Year of Grace 1623, two years before the death of the Scottish King and the enthroning of the Man of Blood. She had been nursed on the old milk of family and place, but she had been weaned on politics and religion. For her father with the authority of the Bible in his hand and the stirrings of change coming on the winds from Scotland, would doff his hat to no man, nor let her curtsey ever. Such a small thing it seemed, but it was that that she brought with her from the morning of knowledge: that she was free born and should doff her hat to no one. There had been other things, long ranting and shouting meetings, part Bible and part bile. There had been little gentleness in the making of the Commonwealth of God. But speeches full of pre-destination and covenants and taxes and prayer books and kings and parliaments made little impact on a child. She had not understood that; what she had understood was the sullen heavy obduracy with which her father would keep his hat on his head, with which he would glare at her if he saw her knee so much as wobble, her head so much as nod, on the town street when the painted whores from the great houses went by. And as she grew his escalating obstinacy cost him his work, his position, his comfort, his liberty and his ears, but not, oh never, his dogged joyless sense of himself as righteous, as justified; upheld by a God as resolute and joyless as himself. It broke her mother's pride and she died of shame – unmoved by his zeal, wearied by his anger, shamed by his politics – and still he was not shaken.

Inevitably, inevitably as the pulling of a tide or the waxing of a moon, he had marched off to join Cromwell's army and the only time in all his life that she saw love in his eyes was when he said the name *Oliver*.

She had been left alone and he had scarcely noticed. He had blessed her in the Lord Jesus, told her to bend her knee to no man, reminded her that Liberty of Conscience was her strength and stay and that the Lord of Armies would uphold his oppressed; and then he had gone marching off to war with his friends leaving her friendless and alone. Alone and desperate, since his choices had isolated her from her community and made it well nigh impossible for her to earn an honest living. Most folk did not want a Ranter Maid, nor the daughter of a stubborn Independent in their service. He must have known and he had not cared.

Maria came. She came to the cottage one morning, neat and plain in brown dress and starched cap, just like all of them, but her brown serge was fresh and smooth and her cap was pure linen. 'Don't bend your knee to me, Sister' she had smiled, 'I think you must be in bad trouble even to consider it.' And after a small pause she added, 'I did not come for him, for your father, though he is fighting with my husband and I must love him. I came for you, because I have seen you at worship and heard your strong silence while too many speak.'

Maria. Dearest sister in Christ. Maria had taken her into her house and into her heart with so little fuss and so few words needed. Barely five years older than herself, but mistress of a great house, empowered by her husband in love and trust to run it while he too, though as an officer, took to the war to defend Liberty of Conscience and the Rights of Parliament. Mistress too of a great learning, a greater kindliness and a still greater passion. Maria had taken her as she was, for love, as daughter, as sister, as companion, as friend. And they had lived togther there and she had learned some things from books that were important, but more from Maria herself – that religion and politics were grounded together not in the Law but in the Love of God.

And together, women alone, they had followed the up and down courses of the war and had prayed daily for the safety of their own, for the safety of Cromwell and for the victory of truth and justice. And they argued from the Bible, from history and from their hearts, for the Liberty of Conscience, and the right management of the State and freedom and the Vote for all men – yes and women too, late one night, with giggles at that daring and at its impossibility – and other things forgotten now. And they cheered the gradual winning and their own men appeared briefly: Maria's husband, jovial and kindly, handsome on his big horse, the modest plume in his hat quivering with delight at seeing his young wife. And her father, lit up now with a fierce light, and transformed, golden, even lovely, in his new hope.

One happy time they both came together, flushed with their success, and stayed two glorious nights. And on the second evening her father had opened his heart and prophesied to them, speaking of the New Time that was coming, when Oliver disbanded the army and every man might sit each under his own apple tree and swords would be turned to ploughshares and the land itself would flourish in the year of Jubilee, and the Spirit would be poured forth in Liberty.

'You're a damned Leveller, man,' laughed Maria's husband.

'No, brother, a covenant man, but a free born one who'll . . .'

'Doff his hat for no man,' the three of them had chanted at him, mocking, loving, laughing all together and magically he had smiled. And her father's smile, gay on his strange earless face, had moved her suddenly to a new knowledge. From that moment she believed in the promise, from that moment she knew in her belly that it must be done, that it must be won: that right to sit at a table and say 'free born' and laugh together.

The news was uncertain but exciting. The Man of Blood captured; the New Parliament – no, the Old Parliament but winnowed by the hand of God, obedient to His holy will – preparing to bring him to justice. The army to be paid and disbanded; the army to go to work to decide how the New Way should best be brought in; great meetings at which any man might speak, and the soldiers choosing for themselves their own spokesman. And Maria with child, and the war soon to be over and the promise borne to fruit by the men who had bought freedom with their courage.

Then in the darkening of a long evening Maria's husband returned. Angry, sullen. And over their supper, not laughing and golden, 'Damn it, wife, they want to elect their own officers. They want to sit in council with us. They want the right to refuse orders they say are against God. Do they think I will take commands from some apprentice brat with a Bible in his dirty paw? They want Liberty of Conscience for ana-baptists and ranters who take off their clothes and wail in the streets. They go beyond God's good order: I swear that next they'll be wanting Parliament; have we come to this, to be ruled by men who have neither property nor interest?'

'I thought,' said Maria, dreamily as though she had heard his words but not the sourness in them, 'I thought it was what we fought for.'

And there was silence.

A silence icy and complete.

But in the night there was not silence. In the night she heard him shouting, shouting that he would be master in his own house, that he'd not be ruled or taught by women or rabble; that he stood with Cromwell and she was out of God's good order to rebuke him; and to get that witch woman out of his house and away from his son to be. And once, just once, she heard Maria cry out, only once, and she huddled in her bed and did not move.

In the morning Maria asked her to leave. Maria's eye was blackened, the bruise spreading, and her lip was cut and she did not raise her eyes from the floor; and neither of them even spoke about it. Maria gave her money and a blessing; she gave Maria thanks and a kiss, but neither of them spoke about it.

Later her father too came home. He came home broken. What the stocks and the ear-cropping and the poverty and his wife's death had never done, Oliver had done. It was love that had broken him.

Her father did not speak of it to her. She could learn what had happened only through gossip, the comings and goings of news in a small town where they did not love the man. He never told her that he had thrown his lot in with the Levellers, with his friends and fellows. The Levellers in the army had said that Cromwell could not disband them without their pay and he could not order them to Ireland, for they were free-born men and God himself guaranteed them their rights. They would not be ordered off to Ireland, and they would not be worn down into sneaking away at night, in despair, carrying their rights and demands, but not their honestly earned wages, with them. They would choose their own officers and their own representatives. They would have freedom of worship and Liberty of Conscience. Cromwell had agreed to negotiate with them and they had trusted him. He had trapped them and rounded them up like cattle and herded them into a Church some place south of Gloucester and he had preached them into submission. He had shot their leaders and broken their wills. He had not defeated them, but broken them and they had defeated themselves. They had penanced themselves like damned papists, they had snivelled and grovelled to him, whingeing like dogs. And they had consented to go to Ireland, or – like her father – had whispered away into the night, returning after the long years of war with nothing, with less than they had set out with, even their pride and their hope taken from them. They had loved Cromwell and trusted him and he had used their love to betray their trust.

She knew only that he was changed. She knew only that faith in a politics argued in righteousness and fought for in blood could not save a person from the betrayal of love.

He drank too much, and one evening at worship when the preacher had said that everyone might ask questions and she had stood up to speak, the minister had said, 'I do not permit a woman to speak in Church. Brother, take your daughter home and teach her respect.' Her father did not look at her; there was silence between them as they walked down the town. He drank all evening and she sat there not speaking. Late, late in the night her waiting came finally to an end. He stood up, 'I'll not have you shame me,' he said wearily. She said nothing. 'It's in Paul daughter, a woman may not speak.' She did not, but slowly she rose too, the pair of them facing each other across the room. 'You lack respect,' he said, still in that tired voice. 'I plead the Freedom of my Conscience,' she said calmly. 'As you taught me, I'll doff my hat to no man.'

So he beat her.

He beat her with the leather strap from the water pail, heavy and cold. He ripped her dress open down the back with one hand and he beat her until the blood came. He beat in dogged, sullen cold fury. He beat her in heavy concentrated silence and she received it in silence, and far away beyond the gateway of pain, of anger, of grief and loss, she knew that for the first time in thirty years she was the most important thing, the only thing, in his life. That his feeling for her was his only feeling and that how she felt towards him mattered to him. She felt a fierce crimson joy and knew that she was no longer free.

He went out the next day, leaving before dawn, with her still crumpled on the floor. Later she got up, washed as best she might, changed her dress, ordered her hair. Then she left the house and never returned, because she knew that her love would betray her and she would plead and grovel as both he and Maria had done.

Soon afterwards she heard Sister Elizabeth Hooton preach and she joined the Society of Friends. She was moved to do so because they let, no encouraged, women to speak. And because the Friends stood for Liberty of Conscience against all the principalities of this world. They held all people free born and would doff their hats to no man. They sought to change not the state, with its complexities and powers, but the inwardness of each person and thus the whole world. And they set no one in authority over another.

But also she was moved to join them because the Truth of Inner Light, the spark of God in each soul, set her free from other people. She did not need them, need to risk them, to know them and their betrayals and their loves, know their needs and their dark corners. She did not need, in the light of that truth, to bother with them any more, and she was relieved.

In the authority of her new freedom she became brave, bold, necessary, serviceable. Her head cleared; within a month she had been arrested in Selby for speaking out in the steeple house, and was imprisoned in York Gaol for six months. Released eventually, she felt full of excitement and power. She and Sister Elizabeth Williams went to Cambridge, to show the hireling shepherds that all their learning was of no use to the souls of the poor, and that thay used their knowledge against their sheep, and their power and wealth against God's own chosen ones. She had stood then in that grey city, in the centre of the dreadful wide-skied Fen country, Oliver's country, and the power of hatred had filled her. She had given a mighty testimony: she had spoken of the things of God to the young men there and had preached justice, freedom and equality openly at the gates of the Prison Houses that were called Colleges. But afterwards they were flogged. She had not anticipated it; it was the first public scourgeing, the first of many, that the Friends were to endure. She had not anticipated either the return of the crimson fire of joy, the excitement, the secret pleasure. Filled with the power of that fire she had indeed sung a triumph song, sung even as they beat her and praised God, but . . . but she had known what that witness had truly been and she had fled north again.

She had preached in Pontefract, but her father had not come to hear her and she did not see him because she was arrested again and returned to York for another six months in prison. And such was her power that they placed her in a cell on her own so that she should not stir up the other prisoners to protest at the injustice that was being meted out to them all. But in the solitude of the cell she could not turn away from the memory of the flogging and the excitement of it. Her hands learned new consolations that were not of the Spirit, and when, after her sentence was completed, she refused to take an oath of good behaviour and so earned herself another three months of solitude, she could no longer be certain whether she proclaimed Liberty of Conscience or was seeking rather the dark and dangerous pleasures of solitude and lustful imaginings.

So, after her release, she fled still further, first to the Barbadoes and then – since welcome and success and kindliness and admiration did not ease her – on to Boston. Here she and Sister Ann Austin declared a judgement on those who had left their homeland for the sake of the Liberties and now denied these to all others. In Boston they had been imprisoned again, and their books all burned, and their cell window barred against the light. But later they had been stripped naked and stood in public and examined for witch-marks; prodded, poked, excavated and she . . . and she for the first time was frightened, for as he pried at her inwardness surely the black clad witch-examiner would feel and know her heat and dampness. For the first time since she kissed Maria in silence she knew real shame. Sister Ann beside her tutted and grumbled, not so much enraged as cross; cross as she might have been if a neighbour had stolen cabbages from her garden. And seeing Ann's simple innocence she had known that she would have to flee still further.

'I am led,' she had told the York Meeting, 'I am led to cross the seas again.' But she had not been led she had been driven. The shadow of her lust was behind her, greedy and waiting to consume her; the shadow of her desire pounding her, hounding her, un-named, unacknowledged while she thought she was led in a glory of inner light. She travelled fast, Southwards to a springtime Italy, then Eastwards across the Mediterranean towards the rising sun, towards the lands of the crescent moon. At sea she had felt easier and the dotted islands on the water beyond Greece had filled her with a sudden happiness as they danced absurdly on the absurdly blue water. She had been full of hope, all troubles forgotten in the pure delight of travelling in unknown lands, towards those ancient countries where Paul and Barnabas, Phoebe and Prisca had once travelled as she did now, in the joy of their own inner light, so freshly and newly revealed.

At Smyrna however she had encountered a new obstacle. Landing she had planned to turn northward immediately and travel up the coast to Constantinople, but she was unexpectedly enchanted by the strange-smelling town, by its colour and bustle, by the extravagant buildings and the flaunting men; she had lingered enjoying herself. And the government officer from England had found her and detained her. She would not of itself have minded prison, but she was shaken by his caring: he was worried about her, concerned for her safety. Not angry or punitive, but anxious. She was confused: she had no experience of paternal affection. But he would not let her continue: a woman, in his well meaning and businesslike scheme of things, could not travel alone, could not wander unescorted, in pagan lands. Neither her will nor her witness could move him. So far away from home he was not concerned with theological niceties, only for her personal safety and his responsibility. He had bundled her back on a ship, Venice bound, while she was still smiling at him, enjoying his fine brown face, his gentle concern and his English voice.

It was a whole day's sailing before she realised what she had done; she had let kindness weaken her. Her smile faded and her obduracy rose. She would not be twisted from her path by affection, softened by gentleness; and she saw Maria's swollen eye, Maria's lip split at the corner, the dry scab cracked, her hair neat but her lip swollen, and neither of them speaking of it at all. So she set her will and bullied the ship's captain without mercy until he agreed to put her ashore as they passed the southern end of Greece. 'He was prevailed upon by the light and by my earnest testimony,' she told herself, practising for recounting her journey to some future meeting in some future town. But she knew that he was prevailed upon principally by his own sloth and by her ruthless determination.

But she had not outwitted the shadow, nor was she any longer sure that she had really wanted to. And in the lonely night she turned at last to meet it, and she named it from her past, from all those moments of making and meaning that she had refused to remember before. She held herself to examine them in all their detail, just as she had held herself before the Examiners in Boston, as she had held herself not to grovel to her father. And the shadow of her past swelled up enormous, black as hell and devoured her utterly. She faced her past and her sin and her filth and she wrestled with them as Jacob wrestled with his angel. But also it was not wrestling because her past moved into her, was her, was herself, was her own inward being – not love and light, but pride and filth. Like Maria, like Maria and her husband, like her own father, she had failed utterly: she had been free born and she had bound herself in chains, bound herself in the chains of humiliation, chains of flesh, of deceit, of cowardice. She had deceived others also, lied and tricked them. Maria had carried her shame openly – her eye bruised, her freedom broken; her father had known himself defeated, and had lived out his shame for all to see without pretence. But she . . . she had carried her defeat and her unloveliness in secret; she had accepted the praise and love that they had given her, she had boasted in her own power: she was the pit of hell, the spawn of Satan, unloving, unlovely, foul and deceitful even to her self.

As she turned to embrace the shadow it lept on her eagerly; on her, in her, over her, and it overwhelmed her. Her inner light, the presence of God, of love within her, from which nothing in the whole of creation should be able to sever her, wavered, flickered desperately, and the darkness overwhelmed it and it was extinguished.

She covered her face with her cloak and wept.

In the silence her tears were enormous and she sank into them and despaired. She drowned in them as her father in the drink, and when all the tears were used up she was a dry, empty shell, a carapace to be consumed into the earth, dead, finished. So she just lay there, and did not even form the question as to how long she might live now that she withdrawn her consent.

She never knew how long, and she never knew what changed. When without thought or preconsideration she pulled the cloak away from her face it was morning. The grey paling time had passed and the sun had risen, but barely. The night was once again completely conquered by the day, but the victory was still perfectly fresh, clean and golden. It was not the sun that had stirred her though. Not five feet away from her a cat was standing – a huge wild cat with rough flecked fur, small ears, low slung belly. It was motionless, but the last few bones of its tail flicked as though with a separate life and its eyes were turned towards her with a totally abstract interest. She assumed numbly that it had come to devour her as the Cities of the Plain had been devoured

for their uncleanliness. And although this seemed right and
fitting, a flicker of sadness somewhere deep inside marked a vast
turning of her heart. She made no movement though, only
waiting and admiring the beauty and the presence of the cat.

Nor did it move towards her; it just stared with open eyes, and
then, turning its head, it walked calmly on and was gone.

Pure gift.

For the great staring eyes said to her, You are who you are. If
you had acted in love and truth you would not have acted other
than you did act. There would have been only one difference –
you would have had more joy.

She knew that this was a gift of truth.

She had been alone for nearly forty years – it was enough. She
could lay it down, let it be. She was washed clean. Gifts are given,
and they are not taken away. She would get up now and go and
bear her witness to the great Sultan and then she would go home.
The cat with the glowing eyes, whose aloneness was as great as
her own, had offered her forgiveness. It was enough. It would be
churlish not to accept it. She accepted.

As she walked that day, beginning at last the long descent into
the great fertile valley where Greece and Asia Minor meet, she
was vouchsafed a new word:

> The spirit immediately drove him out into the wilderness. He
> was in the wilderness forty days, tempted by Satan; and he was
> with the wild beasts and the angels ministered to him.

And a few weeks later, in the great encampment outside
Adrianople, she had an interview with the Sultan himself. It had
not been easy to arrange, because his subjects were all too scared
to raise the matter – the new and extraordinary matter of a pale
woman from far away, who could not speak his language but who
wanted to talk to him of God. She understood their fear, but she
set it aside as she had done so many times before, because she
was determined to finish the task she had chosen. Then she could
go home and start the new, far harder task of learning love and
joy. Her persistence, as so often before, overcame their reluctance. An interpreter was found and a time arranged.

As she was about to enter the Presence, a courtier handed her
a veil and indicated that she should cover her face and kneel on

the ground before Him. She almost giggled as she refused, saying, 'I plead the Liberty of my Conscience, for I am free born and doff my hat to no man.' The courtier looked both confused and terrified, but she was filled with gaiety. And when the Sultan, seated composed and magnificent on his silken cushions, raised his head – his turban glinting in the tent light, his court prostrate, their faces covered, before him – then he looked for the first time in his life into a pair of level eyes that showed neither fear nor desire. He smiled at her. He was only eighteen.

She preached for him, and afterwards they talked a little, although it was hard through the cautious interpreter to know how much they really understood each other. He seemed to agree with much of her witness: 'Yes, yes, that is all true,' he repeated more than once. The important thing was the smile that they had shared. He courteously invited her to stay in his country for a while and to address him or any of his people again.

But she refused and went home to Pontefract in Yorkshire.

Note

Mary Fisher was born in 1623; in 1652 she joined the Society of Friends which had been founded by George Fox and Elizabeth Hooton in about 1646. Because of their interior sense of transformation the Friends were completely unassimilable into their contemporary society: because they believed in the equality of all people before God they refused to use referential titles for monarchs, magistrates, or bishops. They insisted on the right of everyone, including women, contrary to the law of the land, to speak in public if moved by the Spirit. Their rejection of war prevented them from serving in the army or paying taxes that would support a military budget. Their commitment to the importance of Freedom of Conscience meant that they refused to support a state established church by paying tithes – then a part of taxation.

Mary Fisher quickly becames a recognised preacher in the Society, and consequently spent a number of occasions in prison, both in England and in Boston. She also worked in the Caribbean before setting out on her historic journey to preach to the

Sultan of the Ottoman Empire, Mohammed IV. After she returned from this adventure she married, and after the death of her first husband took a second and emigrated to Carolina. She is last recorded living there in her seventies and still offering her active succour to oppressed members of the Society of Friends and to the poor.

The Curator's Tale

SARA MAITLAND

'This,' she said is the most miserable time of all. The hunch is stronger than the observation. The links between the hunch and the observation are clearly there, but at this stage people still think you are quite mad. They are as fearful as if you had cancer. The danger in cancer is to die; . . . and the danger in the scientific process – at least in this society – is the danger of having an idea which is wrong. It's equivalent to death.'

An Imagined World, June Goodfield

The curator had had a tiring day.

A very tiring day.

The reconstruction which had made her name had been dismantled, taken down, thrown away.

She was seventy-two years old. It had been a terribly tiring day.

She stood now, a moment's pause not quite without complacency, at the top of the monumental sweep of staircase, under the shadow of her grandiose museum. Once she had found it ostentatious, vulgar and typically Victorian, but now she loved it. She was powerfully reassured by it and she swaggered almost, her gesture disguised by the outrageous swagger of the building; and the traffic pouring past the foot of the staircase did not pause to notice or care. Normally she would have slipped out of the door at the back – modern, convenient to her office and approximately half a mile nearer home – but today she needed that pause, that assured swagger; she needed all the outdated civic dignity that the ornate brickwork could give her; she needed that moment of standing framed in the massive doorway and looking out over the traffic through the plane trees. She needed to steady herself.

For a flicker of time the pause became a pose. She hitched her voluminous and shabby satchel further behind her back, out of sight, and stuck her hands deep into the pockets of her jacket. Even the noise of the traffic could not silence her mother's voice saying, 'Rachel, I do wish you wouldn't adopt those mannish postures,' and she grinned a defiance nearly sixty years old. There were no cameras; the pose was for her own invisible spirits to admire; for them to congratulate her on her courage and integrity. She could seek no other praise. She not had acted virtuously, only necessarily. There would be no congratulations, nor should there be.

It was a pose though of professional not personal vanity. There was a photograph of her that Phoebe had hung in Amy's room, showing her half a century ago, brown and whipcord slender, wearing shorts and a soft sunhat over her cropped hair and looking, it had to be acknowledged, magnificent. But that was Phoebe's vanity, Phoebe's image, not hers. For herself she had known what had come about one day several years ago when she had been reading a P. G. Wodehouse story. It contained a description of a woman who 'fitted into my biggest armchair as if it had been designed for her by someone who knew they were wearing armchairs tight about the hips that season.' Instead of laughing she had wept. She had, when young, always imagined that she would grow up into a magnificent old lady, tall and gaunt with a craggy but splendid bone structure and fingers like lizards' talons. She had been wrong about that too. Now she bought her clothes at Harrods because they did not distinguish an 'Out Size Department.'

The reconstruction which had made her name had been taken down. She had ordered this to happen and had spent the day supervising the task. Her own, her very own, late Cretaceous carnivorous dinosaur, which she had excavated herself and reconstructed from her own fossils, reconstructed with 'an imaginative intuition amounting to genius' as the Old Man himself had said. The dinosaur named after her father, which had proved her bold and flashy theories, which had stood as a central exhibit in the museum to the delight of school children and the admiration of her colleagues for over thirty years. It had been taken down, torn apart and would now be thrown away.

Because she had been wrong.

She had been wrong when everyone had said she was wrong, and she had still been wrong when everyone had said she was right. Of course, over thirty years, she had been challenged and the details had been filled in, but her central thesis had endured, because the museum liked it, because the public liked it, and because of course, once they had grasped it, the palaeontologists liked it a lot. She could have got away with it too, and that hurt. The museum particularly had waited eagerly for her to defend it, and would have given her every benefit of the doubt, and then some extra – it was a popular exhibit, it fitted in with modern ideas of museumology even better than it fitted with outdated ideas of palaeontology. Even dear Paula, her research assistant (it isn't fair, she always gives jobs to the girls, they said, as though men didn't always give jobs to the boys, except of course their daughters and she had no sons), even Paula had hinted, had half-suggested, that they leave it 'for now', meaning of course until she was dead. And, dear God, that reminded her, she must take care to live long enough for poor dear Maxwell to alter her obituary, perhaps she should write to him; she would hate him to be embarrassed, and he was so old and ga-ga now that he was bound to miss the literature. They were all old and ga-ga now. She was too, probably. She ought to have retired and left someone else to do the job, someone whose professional jealousy could have given him real pleasure in proving her wrong. For it gave her no pleasure. That was why she needed the soft sunshine of a city evening, and all the strength she could draw from the extravagant and outmoded architecture: to steady her, to give her substance, to make acting righteously feel as though it were enough.

Because of course it had been damned expensive. No one knew how expensive. Except Phoebe maybe, and she did not want Phoebe to know. She did not want Phoebe's pity, or her scorn, or to be grist for Phoebe's theories. But being wrong was even more expensive than being right. She had given up too much for that dinosaur. She had not meant to, she had not set out to do anything so complicated. The paths in seemed always joyful and simple, but like a lobster pot you went in easy and did not know until too late the impossibilities of return. For women there was never anyone to hold the thread when they went into the labarynth. And the Minotaur only ate young women. Ambition it was called, but no one ever thought that *she* was ambitious: *she* was just getting on with it, making today's choices,

short term and just for now, for the enormous excitement of an
idea, a find, a discovery, just for fun. No one told you when you
were young and ambitious that all ambition was greed, and that
all greed had to be paid for, or it did if you were a woman, a
woman who wanted to be any sort of scientist and . . . oh, damn
Geoffrey. Damn him. She was too old now for understanding
and forgiveness (always hers of course). All the explanations –
the War, and late fatherhood, and even the simple fact of being
an ambitious man with a more successful (no, no, a cleverer,
more competent, better-at-the-job, she was also too old to lie
about it) a *more intelligent* wife – didn't help and didn't matter.
Just damn him, because he could have been more generous,
because he had promised he would be, and he had not kept his
word. He had lied to her. So damn him. She dealt in truth
becasue she had to. She was seventy-two years old, he had been
dead for nearly fifteen years, and it was he still who had brought
her to this place of pain, this place of holding on to a slim margin
of dignity and professional integrity and making that be enough.

And how to damn him, when there was Amy carrying his genes,
visible in her nose and the turning of her too thin neck. Amy.
Amy. Her legs were so skinny that they filled you with fear for her
on windy days. Her shoulder blades were like wings, trapped
under her shirts, mobile, fluent, fighting their restraint. Sometimes when Amy spoke her silvery words of wisdom you could
almost see the soft smoke and delicate flames emerge from her
mouth and nostrils, not to burn but to illuminate. Phoebe had
grown up repudiating the hard clarity of science, butting her fierce
and stubborn head against the edifice of logical thinking, of a
reasoned and relaxed relationship between facts and conclusions.
Phoebe called it 'masculine modes of thought' and rejected it
conscientiously. It made her a cranky and trying young woman,
frankly, though she was your daughter and you went on loving her.
But Phoebe had produced Amy and Amy was a bell of clarity.
Amy was ten years old and she knew already. The truth was in her.
So deeply and naturally that she did not have to fight it. The
ancient and enduring truth, so that when she sang and danced, and
walked and breathed, the light poured out of her and her shiny
eyes were wide and deep.

She had married Geoffrey in 1935. She had been twenty-one
and had just taken her brilliant degree. Her father had liked
Geoffrey, liked his work and his background and, in fairness,
him, and probably the flattering fact that he was so much older
than she was. Her mother had been deeply relieved that all this
education had not protected her only daughter from woman-
liness. Even so they had both thought she was too young. But she
had wanted to go excavating with Geoffrey, hammers in their
hands and ideas in their heads. They would of course have to be
married or else she could not go. She had tried, quite recently to
explain this to Phoebe and Phoebe had roared with laughter, not
very kindly laughter. Phoebe had no sense of history, unfortunately. Her own father had been on the Central Asiatic Expedition in 1923; he had taken her and her mother with him as far as
Kalgan. So she had spent the end of her first decade in that
strange and colourful city up-country from Beijing. Where her
mother had poured immaculate afternoon tea seated at a camp
table, and where the wind from the desert of Mongolia was held
back by the great and ancient wall that snaked across the wild
lands of the innermost continent. She had stood on that wall in
her neat black stockings and looked northwards into the vast
vaccuity which had spawned the Mongul Hordes and which now
spawned promises and whispers of the most ancient secret, of the
origins of humanity. The wind sweeping in from the waste place
beyond the wall now blew the scent and spice of an even more
deeply hidden past, the dream and the reality of fossils, of
dinosaur memories. Perched there, still spindly like Amy, she
had fallen in love for the first time, with her father and with
palaeontology; ten years later, promising, hopeful and in love
afresh she *needed* to go on Geoffrey's expedition with him.

She was financed by her father as his wedding present to her.
She was described as Geoffrey's assistant and secretary in the
expedition reports, but she had known herself to be his companion, his colleague and his friend. It was from that charmed and
charming field trip that the photograph in Amy's bedroom came.
No wonder she had looked magnificent; she had been magnificent. Africa had opened its arms like a warm mother, though
doubtless Phoebe would say that was racist, and heaped her
sweetness up on them. Sunshine and good luck and wildness still

untamed and friendship and an unexpected abundance of Upper Jurassic and Lower Cretaceous dinosaur fossils and wonderful sex. And Geoffrey so kind and generous and eager to teach and share: mentor, tutor and lover as well. And, although she had not said it then or since, best of all the growing certainty that *this* was what she did, this finding and understanding of fossils was her work, a shared labour and one at which she was easily at home and exceptionally talented: an odd combination of learning and then seeing, guessing and then confirming, and proving both learning and sight with the utter physicality of digging and extracting. She had been made for this. Warmed by Geoffrey's benignity and his own seniority, she could escape the veiled insinuations of some of the young men on the team and concentrate on learning her job. She had been filled and overflowing with joy.

Phoebe constantly told her that it was sentimental to believe that the summers then had been warmer, the sun brighter, the colours of everything fresher – but still she did believe it. They should have known of course that a shadow had fallen over the world and the diluvian rain clouds were gathering, but they had not cared; they had turned their backs on a troubled Europe and plunged into a superficially untroubled Africa, not bothered by the things that should have bothered them. The guilt had come later but she could not now pretend that it had been otherwise; then it had seemed a time of hope. The archaeologists were pushing backwards and the palaeontologists and geologists were pushing forward and there seemed good grounds to believe that they would meet in the middle somewhere, probably Central Asia or Western Africa, and it all seemed more exciting and more important than the fate of Abyssinia, or Spain or even central Europe. And when you leaned forward to examine newly dug ground the sun stroked your back and kissed your naked neck and who could not be pleased with themselves.

They had two seasons in Africa, two seasons of rich and exciting digging; two seasons during whch the white farming community had laughed at them but kindly and warm hearted so they they felt both welcome and superior; two seasons during which she hardly spoke to another woman, but lived slim and vital like a boy, separated it felt from the other members of the expedition more by youth than by sex.

They returned to a cold and changed England that they could not really understand, to find that ancient loyalties had shifted and what seemed strange to them had become daily fare to old friends. They found it difficult to reconnect and were pushed ever more closely into each other's arms. Politically, along with their friends, they opposed appeasement, but in the secret corners of the hearts they did not: they did not want a war, but to spend time with their fossils, time to work and catalogue and assess, to contemplate and to publish. They wanted contact with their German colleagues whom they could not understand as the enemy, but only as the best palaeontologists in the world. They told themselves that the community of scientists was international and beyond political boundaries; but they had to close their eyes to the number of Jewish scientists whose addresses had changed, or whose names were disappearing. They were confused by the world and excited by each other. Nonetheless with considerable solemnity and self-satisfaction, with unspoken murmers of look-at-me-and-my-fine-sacrifice, Geoffrey had joined up in 1939, and she had been alone. 'Take care of our bones,' he said on Waterloo Station, and disappeared.

Almost immediately she took a museum job in London; she would not normally have had such an opportunity and she knew it, but there were not a great number of women palaeontologists around. Later the job became the more dramatic, but less scholarly one of preparing the entire major collection for evacuation. It turned out to be a reserved occupation. It cut her off still further from other women, who could not understand its importance, not like munitions, or nursing, or even real research, just messing about with old bones while other people furthered the War Effort. She spent most of the war alone missing Geoffrey terribly, missing sex and companionship and real work. She practically lived in the basement of the museum because it seldom seemed worth the effort of returning to the flat to be alone there. And for the first time in her life she started reading more widely – history and anthropology first, and later psychology, the classics and mythology. And in between this animated reading and her job she looked endlessly, lovingly, tenderly and hopefully at the beautiful, careful, scholarly sketches that Geoffrey had done of their fossils. They were the nearest thing she had to him and to her own work and they gave her back the feel of an Africa so distant and strange and wonderful that she knew sadly she would never go there again.

And while London burned and she mourned, she conceived her idea. A curious amalgam in a curious time; part Jung, part Franz Nopcsa, part Africa and part inspiration. In 1943 Geoffrey was captured. She wrote the book for him, reaching out to him in prison, in the cold place where he could not touch fossils or her, and she had to tell him stories across the dark, across the dark which was ablaze with the fires of hell; where fire fell from the sky and smoke rose up to meet it. Dragons, she concluded, were not the products of imagination, they were deep race memories of the dinosaurs. The book was called *Fossil Remains and Dragon Lore* and was subtitled 'a scientific fairy story'. It proved that even primal myth should be placed safely in the hands of the natural sciences.

It was an idea for the post-war era, for the New Britain; an idea which fitted into the dreams of a new life of science and technology which was going to arise out of the ashes of a broken world. It was one of the first really accessible books on what palaeontologists had been up to for over half a century; it moved away from text-book publications and the elitism of a profession which was still trying to prove its scientific credentials – not because she had felt a populist mission, but because she had been too young and too professionally privileged to know that struggle, because she had been lucky and beloved. The book was published in 1948 and to her genuine surprise proved immensely popular. Fellow palaeontologists were amused and impressed or challenged and stimulated. Her father was delighted.

Geoffrey was furious.

He expressed his fury in coldness and in his determination to get her pregnant.

He had come home in 1946. She had been so happy to see him. Like all POW wives, and especially those whose men had been in the East. She knew her man had had a bad time, that it might be difficult. Love, they had been told, would conquer all. Of course he needed a home life, and attention, and love; now was not the time to tell him about her work, about what she had been up to while he had been missing all the fun. She resigned her job with scarcely a regret – she had not deserved it anyway, and she knew it. She wanted to be in Oxford with him. If he wanted a big house away from the centre instead of a handy flat that seemed completely reasonable to her. When she showed him her typescript she tried not to mind that it took him a surprisingly long time to read it; after all he had his own stuff to catch up on and it was only apprentice work after all; he was a real scientist, she was just his admiring student. She had dedicated the book to him. He treated it, rightly, as a matter of not much account – an interesting idea possibly, though rather over stretched. He pointed out some minor technical errors. He also corrected her punctuation, but she ignored that. He never discussed the central thesis. And, she noticed, he now always said 'my fossils' not 'our fossils' as he worked on the important task of cataloguing them, ignoring all the preliminary work she had done with them.

'Cassaubon,' she thought one night and was ashamed of herself.

It was not until after the book was published that she realised how angry he was. She tried not to think straight, although it was difficult – it was not until the book was successful that he had really been angry.

'I wish to God,' he said one day, 'that you hadn't dedicated that thing to me; it's so embarrassing.'

When he did not get the job in York he said that he wished she'd used her own name for her 'so-called professional' publications – 'I'm afraid they may have got me confused with your visionary ramblings.' She never told him that she had been invited to apply for the job herself and had refused because she knew that he wanted it. It was not fair on him and his colleagues that they had had to go and fight a war while she had done their work and had time to do her own.

'Look,' she said, 'I'm just a populist, a communicator; it's the real academics whose work matters.' But she was publishing academically too, steadily. She had to defend her idea, which argued for a later extermination of carnivorous dinosaurs than was generally held; she had to describe her sources and compare finds. In 1948 the Russian expedition to Mongolia through Ulan Bator discovered the 'The Dragon's Tomb' – an extraordinary collection of late dinosaur remains. They sent her their technical notes, and some queries about how she would interpret some of their data. She took the material to her father, although his memory was not as good as it should be any more, and they had a happy time working through it. But to Geoffrey she said, 'Of course they only sent it because Daddy was with Andrews,' or 'Only because I have more time to publish, I don't have all the department headaches,' or 'They can't have read the book, it's only the association of dragons in both titles.' But he stopped bringing his visiting colleagues home to meet her and he started insisting on the baby.

Well, of course she wanted a baby. She wanted Geoffrey's baby; before the war it had been him saying wait, wait, and there's no hurry and we've got so much work to do together. She still wanted to have his baby. They had a house and he a secure job. So why was she so frightened? No, frightened was not the right word. But there was still time, and she had been invited to go to the USA. But Geoffrey had been through the war; and of course he was older than she was.

In 1951 her father died. Within eight weeks she was pregnant.

She thought she was bound to have a son who would be like her father. Instead she had Phoebe, who from birth onwards looked exactly like Geoffrey.

The problem was not Phoebe who happened to be a complete delight and very easy baby. Influenced by modern psychology she did not employ a nanny, so she had all the pleasure of Phoebe's growing and although it did cut into her work time this was not such a bad thing, because she had run out of steam a bit. What she needed, desperately needed, was some proof. She needed one, just one, suitable dinosaur, later, not even a lot later, than anything they yet had. She was sure it was there, waiting for her; all the evidence suggested that it was bound to be there. Indeed the profession was coming round to her way of thinking, they all now wanted it to be there; once they had grasped the notion they tended, those who liked grand theories, to like hers. It made them important for one thing, though she had not realised that then, it kept attention focussed on them, rather than on the climatologists, or the origins of man people who were grabbing the lime-light, the influential positions, the publishing space, the best jobs.

She wanted to go and look for it. Too frustrating to wait for someone else. She wanted field work to refresh her mind. She wanted the stimulation of travel and the reality of a spade and a hammer in her hands. Geoffrey wanted her to stay at home with Phoebe. Geoffrey was suddenly extraordinarily well read in child psychology for someone who had dismissed its use in her own work. 'I'll take her with me.'

'Too dangerous.'

'Don't be silly.'

'I'd miss her too much,' he said, 'I'd miss you too.'

'Come with us,' she said, sudden memories of the warmth of the sun and his kisses on her neck.

But he had forgotten. 'I've got too much work to do, real work' and 'I've got neither the time nor the patience to hang around some god-forsaken dust hole, trying to keep some uppity camp boys under control while you try and bend scientific fact to match your crazy theories.'

'Geoffrey,' she had pleaded, 'If you're so sure I'm wrong, can't you show me where.'

'Oh God,' he said, 'if you can't see the problems for yourself, what on earth is the point?' and after that he would not talk about it anymore. If her work came up he simply looked distant and a few hours later he would complain about the state of the house or the inadequacies of her cooking. She made sure it came up as seldom as possible because she could understand how he felt, how it would hurt her if he had a theory that she sure was wrong. And of course if things were bad between them then it was bound to affect Phoebe. And of course she loved him very much.

In 1957 he was finally offered an expedition of his own. He was pleased and sunny and laughed and said that it just showed that careful, conscientious, scholarly work payed off in the end. He had forgotten how much he would miss her and Phoebe. She decided that she would go to. She knew he did not want her to. She thought it through and played her cards with care. She never said she was going, but she let all his colleagues and her correspondents assume that she was, that she was excited, and that he and she both believed there were great hopes in the site. She put him in a position where he would look silly, petty and needlessly fearful if he refused point blank to take her. She hated herself and him and felt guilty, but she could barely suppress her excitement at the thought of once again doing what she did best, digging up new fossils, being a field palaeontologist.

He won though. She went with him to Africa, and she was deftly confined as a camp follower. Her reputation was not big enough to follow her into the bush; he, as leader of the expedition, had every right to bring his wife and delightful baby with him, what fun for them, and always useful to have a woman in the camp to oversee the cook and the boys.

She won too, because she found it. She wanted it so badly and despite everything she found it, or enough of it anyway. Not fifty yards from the camp, a good mile from where the proper digging was going on, in a rock formation that no one else would have considered, she found it: a good part of the skull and several vertebrae in good condition, plus some not very easy fragments of major bones. Not articulated, not properly *in situ*, but late, late, late, and exactly what she had predicted. She had wanted it too much. She should have known that you must not want too much, that you must not be greedy, that greed distorts judgement. But she had said she would find it, and she had found it. She would have liked some teeth as well, of course, but no one gets everything: she had enough.

She did not even tell them. Waved them off each morning holding Phoebe's hand and smiling; then a quick turn around, leaving Phoebe playing happily in the camp, but with her glasses on and her hammer in her hand. She extracted it damn near single-handed. If she hadn't been so good . . . But no, she must not think that, must not boast, it did not matter and it was probably not true anyway.

When Geoffrey found out she knew it was the end. He would never forgive her. It made her fragments matter more not less. Back at home, two years and two important papers later, she had brilliantly produced her reconstruction of a previously unkown, late Cretaceous carnivorous dinosaur, named after her father, but better know in the museum and in the literature as the 'Dragon Type,' which was generally agreed to prove the theory she had first suggested ten years previously. Natural science laid claims through her work to a whole new territory and everyone, except Geoffrey was delighted.

She had never gone on another field trip – there was Phoebe's education to be thought of. Gradually, without specifically planning it she moved out of pure research, and finally when Phoebe was old enough, she took a musuem job again. The new skills of museumology, the presentation of material so as to delight and edify, seemed a more suitable area for her to operate in, especially since having a child she would naturally understand the educational aspects. The museum was properly very proud to have her: it was a good, eminent and relatively well paid job, one that she found increasingly pleased her – after all she had always been primarily a communicator, a populariser of the important work that academics like her husband did. Also it eased the tensions between Geoffrey and she, and they managed to get along all right. When he died in 1973 she was sad for quite a long while, and then when Amy was born in 1976 she and Phoebe had bought the Bayswater house together, divided it into the two flats and it had worked very well. But she had been proud of her dinosaur, painfully proud of her dinosaur, because it had been so expensive for her; it had to be good, it had to be. She needed so much to prove that the world of science was stronger and more real, more important than the world of the heart, of love and of joy.

But recently she had become convinced that the facts should not be made to accord with her original conclusions. Damn. This had been borne in on her from two distinct sources. There were the scientific data. A very bright young woman in Philadelphia had written an important critique, and although she had dismissed it in print, though without malice, and to everyone's apparent satisfaction . . . well it gave her pause. There was a problem with the age of the sediment; and worse, the possibility – overlooked, she now knew, in her enthusiasm – that the dinosaur had not been fossilised where she had found it, that it was older than she wanted it to be, and that her reconstruction was shaky, was wrong. Palaeontologists had been wrong before; Gideon Mantell had placed the *Iguanadont's* spiked thumb on its nose as a horn. Being wrong about detail did not necessarily matter. But her belief in the theory collapsed entirely under the pressure from Amy and Fenna.

Fenna was Amy's imaginary dragon.

Amy was the most purely joyful thing in her whole life, the absolutely wanted child, the golden speck at the bottom of the

Pandora's box of her life. Amy was sweetness and light when she had finally ceased to expect it. Amy had reconciled her to Phoebe's morals and politics, since without those Amy would not have existed. Amy was Amy and was also the means of her steady comradeship with Phoebe, and therefore her home and her happiness.

Fenna was the most purely joyful thing in Amy's life. And Amy was more generous than her mother or grandmother; she was determined to share her joy.

Fenna had appeared when Amy was about five years old. At first she had been flattered that Amy had turned not to an imaginary brother or sister or friend, but to her grandmother's work.

But over the next five years she had come to realise that Fenna was no compliment.

Fenna was her enemy. She was Fenna's enemy.

Fenna was an assault, an attack, on all that she had stood for.

Fenna was the wilful instrument of her own professional dis-integration.

Fenna was flame and fire, and moved on the wings of the night that were dragon wings to dance with taloned claws and mock scientific theory.

Fenna was the dark force of the imagination as well as its golden dancing; Fenna was chaos as well as order, and brought, on fiery dragon breath, the full danger of the chasm.

Amy could play safely with Fenna and explore the land of dark flames and reversed colours that lies in the pit of disorder; Amy could ride the rough neck clinging to the glittering scales and interpret the wreaths of smoke that drifted from Fenna's nostrils when the great beast played at being tame. Amy was safe because she never thought to deny Fenna's powers and floated with them, but the two older women suffered under the assaults of this strange visitor from within the dreaming self. Phoebe could learn in the end to smile and shrug off as a game the tickling of Fenna's wrath, because she still played fast and loose with the disciplined structures of convention and rules which are supposed to protect women from their dreams. But she could not. Amy was as gentle as she could be, as gentle as any child who has grown up loved, loving and thoughtful, but Amy delighted in Fenna and could not understand why her grandmother was afraid of the long scorching breaths, the flailing tail that swept the stars across the sky on windy nights and hurled them down beyond the horizon in exploding fireworks, the vast wings that shaped the storms of the universe. And Fenna had taught her a toughness, a scaled cladding against delusion so that she knew quite well that unless and until her grandmother truly recognised and respected the powers of which Fenna was the prophet, then she could not really hope to be safe.

So Fenna unknotted the scientific shapes of her mind and each knot severed or untwined hurt her head. And the ones that she would not let Fenna melt with steaming breath hurt even more; they swelled into ugly lumps in her brain and kept her awake at night; they tangled themselves around all the words that she wanted to read, or the scholarship she wanted to consider, and there was no peace for her at all.

Fenna and Amy persuaded her that she could no longer claim for science the priority over life and death and dreams that she demanded for it. Fenna and Amy persuaded her, very simply, that dragons were entirely real, were real products of the mind and eye and hopes and desires and loves and hates of life. Their reality was more central than hers.

So being committed – more lovingly and more clearly than at any time since she was twenty – to the disciplines of scientific truth, she ordered her life work to be torn apart. The paper denouncing it, which she had the arrogance to insist on writing herself, though she printed it as co-written by Paula, because Paula was going to need to detach herself from her past professionally, had been as calm and reasoned and sparkling with accuracy and detail as anything she had ever done before. She did not mention Fenna and Amy in the paper because she was afraid it might confuse things and she had wanted there to be no possibility of mistake. But she had known, and so had they.

She was very tired and paused now on the monumental steps of her museum, because she had spent the day supervising the destruction of her meaning. She would cling to her professional integrity as she had done for fifty years, and she would, as she had always tried to, make that sufficient. The pose, the swagger, the moment of pride was solitary, an indulgence for herself alone, and there would be nothing more. She would go home. And also it was high time that she retired.

She shook herself slightly and took a final look down the proud granite staircase towards the traffic. Then running her eyes along the trees she suddenly noticed, for the first time, a medium sized green and scarlet dragon sitting in the upper branches of a particularly fine plane tree and munching a green leaf. It looked directly at her, its ancient and mischievous eye almost tender, and the smoke furling gently from its navy blue nostrils wafted gently into the evening, almost indistinguishable from the exhaust fumes of the cars below it. She had never seen a dragon before, and now she was liberated into joy.

For someone over seventy her descent of the great staircase was as good as a frolic; her satchel swung wildly round, merrily bumping her large bottom, her sensible suede shoes skippetty-hopped like the finest quality glass slippers, while her honest tweed skirt flirted up her legs in order to give her long beige knickers their first sight of the sunshine in fifty years.

By the time she reached the bottom the dragon had vanished, but this, far from mattering, only added to her amusement. Quite suddenly she felt a generous relief, as though she'd given science and herself new hope of heaven, and set out through the coming dark, home across the dragon haunted park.

The Wicked Stepmother's Tale

SARA MAITLAND

The wife of a rich man fell sick and as she felt that her end was drawing near, she called her only daughter to her bedside and said, 'Dear Child, be good and pious, and then the good God will always protect you, and I will look down from heaven and be near you.' Thereupon she closed her eyes and departed. Every day the maiden went out to her mother's grave and wept, and she remained pious and good. When winter came the snow spread a white sheet over the grave and by the time the spring sun had drawn it off again the man had taken another wife . . .

Now began a bad time for the poor step-child . . . They took her pretty clothes away, put an old grey bedgown on her and gave her wooden shoes . . . She had to do hard work from morning to night, get up before daybreak, carry water, light fires, cook and wash . . . In the evening when she had worked until she was weary she had no bed to go to, but had to sleep by the hearth in the cinders. And as on that account she always looked dusty and dirty, they called her Cinderella.

You know the rest I expect. Almost everyone does.

I'm not exactly looking for self-justification. There's this thing going on at the moment where women tell all the old stories again and turn them inside-out and back-to-front – so the characters you always thought were the goodies turn out to be the baddies, and vice versa, and whole lot of guilt is laid to rest: or that at least is the theory. I'm not sure myself that the guilt isn't just passed on to the next person, *intacta* so to speak. Certainly I want to carry and cope with my own guilt, because I want to carry and cope with my own virtue and I really don't see that you can have one without the other. Anyway it would be hard to find a version of this story where I would come out a shiny new-style heroine: no true version anyway. All I want to say is that it's more complicated, more complex, than it's told, and the reasons why it's told the way it is are complex too.

But I'm not willing to be a victim. I was not innocent, and I have grown out of innocence now and even out of wanting to be thought innocent. Living is a harsh business, as no one warned us when we were young and carefree under the apple bough, and I feel the weight of that ancient harshness and I want to embrace it, and not opt for some washed-out asceptic, hand wringing, Disneyland garbage. (Though come to think of it he went none-too-easy on stepmothers did he? Snow White scared the socks off me the firt time I saw the film – and partly of course because I recognised myself. But I digress.)

Look. It was like this. Or rather it was more like this, or parts of it were like this, or this is one part of it.

She was dead pretty in a Pears Soap sort of way, and, honestly, terribly sweet and good. At first all I wanted her to do was concentrate. Concentration is the key to power. You have to concentrate on what is real. Concentration is not good or bad necessarily, but it is powerful. Enough power to change the world, that's all I wanted. (I was younger then, of course; but actually they're starving and killing whales and forests and each other out there; shutting your eyes and pretending they're not doesn't change anything. It does matter.) And what she was not was powerful. She wouldn't look out for herself. She was so sweet and so hopeful; so full of faith and forgiveness and love. You have to touch anger somewhere, rage even; you have to spit and roar and bite and scream and know it before you can be safe. And she never bloody would.

When I first married her father I thought she was so lovely, so good and so sad. And so like her mother. I knew her mother very well, you see; we grew up together. I loved her mother. Really. With so much hope and fondness and awareness of her worth. But – and I don't know how to explain this without sounding like an embittered old bitch which I probably am – she was too good. Too giving. She gave herself away, indiscriminately. She didn't even give herself as a precious gift. She gave herself away as though she wasn't worth hanging on to. Generous to a fault, they said when she was young, but no one acted as though it were a fault, so she never learned. 'Free with Kellogg's Cornflakes' was her motto. She equated loving with suffering I thought at one time, but that wasn't right, it was worse, she equated loving with being; as though she did not exist unless she was denying her existence. I mean, he was not a bad bloke her husband, indeed I'm married to him myself, and I like him and we have good times together, but he wasn't worth it – no one is – not what she gave him, which was her whole self with no price tag on.

And it was just the same with that child. Yes, yes one can understand: she had difficulty getting pregnant actually, she had difficulties carrying those babies to term too. Even I can guess how that might hurt. But her little girl was her great reward for suffering, and at the same time was also her handle on a whole new world of self-giving. And yes, of course she looked so lovely, who could have resisted her, propped up in her bed with that tiny lovely child sucking, sucking, sucking; the mother who denied her little one nothing, the good mother, the one we all longed for, pouring herself out into the child. Well, I'll tell you, I've done it too, it is hell caring for a tiny daughter, I know. Everything, everything drags you into hell: the fact that you love and desire her, the fact that she's so needy and vulnerable, the fact that she never leaves you alone until your dreams are smashed in little piles and shabby with neglect, the fact that pleasure and guilt come so precisely together, as so seldom happens, working towards the same end and sucking your very selfhood out of you. It is a perilous time for a woman, that nursing of a daughter, and you can only survive it if you cling to yourself with a fierce and passionate love, *and* you back that up with a trained and militant lust for justice *and* you scream to the people around you to meet your needs and desires *and* you do not let them off, *and* when all is said and done you sit back and laugh at yourself with a well timed and not unmalicious irony. Well she could not, of course she could not, so she did not survive. She was never angry, she never asked, she took resignation – that tragic so-called virtue – as a ninth-rate alternative to reality and never even realised she had been short-changed.

So when I first married my husband I only meant to tease her a little, to rile her, to make her fight back. I couldn't bear it, that she was so like her mother and would go the same way. My girls were more like me, less agreeable to have about the house, but tough as old boots and capable of getting what they needed and not worrying too much about what they wanted or oughted, so to speak. I didn't have to worry about them. I just could not believe the sweetness of that little girl and her wide-eyed belief that I would be happy and love her if she would just deny herself and follow me. So of course I exploited her a bit, pushed and tested it, if you understand, because I couldn't believe it. Then I just wanted her to *see*, to see that life is not all sweetness and light, that people are not automatically to be trusted, that fairy-godmothers are unreliable and damned thin on the ground, and that even the most silvery of princes soon go out hunting and fighting and drinking and whoring, and don't give one tuppeny ha'penny curse more for you than you give for yourself. Well she could have looked at her father and known. He hardly proved himself to be the great romantic lover of all time, even at an age when that would have been appropriate, never mind later. He had replaced darling Mummy with me, after all, and pretty damned quick too, and so long as he was getting his end off and his supper on the table he wasn't going to exert himself on her behalf, as I pointed out to her, by no means kindly.

(And, I should like to add, I still don't understand about that. I couldn't believe how little the bastard finally cared when it came to the point. Perhaps he was bored to tears by goodness, perhaps he was too lazy. He was a sentimental old fart about her of course, his eyes could fill with nostalgic tears every time he looked at her and thought of her dead mother; but he never *did* anything; or even asked me to stop doing anything. She never asked, and he never had eyes to see, or energy or . . . God knows what went on his head about her and as far as I'm concerned God's welcome. She loved him and trusted him and served him and he never even bloody noticed. Which sort of makes my point actually because he would never treat me like that, and yet he and I get on very well now; like each other and have good times in bed and out of it. Of course I'd never have let him tell me how to behave, but he might have tried, at least just once.)

Anyway, no, she would not see. She would not blame her father. She would not blame her mother, not even for dying, which is the ultimate outrage from someone you love. And she would not blame me. She just smiled and accepted, smiled and invented castles in the air to which someone, though not herself, would come and take her one day, smiled and loved me. No matter what I did to her, she just smiled.

So, yes, in the end I was cruel. I don't know how to explain it and I do not attempt to justify it. Her wetness *infuriated* me. I could not shake her good will, her hopefulness, her capacity to love and love such a pointless and even dangerous object. I could not make her hate me. Not even for a moment. I could not make her hate me. And I cannot explain what that frustration did to me. I hated her insane dog-like devotion where it was so un-deserved. She treated me as her mother had treated him. I think I hated her stupidity most of all. I can hear myself almost blaming her for my belly deep madness; I don't want to do that; I don't want to get into blaming the victim and she was my victim. I was older than her, and stronger than her, and had more power than her; and there was no excuse. No excuse, I thought the first time I ever hit her, but there was an excuse and it was my wild need, and it escalated.

So in the end – and yes I have examined all the motives and reasons why one woman should be cruel to another and I do not find them explanatory – so in the end I was cruel to her. I goaded and humiliated and pushed and bullied her. I used all my powers, my superior strength, my superior age, my superior intelligence against her. I beat her, in the end, systematically and severely; but more than that I used her and worked her and denied her pleasures and gave her pain. I violated her space, her dignity, her integrity, her privacy, even her humanity and perhaps her physical safety. There was an insane urge in me, not simply to hurt her, but to have her admit that I had hurt her. I would lie awake at night appalled, and scald myself with contempt, with anger and with self-disgust, but I had only to see her in the morning for my temper to rise and I would start again, start again at her with an unreasonable savagery that seemed to upset me more than it upset her. Picking, picking and pecking, endlessly. She tried my patience as no one else had ever done and finally I gave up the struggle and threw it away and entered into the horrible game with all my considerable capacity for concentration.

And nothing worked. I could not make her angry. I could not make her hate me. I could not stop her loving me with a depth and a generosity and a forgiveness that were the final blow. Nothing moved her to more than a simper. Nothing penetrated the fantasies and day-dreams with which her head was stuffed so full I'm surprised she didn't slur her consonants. She was locked into perpetual passivity and gratitude and love. Even when she was beaten she covered her bruises to protect me; even when she was hungry she would not take food from my cupboards to feed herself; even when I mocked her she smiled at me tenderly.

All I wanted was for her to grow up, to grow up and realise that life was not a bed of roses and that she had to take some responsibility for her own life, to take some action on her own behalf, instead of waiting and waiting and waiting for something or someone to come shining out of the dark and force safety on her as I forced pain. What Someone? Another like her father who had done nothing, nothing whatever, to help her and never would? Another like him whom she could love generously and hopelessly and serve touchingly and givingly until weariness and pain killed her too. I couldn't stand it. Even when I beat her, even as I beat her, she loved me, she just loved and smiled and hoped and waited, day-dreamed and night-dreamed, and waited and waited and waited. She was untouchable and infantile. I couldn't save her and I couldn't damage her. God knows, I tried.

Now of course it's just an ancient habit. It has lost its sharp edges, lost the passion in both of us to see it out in conflict, between dream and reality, between hope and cynicism. There is a great weariness in me, and I cannot summon up the fire of conviction. I do not concentrate any more, I do not have enough concentration, enough energy, enough power. Perhaps she has won, because she drained that out of me years and years ago. Sometimes I despair, which wastes still more concentration. We plod on together, because we always have. Sweetly she keeps at it, smile, smile, dream, hope, wait, love, forgive, smile, smile, bloody smile. Tiredly, I keep at it too: 'Sweep that grate.' 'Tidy your room.' 'Do your homework.' 'What can you see in that nerd.' 'Take out those damn ear-phones and pay attention.' 'Life doesn't come free, you have to work on it.' 'Wake up, hurry up, stop day-dreaming, no you can't, yes you must, get a move on, don't be so stupid'. And 'You're not going to the Ball, or party, or disco, or over your Nan's, dressed like *that*.'

She calls it nagging.

She calls me Mummy.

I Was a Teenage Novelist

ZOË FAIRBAIRNS

'Autobiography, written in 1985'

I started work on my first novel *Live As Family* when I was seventeen and recovering from glandular fever. Glandular fever, if mild, is quite a good disease for novelists to have, because one thing that everybody knows about it is that it is very important to sit quietly for as long as possible afterwards. People who are convalescing after glandular fever should not be expected to do much in the way of housework or homework.

A year later, my brain still in top gear from my recent A-levels and only the fag-end of the term remaining before I left school, I finished the novel and gave it to a friend, the writer Michael Baldwin, who had agreed to read it. He passed it on to his agent, Michael Thomas of A. M. Heath and Company.

School ended and I started my holiday job as a filing clerk. One day as I was setting off for work, a letter came for me marked A. M. Heath. I put it in my handbag and made a deal with God. 'If I don't open it until the bus comes,' I proposed, 'this letter will say that somebody wants to publish my novel.'

God agreed. I didn't, it did and Macmillan did.

I was under age, and fathers were the supreme legal guardians of (legitimate) children in those days, so mine had to countersign my first publishing contract. I began my first year at university knowing that within nine months my novel would be in the shops. Great, I thought, this is going to be easy, and I set aside two hours a day to work on my second.

It was to be a feminist updating of the myth of Iphigenia. I did not call it that (this was 1967) but that is what it was. Iphigenia, in Greek mythology, was sacrificed to the gods by her father, in return for a favourable wind to enable him to go to war. I had no idea why this story moved and disturbed me so much. It found no reflection in my life. As an eleven-plus beneficiary from a middle-class home, I had had every opportunity to be what I could be. If I was uneasy about the future (nearly every adult woman I knew was either a nun, a housewife or a single career woman whom, I understood, nobody loved) it was only because I was not yet mature enough to understand the reasons why women had to choose between career and family while men could have both. I was sure that all would become clear in time . . . after all, no one else seemed bothered by this. In my *Iphigenia* some of my fears and feelings about what I would have called patriarchy if I had known the word were expressed in a story whose details I do not remember. I no longer have the manuscript, I tore it up.

Live as Family came out in July 1968 when I was nineteen. It received a great deal of attention, both reviews and features. I no longer have them (I tore them up too) but my recollection is that they concentrated on:

(1) my age.

(2) the fact that, while some students were out throwing cobblestones at policemen, here was a good student who had stayed at home writing novels.

(3) my looks. One reporter described me as 'an attractive brunette.' Sadly for my ego, I was forced to conclude that this was either a formality or a guess; he had interviewed me over the phone, asking me what colour my hair was.

(4) the fact that the novel was autobiographical.

(5) the fact that it wasn't too badly written, considering.

Actually the novel wasn't autobiographical. I couldn't understand why journalists, of whom I was in considerable awe, having read in careers leaflets that they must be meticulously accurate over even the smallest detail, would make up such a thing and print it as a fact.

Eight weeks after they published *Live as Family*, Macmillan rejected *Iphigenia*. I was distraught. Was my career over so soon? Of course not, said my editor, who was immensely kind. On the contrary: it was *because* he had such faith in my future with the company that he wasn't going to take the easy way out and publish a book that was so melodramatic and whose male characters were such cardboard cutout stage villains.

To do so would be to do me a grave disservice. He recognised that my immediate temptation would be to offer the manuscript to another publisher. And it was quite possible that there were publishers – less concerned than Macmillan were for my long term best interests – who might publish it as a cunning and unscrupulous way of capturing me for their lists. But *Iphigenia* would do my literary reputation no good at all. And Macmillan hated the thought they might lose me. There was no dishonour in recognising that a manuscript had failed and putting it aside. Nor did an abandoned manuscript represent wasted time. One learned so much from them. Would I do the brave, the honest, the difficult thing, and forget about trying to publish *Iphigenia*?

That odd summer, which began with the student riots in Paris and the publication of *Live as Family*, and ended with the Soviet invasion of Czechoslovakia and the rejection of *Iphigenia*, somebody gave me *The Bell Jar* to read. I drew enormous comfort from the realisation that this woman Sylvia Plath knew what it was to ache for recognition as a young writer, to think you had it, and then to discover that all the fuss had been a joke at your expense. Then I read on and discovered the depths of self-destructive despair to which such treatment could push you. At least, I thought, if I took my Macmillan editor's advice and didn't offer the book again, it couldn't be rejected again.

My agent was, and still is, a very wise man. He took the time to explain to me that 'a grave disservice' and 'put it aside' are cliches frequently used by publishers when they reject the work of their own authors. All they mean is that the publishers don't want the embarrassment of being proved wrong by having the book successfully published by someone else. (When this happens, publishers sometimes speak of having had an author 'stolen' from them.) My agent doubted that *Iphigenia* would be as easy to place as *Live as Family* had been, but if I wanted him to try, he would.

He tried, but sadly the unscrupulous publisher of Macmillan's fears was nowhere to be found, and soon I asked him to stop trying. I was feeling such a fool. Here I was, still in my teens, a university student with a published novel in the shops and the possibility of a scholarship to America on the horizon . . . the whole world was open to me, how could I imagine otherwise? How could I have written anything so pompous, so ungrateful, so *outdated* as a story that implied that all was not fair and equal between the sexes?

It was time to turn my attention to more serious matters. Deeply influenced by *The Catcher in the Rye*, I wrote *Down*, the story of a young man in search of himself, and Macmillan published it. On the dust jacket they put the following quotation from one of the *Live as Family* reviews:

'By the time she comes of age, she will be one of our established women novelists.'

That is quite a thing to have said about you in a public place when you are twenty, particularly when the people who quote it show no further interest in your work. Macmillan rejected (and advised me to put aside) *A Publicity Stunt,* a novel about a young woman coming under the influence of the new Women's Liberation Movement which I had joyously discovered while in the USA; they rejected *Thank You For Having Me,* which was about a group of women and men coming under the influence of the not-quite-so-new Women's Liberation Movement; and they rejected *Tales I Tell My Mother,* the collection of feminist short stories which I co-wrote with the other authors of this book. In fact, after *Down* (1969) I was never to be published by Macmillan again until 1985, when lo! They launched a Women's Studies list! And included an extract from one of my later, published (but not by them) novels in an anthology. Macmillan very properly obtained permission to do this from the book's publishers, but nobody bothered to tell me, so the first I knew of it was when I walked into a bookshop, picked up a new Macmillan volume and found that it contained fiction by me. Imagine my surprise at Macmillan's unexpected re-entry into my fiction writing career. If I had known they were coming, I'd have baked a cake.

The story is running ahead. I return to 1974, which was the year when I decided to retire from novel-writing. *Down* and *Live As Family* were out of print, *Iphigenia* was in the bin, *A Publicity Stunt,* with its collection of rejection letters was stowed in a suitcase, and *Thank You For Having Me* was still being hawked around by my indefatigable agent and getting nowhere. I had left university and got my first full-time job, as editor of the CND newspaper, *Sanity*.

I brooded on the monstrous trick that had been played on me. As little more than a child, I had been led to believe that I could be – that I already was – the thing I wanted most to be: a successful novelist. As an adult, with serious thoughts in my head, I was no longer of interest. There seemed no way that I could combine my three passions – feminism, left-wing politics generally, and novel-writing – in a way that would give me my heart's desire: my name once more on the spine of a book.

But now I could stop trying. My job – as a journalist for a good cause – would satisfy my hungers to write, to be published (no more rejection slips – I was the editor), to be paid and to be politically active. I could have all those things without ever again going through the miserable cycle of novel-writing – the dazzling idea, the months of work, the elation of 'The End', the confidence as the thing is sent off, the thud of despair as it comes back, and then the growth, in the soil of the despair, of another dazzling idea – and this one really *will* wow them – starting the whole thing off again. Goodbye to all that. I embarked on my new career with a deep sense of peace.

It was Valerie who spoiled it: Valerie Miner, a freelance journalist from the USA who was working in London. We were good friends, but I wished she wouldn't keep going on about feminist fiction and why didn't she and I and a few other friends of hers get together and see if we could write some? And when I explained that (a) there was no such thing as feminist fiction, and (b) even if there were, nobody would publish it, and (c) even if they did, journalism was more important, and (d) I didn't write fiction anyway, she kept giving me funny looks.

I met the other members of the proposed group. There was Michele, who was already known as a poet; Michelene, whose plays I'd seen and who had edited *The Body Politic*, which my women's group at university had devoured with awe and delight; and Sara, who had been published in a Faber collection of short stories and who believed in God. There was another woman, a novelist, but she left. I thought I would too. It wasn't that I didn't like the group, I did; but their enthusiasm for putting together a collection, *and publishing it,* filled me with dread.

Nor was this all. *Acts of Violence*, a story I wrote while in the group (just to show willing; I wasn't staying) kept worrying me with the thought that the themes it touched on were much too big for a short story, and it might be a novel called *Benefits*.

And then Michael Thomas, my agent, had to go and put his oar in. (Or my former agent, as I would have said then. Since I did not write books, I did not need an agent.) After a long period of silence between us, he wrote to me on some pretext or other, adding at the end, as if it were an afterthought, that he hoped that one day, 'sooner rather than later' I would let him have another novel.

'You'll be lucky, mate,' I thought. I did not blame him for what had happened, but his words and his persistent confidence opened deep wounds.

Tales I Tell My Mother was offered to Virago and The Women's Press, the only two feminist publishing companies then in London, and turned down by them; then it was sent to every mainstream publisher where a feminist editor was rumoured to be lurking, and they all said no too. I pretended to share the shocked indignation and disappointment of the other group members at each fresh rejection, but secretly I was rather relieved. Publication, I thought, always ends in tears. It is thanks to the energy and commitment of the others that the book finally found a publisher in Journeyman. And of course when the book came out, I was as delighted as anyone. I started writing *Benefits*.

An editor at Methuen had been more enthusiastic than most about some of the *Tales* . . . and had asked to see any novels that any of us might write. So when *Benefits* was written, I sent it to her. I was full of confidence. She had asked to see it, she liked my stories, she was actively looking for feminist novels and this one really would wow her . . .

It didn't. She sent it back.

Then there was wailing and gnashing of teeth! I was furious that I had set myself up for this. Would I never learn? How many times did I have to be told? Why hadn't I stuck with my earlier decision to abandon novel-writing, since I clearly did not have what it took? I told my agent that I had decided to fling the manuscript of *Benefits* into the Thames from Hungerford Bridge. I might or might not let go of it. He thought we ought to offer it to Virago first.

I already knew the women at Virago, and over the next two months we had intermittent discussions of *Benefits*. They made favourable sounds but didn't feel able to commit themselves. Finally, one Tuesday, they gave me their firm decision, which was . . .

. . . that they would give me their firm decision next Monday. They liked the book, but it was one of many. They were still a small company and could only do a few new titles each year. They would phone me on Monday with a definite yea or nay.

The Friday before the Monday brought a letter from Virago. At first I did not bother to open it, since it was perfectly obvious what it was going to say. Why would anyone, having promised to phone on a set date to give someone either the worst or the best news of their life, send them a letter three days early? The only possible explanation was that the decision had gone against me, and an early letter seemed kinder than phoning . . .

Fifteen months later, in October 1979, exactly ten years after *Down*, Virago published *Benefits*, my second first novel. I was thirty. Virago was making its name by launching new women writers and rediscovering forgotten ones. I felt I was both, so it seemed doubly appropriate to be published by them. Everything went very smoothly, the book was well received, and Virago actually offered to commission my next book.

Commission? I thought. Commission? After all those years of rejection slips, someone was now offering to publish something of mine that wasn't even written yet? It couldn't be true. It was true.

It is probably just as well that I and the two Virago editors with whom I worked were so euphoric about the project (a big, fat family saga, full of feminist history, *Stand We At Last*) that it never occurred to us to sit down and hammer out exactly what we expected of each other. If we had, it is unlikely that we would have gone ahead, and even in my gloomiest moments about this book I have never wished it unwritten.

If we had discussed things properly at the start, they would have discovered that, commission or no commission, I reckoned that it was my book. I took it for granted that as long as I kept to the agreed deadline I could work at my own pace, and that, although I should pay full attention to editorial criticism and advice, the last word on what went into the book would be mine.

I would have discovered that they, on the other hand, wanted to exercise much more control than I would ever willingly accept, including the right to see and criticise early drafts before they were ready to be seen by anyone (which is a bit like having someone insist on sampling a half-cooked meal, and then having them get angry because it doesn't taste nice); the right to have a synopsis of what was going to happen in the story at a time when I didn't know because I hadn't written it yet; and the right to demand radical rewriting in line with their ideas and preferences, whether or not these were the same as mine.

They also reserved the right to change their minds in the most disconcerting ways. After three years of hard work, frequent rewrites and sometimes very tense meetings, Virago finally accepted the manuscript and sent it to their typesetters. Then Pan and Houghton Mifflin made offers for, respectively, the British paperback and the US hardback rights, subject to certain revisions. Virago promptly revised their opinion of the book being ready for publication, turned off the typesetting machine, postponed their publication date and returned the manuscript to me. We all found that this concentrated my mind wonderfully (my publishing history has made me acutely aware of the power of publishers to consign me to the wilderness where ex-novelists go) and I did as I was told, expanding the book by about thirty pages. Everyone agreed that it was an enormous improvement . . . but when, a few months later, a French publisher asked for the entire novel to be cut by 20% to enable them to do a cheap edition, Virago thought I should do that too. (I refused, and the French publishers published in full.)

It wasn't like this all the time: most of the time we got on quite well – remarkably so, considering we were at cross purposes. Parts of the book are immeasurably stronger than I could have made them on my own, thanks to help from Virago editors. Nor is it a case of pointing to bits of the book that I dislike and saying 'Look what they made me do.' I wrote every word. But there is an overreliance on cliché, a lack of conviction, especially in the insipid last section, which arose from the impossibility of writing *with* conviction when the whole exercise had started to feel like an obstacle course whose judges kept changing the obstacles and sending me back to the beginning when I fell over them.

A Virago editor said: 'If you want to be a best-selling novelist, you have to put up with this kind of thing.' I believed her but I saw a corollary: if I was content just to be a novelist, full stop, then I didn't have to put up with this kind of thing. I don't have any moral objections to writing formula fiction (this is the approach whereby the novel is tailored to fit the marketing strategy, rather than vice versa); it strikes me as a relatively innocuous way of making a living; it's just that it isn't any fun. Either you bleed to death or you stop caring. And writing a novel without caring is drudgery. And if I have to take on drudgery in order to make my living, I would prefer that it be something completely different from novel-writing, because novel-writing is special to me. If I have to treat it as a loved but expensive hobby – well, I have before and I will again. I prefer, of course, to make money – as much as possible – from my novels, but I don't want to write novels for money.

While *Stand We At Last* was still being argued about, I mentally abandoned it to its fate and started work on the next book I wanted to write, which was *Here Today*. I did not seek a commission or advance for it, preferring to support myself as a creative writing tutor and a temp typist. This latter occupation helped me research the book, which is about office workers. I told Virago that I would not discuss it until it was written. Until it was written, there was nothing to discuss. When I did show it to them, they rejected it. (They said that to publish it would be to do me a disservice. They advised me to put it aside.) Once again I knew what it was to be flavour of the month when the month ends. Once again a publisher had published two of my novels and then, when I wanted to do something a bit different, shown me the door. I wondered if it would be another ten years before I found another publisher . . .

Actually it took ten weeks. I took *Here Today* to Methuen, where it was warmly welcomed, supportively and co-operatively edited, and published in hardback in 1984 and as a mass-market paperback in 1985. It sold well, got varied but mainly favourable reviews, won the 1985 Fawcett Book Prize, and a film company has bought an option to turn it into a TV series. And that is my publishing history to date.

You will have decided by now whether I am what the literary critics call a reliable narrator. But even those of you who take sides on principle with rejected authors throwing buns at their tormentors (possibly because you are or have been a rejected author yourself) may be wondering: what about those unpublished novels? What if they weren't worth publishing? (On the published ones you can, of course, make up your own minds.)

For what it's worth, here is my assessment of my novels. *Benefits* and *Here Today* are my favourites. I can see faults in them but I love them: *Benefits* for its guts, *Here Today* for its heroine who I wish existed and was a friend of mine.

Of *Stand We At Last*, an acquaintance in the book trade said: 'It was a brilliant piece of publishing.' It depends what you call publishing. It was certainly a brilliant piece of marketing. But as a piece of *writing*, viewed from a distance of four years, it strikes me as a fair-to-middling camel: a horse designed by a committee. Like most camels, it is functional, big and has its moments. But it is clumsy-looking, unbalanced. It looks as if it has had bits stuck on and pulled off at random. Its skin is not all that thick, though, and sometimes when I go on like this it kicks me with its hoof and says 'Oh yes? And just who pays the rent around here while you lay down the law about what you will and won't write?' So all right: a fair-to-middling camel, and a nice little earner as well.

I am not the first author to discover that her most commercially successful book is the one that she herself loves least. There may be all kinds of reasons for this, of which the more alienating aspects of bestseller marketing may only be one. Others may include fear of success, and reluctance to accept its responsibilities. I know this. I also know that more people worldwide have bought copies of *Stand We At Last* than have bought all my other books put together, and that it has been enjoyed by a great many people who do not consider themselves feminists, as well as many who do. Several feminists of my age have told me that they liked it so much that they gave it to their mothers. I'm delighted to think that mothers and daughters (and fathers and sons, for that matter) enjoy the book, and I hope they will go on doing so. I might enjoy it myself, if I had not written it.

Of my unpublished novels, I remember *Iphigenia* as an authentic feminist statement that did not know it was that. It may have had its moments of melodrama and overwriting, but nothing that could not have been put right with the right editorial support. *A Publicity Stunt* knew damn well that it was a feminist statement: it was a roar of anger and, as such, made me feel better but possibly wouldn't have communicated much to an uninvolved reader. *Thank You For Having Me* said similar things in a much more controlled and accessible way. All three books would have benefited from supportive editing, had it been offered. All three were better than *Live as Family* and *Down*. If this immature pair represented the standards of publishability, then all three others should have been published. But for many publishers there is no such thing as an objective 'standard of publishability.' There is what can be marketed and what can not. A smiling teenage girl novelist in the late sixties was easy to market. An angry feminist one in the early seventies would have been more difficult.

I mentioned 'supportive editing.' This is what the editor does who, instead of saying 'this doesn't work, put it aside' or 'this doesn't work, do it my way' says 'this doesn't work, let's see how we can make it work.' It involves the kind of creative engagement between author, editor and text that we gave to each other in the *Tales* group, and which Ursula Owen of Virago and Elspeth Lindner of Methuen were later to give to *Benefits* and *Here Today* respectively: a willingness to tease out meanings that are not immediately clear, to see beyond flaws in the writing into the hearts of the ideas, to reconstruct on the basis of what is already present. Publishers do not, of course, have time to do this for every author whose work fails to meet their standards, but if they decide not to do it for a particular author they can hardly claim to be rejecting her work in her own best interests.

Strangers say to me: 'I know who you are.'

'Oh really?' I reply modestly.

'Yeah, I sent my poems to *Spare Rib* and you rejected them.'

Between 1978 and 1982 when I was *Spare Rib's* poetry editor, I must have returned manuscripts to around 1,500 poets. So how, you wonder, can I say these terrible things about publishers rejecting my work when I have done the same to others? Is it the case that I can dish it out but I can't take it?

Of course it is. But it is not that simple.

I did not 'reject' anyone's poems from *Spare Rib*. I may have decided not to shortlist them (we received around 80 each month, and had room for one or two) but that is different.

I'm grateful to Valerie Miner for pointing out how absurd yet telling it is that writers use the language of sado-masochism in describing our dealings with publishers. We 'submit' our manuscripts, and wait anxiously to hear whether they have been 'accepted' or 'rejected', possibly with a 'rejection slip', which sounds like the sort of garment one might buy from an Ann Summers Sex Supermarket for wearing under a Naughty Maid's Outfit.

Rubbish. We offer our work for sale and the publishers either buy or they don't. Of course it is disappointing, even devastating, if they don't, but in the interests of our own mental health we should no more think of it as 'rejection' than does the greengrocer when we pass over her tomatoes because we don't need tomatoes today. She just offers them to the next customer and goes on doing so for as long as she knows they are saleable.

Tomatoes? BOOKS? *Customers?* This is worldly talk. It is indeed. I think writers should try to be as unworldly as possible, but not all the time. Only when writing. It's an expensive business, being unworldly, and one way to finance it is to be a worldly as possible when selling. This means many things, such as employing an agent, joining a union and having as little truck as possible with editors and publishers who, themselves on a living wage, urge freelances to work for peanuts (or less) in the interests of the Women's Movement. (If Journeyman, a small, radical publishing company can give its authors Writers' Guild terms, why can't the feminist presses?) But before that it means keeping faith with our own work and not taking no for an answer when we believe the answer should be yes. I hope those poets whom I disappointed at *Spare Rib* by choosing someone else's work, published their own elsewhere.

The feminist publishing boom has not been caused by feminists publishing books as a way of being nice to each other. What happened to start it off was that a number of talented feminists working in the publishing industry realised, *because* they were feminists, that there was an unfilled demand for a certain kind of book, and linked up with feminist writers (many of whom had been struggling for years to write feminist literature and get it published) to meet that demand, before most of the boys realised what was happening. It's wonderful for all of us – writers, publishers and readers – but it has not changed the situation of writers (feminist or otherwise) who know that publishers (feminist or otherwise) may say no to their books (feminist or otherwise) because they don't like them or they don't think they will sell or because they've already got something like this on next year's list or because they've never done anything like this before . . . the important thing for writers to keep in mind (the only thing that keeps us going sometimes) is the knowledge that they might be wrong.

They might be wrong, but their power to say yes and no is absolute. It is this power – and the anxiety it generates in writers – that is at the root of much of the tension that exists between writers and publishers. Publishers are buyers in a buyers' market. They can grant or withhold what we crave and need, the fulfilment without which our work may seem meaningless: an audience, recognition and money.

The trouble is that the only way out of this unseemly dependence is to become a publisher yourself. Others have done this successfully, but for me it would be unbearable. I would have to choose between manuscripts, I would have to send out rejection slips, I would have to deal with authors.

Mrs Morris Changes Lanes

ZOË FAIRBAIRNS

The names of some of the bikes – Footpad, Puma, Ripper, Axe – aroused deep anxiety in Mrs Morris, and the tone in which the salesman asked if he could help her sounded more like an accusation of trespass. She would prefer him to order her from the showroom rather than press her to buy. She hadn't even chosen a colour yet. Some shades were definitely unacceptable. Black was difficult to see at night and red suggested anarchy and toughness.

'I'm just looking,' she said.

The Puma was a 700 and the Footpad a 650. The Ripper and the Axe came in various sizes, if size was indeed what those numbers referred to. They might be quantities. Quantities of what? Was it good or bad to have a lot of them, or were they just reference numbers like bus routes? Was it just a matter of design that dictated foot-brakes on some models, hand-brakes on others, or was it more important than that? Where did the petrol go? What kind of petrol?

'Was it for yourself?' the salesman persisted.

She was glad of the opportunity to explain. 'They've cut my buses down to one an hour.'

'These,' he said, 'are very popular with the ladies.'

It was called a Polka Pop 49. It was lilac in colour, and had wheels like old sixpences. An enormous shopping basket was attached to the front, and there was more luggage space at the rear. It looked as if it could be carried home under someone's arm. It looked as if, once there, it should be placed on the table at a children's party, covered with candles, and sliced.

'It has an electric start.'

'Very nice.'

'And it won't start unless the brake's on.'

'Off, you mean?' said Mrs Morris.

The salesman looked puzzled. 'No, I meant on. It's a safety feature.'

Mrs Morris still didn't understand. 'Why would I want to move off with the brake on?'

'Dear oh dear oh dear,' said the salesman, giving her some leaflets. He wandered off to chat happily with a knowledgeable new customer who appeared to about the same age as Mrs Morris's son, and ought to be at school.

Mrs Morris read the leaflets and spent a considerable amount of time observing motorcycles on the road. One day she approached a Hell's Angel who was parking his Throbber 1100 in a car park, and he was kind enough to give her a good deal of advice.

She went to another showroom.

'Was it for yourself?' the salesman began. 'Because these are very popular with the –'

'I have heard,' said Mrs Morris, 'that these Polkas guzzle oil and you're always having to change the spark plugs.'

'Well, I wouldn't say –'

'It's no more than you'd expect with a two-stroke engine, is it?' said Mrs Morris. 'Show me a four-stroke, 50 cc's.'

'There's this one,' said the salesman.

'Electric start, I see,' said Mrs Morris. 'Not always reliable, are they? Is there a kick start back-up?'

'Yes,' said the salesman.

'Automatic transmission?'

'Yes.'

She asked a few more questions and then she said, 'Fine. Now I'll need L-plates and a crash helmet.'

'Were you planning to ride it away now?'

'No,' said Mrs Morris. 'I would like you to deliver it to the town hall on Sunday morning.'

'If it doesn't arrive,' thought Mrs Morris as she waited in the car park of the town hall on Sunday morning, 'I can always pretend I'm here in an administrative capacity. Or,' she added to herself as more of her fellow students, average age nineteen, turned up, 'or that I am a parent, come to watch.'

She was surprised to find herself the only person without a motorcycle. Everyone else had ridden here with no apparent difficulty, and Mrs Morris wondered why they were bothering to take training at all. She also wondered whether she was the only person to have read the Motorcycling Safety leaflet which said that your first ride should be a properly supervised training ride, and that the shop should, therefore, deliver the machine to the training area. Certainly the youth who drove up with her shiny new Handy Rider in the back of his van had a slightly resentful air, as if he did not expect to have to do this kind of thing on Sunday mornings.

He set the bike on its stand and asked her to sign for it. He smelled of coffee, as if his breakfast had been interrupted. Mrs Morris remembered with a pang the pile of pancakes she had left in the warm oven at home and thought of the family sitting round to enjoy them. Pancakes were a treat.

'*Where's* she gone?'

'To church, she said.'

(Mrs Morris wasn't happy with this, but it was all she could think of.)

'She doesn't go to church. I think she's got a lover.'

'She does at Christmas.'

'It's July and she was wearing trousers. It's a lover, I tell you.'

Perhaps. Mrs Morris sidled round her Handy Rider, viewing it from all angles. For now she felt a little shy.

The instructors were arranging orange and white cones in lines and shapes in the car park. Mrs Morris had often seen similar cones on busy roads, marking off the sites of accidents.

'This is the figure of eight,' said an instructor called Dave. 'And this is the slalom. Find your own speed, don't hit the cones, pick them up if you do and try not to put your foot down. One at a time now, off you go.'

'Er, David,' said Mrs Morris, approaching him on foot.

'Yes, my love.'

'That's my moped.'

'And a very nice moped it looks too.'

'Could you show me how to start it?'

He looked at her in amazement. She pulled off her helmet, hoping her grey hairs would provide sufficient explanation.

'You do drive a car?' he said suspiciously.

'No. Only a push-bike,' said Mrs Morris. 'I'm a family joke.' The youngsters were sailing round the cones. What was she doing here?

Dave seemed to be asking himself the same question. He went to consult his colleagues about it, having first said, 'Wait there.' Where did he think she would go?

'I think a spot of one-to-one tuition is called for,' he said, returning.

She was grateful but she said: 'What about the others?'

'Don't you worry about them. Now, before we learn to start, we learn to stop. This is the front brake and this is the back brake. Be sure and apply the front brake a fraction of a second before the back otherwise the wheels may lock, particularly if you're travelling at high speeds.'

'But I wouldn't.'

'Wouldn't what?'

'Travel at high speeds. This is a moped, it only does thirty.'

'Dangerous, that,' said Dave.

'What?' gasped Mrs Morris.

'To look at it, you'd think it had more poke. If a motorist overestimates how much acceleration you've got, you could be in trouble. Ever think of getting one of those Polka Pop Pop things?'

'They look like toys,' said Mrs Morris.

'Exactly, so there's no danger of motorists taking them seriously. Never mind, what's bought's bought, this is your throttle. You move it slowly towards you for more speed. If you take your hand off it it slows down automatically, like the dead man's handle on a train.'

Mrs Morris rode her moped across the car park. Dave had to walk quite fast to catch up. 'Didn't hurt, did it?' he grinned.

'Oh!' breathed Mrs Morris, her cheeks burning, hair escaping from her helmet. 'Oh!'

'Now you can have a try at the cones. Get yourself a pair of gloves for next time. Even cheap ones'll save you a layer of skin if you come off.'

Steering round the first cone was exhilaratingly easy. But she misjudged the second. Realising she was not going to get round without hitting it, she put her foot down but forgot to decelerate at the same time. The asphalt came up to meet her.

She lay beneath her Handy Rider. Dark drops of liquid spattered the ground. Blood? No, petrol. The engine had stopped running too, so the bike was obviously damaged. It might even be a write-off, and her insurance was only Third Party, Fire and Theft, so she would not be able to replace it. Ah well. Buying it had been as good a use as any for her nest-egg, a brave try that had taught her something about herself – or rather, confirmed what she had long suspected. There were some people in the world who were meant to travel under their own steam, and others who were meant to accept lifts and use public transport. Mrs Morris belonged to the latter group. She tested her limbs one by one, preparatory to getting up. They seemed to work. Her hands were not even grazed.

She hauled the bike upright. Dave grinned, arms folded. He did not help her.

'It works,' he said.

'What does?' She tried to glance unobtrusively at her watch.

'The Automatic Impact Cutout on the engine. You were just testing it, weren't you?'

'No,' said Mrs Morris.

'Yes,' said Dave. 'You're not hurt.'

'But shouldn't I get the, er, alignment checked, before I ride it again?'

'Get on,' said Dave, 'and ride round those cones.'

'The mirrors are bent.'

'Good. Let them stay bent. They're the most dangerous part of a motorbike, in my opinion. The mirrors.'

'Why?' said Mrs Morris, with great interest. 'What if I want to see behind?' At least while they were discussing mirrors, she wasn't having to ride.

'If you need to see behind, look behind. Get your head on a swivel. Keep looking behind. I'll show you what I mean. If I hadn't forbidden you to use mirrors, how would you use them?'

Mrs Morris recognised a trick to get her sitting on the bike again. Reluctantly she got on, but she kept her feet on the ground and the keys in her pocket. Dave stood behind her, and told her to adjust her mirrors until she had them the way she thought she wanted them. She had a feeling she was being set up.

'I'm a car,' he said. 'Coming along behind you, wanting to overtake. Can you see me?'

'Yes.'

'I'm getting closer. Can you see me now?'

'Yes.'

'Now?'

'No.'

'There you are then. I'm in your blind spot. According to your mirror, I'm not here. Suppose you decide now to pull out or turn right. Whoomph!' He drove his clenched fist into his palm with a loud smack. 'Our time's nearly up. Ready to ride home?'

'What?' said Mrs Morris. 'Pardon? I couldn't even stay on in the car park.'

'That was nothing. Ride it home, go on, if you leave it here you'll never see it again.'

If it gets stolen, she thought, *I'll get my money back.*

'It probably doesn't work any more,' she said.

'You hope,' he jeered. 'All right, I'll make a deal with you. Ride three perfect figure-of-eights, now, and I'll take your bike to my place and look after it for you till next week. And *next* week, *you* will *ride it home.*'

It worked perfectly.

'I want to see the whites of your eyes,' said Dave, the following week, preparing her to ride round a block of left turns. 'I want those mirrors bent so that you can't use them, and I want to see you turn round and *look*. I'll be driving behind you so you're quite safe, but forget it's me. Pretend it's a lunatic. Pretend everyone else on the road is a lunatic.'

Pretend! she thought, chugging round the block. People hooted at her and whizzed by. She approached the corner. She wobbled as she looked behind but the sight of Dave's car steadied and reassured her. She flicked on her left indicator. In the time it took her to do this somebody might have sneaked in, so she looked again. She made her turn.

'Fine,' said Dave. 'Two things. You're a bit unsteady.'

'I can't help wobbling when I look behind.'

'And you're riding in the gutter.'

'But people get annoyed if they can't overtake.'

'You own that thing,' said Dave, 'and you're licensed to ride it. It's taxed and insured, you pay income tax –'

'Well, my husband does,' said Mrs Morris.

'– and you have as much right to your bit of the road as a bus, the Prime Minister's Rolls or a tanker full of phenol. Is that understood? You can do some right turns now.'

Mrs Morris set off with gritted teeth. Word perfect on her Highway Code, she knew that the correct procedure before turning right was to position yourself just to the left of the middle of the road. That meant pulling out in front of the following car.

Still, as long as she knew that the following car was driven by Dave –

But it wasn't!

She had only shot a quick glance over her shoulder (to save wobbling) but she knew it was not Dave. Dave's car was green and this one was red.

Why had Dave abandoned her?

He wouldn't do such a thing. It must be her fault. She must have taken a wrong turning and lost him. But she hadn't taken any turnings yet. Soon she must: at the T-junction ahead she must go right, with a strange red car following her.

She forced herself to think calmly. Her memory of the red car was that it had been sufficiently far away that she could safely signal and pull out. But that had been when she looked . . . it might have put on speed since. Her mirrors, their stems bent as instructed by Dave, told her nothing. She looked again. The red car was still a fair distance away, but was it getting nearer? How could she tell with the quick look which was all her need to remain upright allowed her? To be on the safe side she decided to let it overtake her first. But it didn't. What was it waiting for? The driver couldn't know that she meant to turn right, she hadn't signalled yet. The junction was almost upon her. She *must signal her intentions*. She flicked on her right indicator but still she dared not pull out. She had no idea how the red car was progressing, or whether the driver had finally lost patience and was making a dash for the junction, and she dared not risk losing her balance at a corner by looking again. 'Sorry,' she muttered, changing indicators, 'I meant left.' And she turned left. The driver of the red car came left too, giving her a wide berth, a friendly beep and a wave as he went by. She realised then that he hadn't been impatient at all; he'd seen her L-plates and had been waiting for her to do what she wanted. But how could she have known that?

Mrs Morris stopped by the road. She wiped her brow and thought for a long time. She knew exactly what to do. The question was, when would she do it?

Dave's familiar green car went by and pulled up ahead of her. He got out and approached her with an irritable expression, '*Now* what are you doing?'

'Sorry, Dave, I lost you and then I lost my nerve.'

'What are you doing with those mirrors?'

'Adjusting them,' said Mrs Morris. 'I've decided I'd like to use them after all.'

'I've told you not to use them! There's no point in you coming on this course if you're just going to go your own sweet way. The mirrors are the most dangerous –'

'Not for me,' said Mrs Morris.

Dave stared.

'Dave, I'm sure your advice is very good advice, a life-saver in fact, for some people. Those youngsters who look as if they were born on motorbikes must be taught caution. But I'm so cautious it's taken me forty years to get this far.'

'Yes, and if you want to live another forty, you'll do as you're told!'

'Dave.' She patted his arm. 'If I ever have an accident, do you think it will be caused by my reckless riding?'

'You obviously weren't listening when I told you about the blind spot,' he grumbled, watching her adjust her mirrors. 'You can't eliminate it so there's no point in trying.'

'Here's what I have in mind,' said Mrs Morris. 'I'm riding along and I want to turn. I look in my mirror and if I see anything even slightly dangerous I'll postpone the manoeuvre.'

'You'll never get to where you want to go.'

'I shall. I might be late, but the buses were always late anyway. Now, if the road appears to be clear, *then* I'll look round. As a sort of final check. But in the meantime the mirrors will give me a general picture and increase my confidence. And I won't lose my balance.'

'Perhaps you'd like my job.'

'No, you're a very good teacher, Dave.'

'Thank you.'

'It's just that you've been teaching me the wrong things.'

For the rest of the session, the mirrors were not discussed. He put her on roundabouts, left turns, right turns and straight on. He stood glaring on the central island. She used her mirrors in the way she had planned, but as long as she glanced over her shoulder as well, he made no comment.

'You going to ride that thing home today?' he enquired.

'I think so,' said Mrs Morris.

'See you next time, then,' he grinned. 'Be brave.'

It was something that he said *be brave*, and not *be careful*.

Brave! Compared with what she'd said to him, the dual carriageway and the three-lane roundabout ahead were as nothing. She'd actually looked him in the eye and said *you've been teaching me the wrong things!* But he *had* been. He'd been so busy telling her to look behind that he'd neglected to mention what for. He'd stated the obvious – that you shouldn't pull out when something was in the act of overtaking – but who would, for heaven's sake? Those eager youngsters might, but not Mrs Morris. He'd been teaching her as if she were an entirely different person. He hadn't mentioned, in all his fussing over the different ways of looking behind, that if, however you looked, you *saw* something, it didn't necessarily mean that you had to abandon the manoeuvre, as Mrs Morris had abandoned her right turn when she saw the red car. The fact that a vehicle was visible in your mirror might, on the contrary, mean that it was safe to proceed, for if it was in your mirror it followed that it was not in your blind spot! And if it stayed in the same place in your mirror, it followed that it was not accelerating. And if you watched it for several seconds in your mirror you would see whether or not it was signalling, a point you might miss with a swift glance. And there was another point he had not made with regard to her own signalling: that a signal was a declaration of intent, not a request for permission.

Her mirror was clear. She glanced behind and moved off. The roads were quiet. She tried not to think about the dual carriageway ahead, and the three-lane roundabout that lay unavoidably between her and her home. 'No two roundabouts are alike,' Dave's voice warned in her head. There he went again. It was probably the right thing to say to a youth on a Throbber, but what Mrs Morris needed to remember was that the same Highway Code rules applied to all roundabouts, and everyone had learned them, and no one wanted to die, and no one wanted to kill Mrs Morris.

Before she reached the dual carriageway, there was one more thing she had to do. She stopped at a call box and phoned home.

'It's Mum,' she said.

'Hello, Mum, where are you?'

'Nowhere. I want you all in the front garden in fifteen minutes.'

'What for?'

'What for, what for? Why don't you do as you're told, for once?'

There wasn't much traffic on the dual carriageway, but what there was was moving fast. Twice she considered moving into the right lane in preparation for the roundabout, but abandoned the idea having spotted something coming at speed in her mirror. She almost resigned herself to staying in the left hand lane, going left at the roundabout, going round the block and trying again, but the thought of her family waiting, impatient but expectant and all unbeknownst, for the most astonishing spectacle of their lives, spurred her on.

They wouldn't wait for ever.

They'd say, *oh, it's just Mum being silly again. She's probably bought herself a new dress. We can admire it just as well inside.* And they'd go in.

I will let one more car overtake me, she thought. *And then I will signal to announce that I intend to pull out and then I will do it.*

They've no business going so fast near a roundabout. I have a perfect right to change lanes.

Flinching from the imagined impact of a fast-moving car in the rear of the Handy Rider, Mrs Morris pulled out to the right and took the roundabout exactly as the Highway Code said she should.

The rest of the journey was like falling off a log.

Riding a moped, she chuckled to herself. *It's like falling off a log! This is ME!*

She turned the corner of her road and saw her family standing in the garden.

She checked her mirror, glanced behind, signalled left and came to a smooth halt by the kerb. They seemed not to notice. She switched off her engine. They were still staring along the road. She took off her helmet.

'Hello,' she said.

For a long time nobody spoke.

Then her son stepped forward and inspected the controls on the Handy Rider.

'Hey, Mum, can I have a go?'

'No,' she sighed. 'You have to have lessons.'

Lots of Love

ZOË FAIRBAIRNS

Eva was still in America when news came of her sister's engagement to ' . . . Andrew Pearce, remember? They've fixed the day for a month after you get back, so we're wondering if you and Steve would like to save us a few quid by making it a double!! Can you send your measurements so that we can get started on your dress and specify whether it is to be for a bride or a bridesmaid. Longing to see you again, lots of love, Mummy.'

Andrew Pearce, thought Eva. *Andrew Pearce. Which one was he?* She ran her eye along an identity parade of her sister's many short-haired and usually short-lived men.

THAT one? Oh.

Well, good for her. Good for both of them.

Must send a card.

The college year was ending and the campus stationery store had an enormous variety of engagement cards to choose from. She selected a small ornate one with little space for writing. In large letters she put 'Lots of love, Eva.' She considered adding '. . . and Steve,' but it seemed a bit presumptuous to include him, without his prior agreement, in such an extravagant salutation. He was in Manchester, doing his finals. Did he feel lots of love for Liz? No doubt he would come to, everybody did, but as yet he'd only met her two or three times. And what about Andrew Pearce? How could she be sending him lots of love when a few minutes ago it had been a struggle to work out who he was? It was too late now. She could hardly cross out 'lots of love' and substitute 'best wishes' on an engagement card.

She filled the back of the card with the words: 'Re Steve and me and measurements: letter follows, no room here.' She sealed the card up and posted it.

She queued at the cafeteria for lunch. A uniformed security man checked her identity card and her entitlement to eat. Windows broken during the sit-in were being mended. Hammering and the tinkle of glass echoed round the nearly-empty hall, only half of whose tables were laid up and ready for use. The rest were stacked for cleaning and repair.

Nearly everybody had gone.

A gang of tall fraternity brothers loomed and lurched ahead of her in the queue, draining half-pint cartons of whole milk down their throats to fend off starvation while they waited for their steaks, their meatballs, their hamburgers. She asked for a scoop of chicken salad on a lettuce leaf, and helped herself to lemon tea.

It had been easy to lose weight in America. Everyone knew the calorie counts of everything and there was an enormous variety of permissable foods. Hunger, and the cautious assuaging of it with scientifically-selected morsels of this, of that, had become sweet, sharp sensations. And she had watched the shrinking of her body with awe and fascination. Sometimes, when her roommate was out, she would climb into enormous clothes that only months ago had been too tight, and wonder where the missing chunks of her had gone.

She'd been looking forward to amazing everybody when she went home and they came to meet her at the airport. If she sent her measurements, that would all be spoilt.

The fierce heat of the Virginia afternoon roared along the road outside the women's dormitories. She dawdled, stopping to say goodbye to departing students, and to be introduced to the parents who had come in a panic to collect them. Cars with their backs open gleamed and sent up hot rubbery smells. The cars were loaded with suitcases, lampshades, record-players, books. Students and parents trekked back and forth, bringing more, like a line of ants when a stone is lifted.

The girls still remaining in Eva's dormitory were enchanted to hear that her sister (whom they had never met) was engaged. They had found it incomprehensible that Eva herself should have got engaged and then left her fiancé to come to America for a year. But they had agreed that the ring Steve had given her was

beautiful, unique. It was an antique, gold, with red-brown
garnets which changed colour when held up to the light. If she
didn't wear it any more it was only because she feared losing it.
She had to take it off to wash her hands, and she'd left it several
times in the dormitory washroom. The girls who found it had
always recognised it at once and smilingly returned it.

Now they asked: 'Will it be a double wedding?'

'That's an idea . . .' said Eva thoughtfully.

Her room-mate offered to ask the house-mother if she could
use the dormitory phone to call England and congratulate Liz.
The payphones could not make international calls.

'I can't really afford it,' said Eva. 'Unfortunately.'

The girls whispered together. 'We'll pay! Just three minutes,
though!'

'I haven't time, I have to pack,' she said.

'But you're not going back to England today?'

'Of course not,' she said. 'I'm going to see America first. I told
you.'

'Is it true you closed down your campus?' were Danny's first
words when she got through to him in New York.

'Not personally. But they're cancelling exams and sending
everybody home to, er, prevent further disorder.'

'Far out,' he said.

She waited and so did he. 'I have to decide something,' she
said.

'What's that?'

'I don't want to go straight home. I want to see America.'

'Come to New York,' he said. 'It's all here.'

On the Greyhound Bus to New York she took an Ortho-
Novum from its foil packet and swallowed it. She normally took
them in the evening, but this evening she might forget. And she
enjoyed her own bravado. She checked that she still had her
spare packet. She always kept a spare seperate from the one
currently in use. She had one packet in her rucksack and one in
her pocket. Like the royal family never travelling together in the
same aeroplane.

She was proud to have been part of the women's campaign to

have the pill made available at the campus Medical Center, but she hadn't been expecting, at that point, to make use of the facility herself. She'd brought one packet with her from England, to take in her final month in order to prepare herself for her return to Steve. She'd welcomed the thought of a year's break from it. It had seemed medically wise.

Danny met her off the bus at the New York terminal. They kissed and hugged and she fingered the key that he always kept round his neck on a piece of string. It wasn't the key to any door he knew of. He just liked it.

They travelled by subway to his home. He said his car was out of commission.

'That's a nuisance,' she said.

He raised his eyebrows.

She said, 'I meant, I thought you'd drive me round and show me the sights.'

'You'll see all the sights you want on the subway,' he promised. 'I'll get the car fixed tomorrow.'

She wondered why he couldn't have got it fixed for today.

The subway was a disappointment. Nothing happened.

'My sister's getting married,' she said.

'Why?'

'Don't know. Loves the guy, I suppose.'

'That's no reason. I love you, I love lots of people, doesn't mean I go around marrying them.'

She felt embarrassed by his declaration in a public place. Ought she to say *I love you* back?

'It's just that I don't have much time,' she said. 'I have to be back for the wedding. And before I go I want to do things, see things.'

He let her into his apartment with a key from his pocket, put his hand inside her jeans and asked her to tell him about the things she wanted to do and see.

In the week that followed she fantasised that he was keeping her prisoner, a sexual slave. It was almost a disappointment to wake up in the mornings and realise she could go out, go any-where. He didn't care, he needed the days to sleep off their energetic nights. She hardly slept at all. She sat about thinking, or cleaned up or went for walks or made visits like a tourist. She tried cups of coffee, cans of beer and cigarettes as strategies for getting him to wake up and take the car to the garage before it closed but he wouldn't open his eyes. He wasn't doing it on purpose. Some people's need to sleep was like that.

'It's a funny thing, hospitality,' she said one evening.

'Yeah?'

'I have all these people all over the country who've said I can go and stay with them, any time. But I don't know if they mean it.'

'If they said it, they mean it.'

'It's not that simple. I think people sometimes say things just because it seems like the next thing to say. I'd hate to feel I was disrupting their routine.'

'You think you're disrupting my routine?'

'No.'

'So where's the problem?'

It was only his idiom, but his choice of 'where's the problem' rather than 'what's the problem?' which was how she would have put it, disturbed her. Where? was right. She realised she'd been thinking that by travelling long, aimless distances, she would find where the problem was and solve it. She was trying to make her own personal frontier myth in the absence of any others that seemed to fit her situation. She could not be Huck Finn on a raft or Easy Rider on a motorbike. She couldn't even be a Kerouac, she didn't know how to drive. She was waiting around for Danny to get his car fixed.

'I'm running out of time,' she said desperately. 'We all are, how can you sleep your life away?'

'Go on your trip, then,' he said bitterly. 'What do you think I am, your chauffeur?'

'Can I come and see you on my way back?'

'Sure,' he said. 'You have a nice ass,' he said, running his hands over what remained of it. It was amazing. To her own eyes there seemed to be nothing there at all, just a corner. Yet Steve had liked to grab her in handfuls. Danny was angry again, as if he'd read her mind. 'Think of me as a rest-stop,' he said, 'on the way to your wedding.'

'You always said you didn't mind about me being engaged,' she said.

'Mind, why should I mind?' he said.

She had no itinerary. Her 'See America' ticket was a book of vouchers. Each voucher could be exchanged for a bus-ticket to anywhere in the US or Canada, and if the book ran out within the thirty-day time-limit a new one could be obtained free of charge. Several times she selected a city – from the words of a song or the name of a film – and headed there, but then at a rest-stop in a terminal she would hear of a bus just about to leave for somewhere else so she would go there instead. She travelled day and night, wide-eyed, unsleeping. Even if she found herself in a city where she had an offer of accommodation she travelled on, but she knew she would have to stop some-where soon if only so that she could borrow a tape measure and send home her measurements. She had no idea what was happening to them. She was committed to continuing with her regime of low calorie foods, and had invested in a spoon so that she could buy pots of cottage cheese and eat it as she went along; but the spoon became smelly and so did the cheese, and then she would tell herself that she wasn't really seeing America if she wasn't tasting Greyhound Terminal food and she would buy pancakes with maple syrup and hamburgers to go. Whoever heard of a character in a frontier myth worrying about their figure?

She knew too that, to be properly picaresque, her journey must be unstructured, uncomfortable, possibly even unsafe, but somehow she must have a bath soon. She was quite glad when people avoided sitting next to her, but the thought that she smelt was humiliating. Another point about picaresque journeys was that you were supposed to have adventures. She wasn't even having conversations.

She walked with determination from the bus terminal some-where in Georgia. It was early evening and she searched for an adventure. The sun was going down but the heat of the day still muffled the streets and nothing seemed to be open. She wondered if it was Sunday. A notice outside a hall advertising a prayer meeting suggested that it might be.

She was courteously welcomed to the prayer meeting, and curiously questioned. She was asked to go up on the stage and sing an English hymn. She declined. 'They're no different from yours,' she explained.

After the prayer meeting she wandered the dark streets until a car glided to a halt beside her. It was only a police car. The officer asked her her name and whether her parents knew where she was. 'I'm twenty-one,' she said. The officer repeated his question. She said yes, feeling truthful; her parents knew she was in America.

The policeman wanted to satisfy himself that she had money and proof of her identity. She showed him her passport, letting it fall open at the page where the Foreign Secretary demanded that she be allowed to pass without let or hindrance.

'Where y'all staying the night?'

'On the bus, someone's meeting me at –'

'I didn't hear what you said.'

'I always sleep on the buses.'

'Can't hear you. Get in.'

Sweat froze on her skin as the police car cruised the streets.

'I've got a daughter just about your age.'

'That's nice,' she said.

'The Southern Christian Women's Hostel is where y'all said you were staying, ain't it?'

'Yes.'

At the Southern Christian Women's Hostel he rang a bell on a desk and said to the woman who came out: 'I have a young lady from England, ma'am, needs a bed for the night.'

'*England*,' beamed the woman. But when the policeman had gone, her face tightened. 'Why did you come in with the police?'

'No reason. He just picked me up and brought me here.'

'Unfortunately,' she said, 'we don't appear to have a vacancy.'

When Eva found the bus station again, the last bus of the evening was about to leave. It was bound for St Louis, Missouri.

She had a phone number there.

It seemed the longest of long shots. They were called the Leffmans. They were the parents of one of her sister Liz's former boyfriends. Eva had never met the son and Liz had never met the parents, yet they had taken the trouble to write to Liz, via their son, urging her to urge Eva to be sure and call on them should she ever be in St Louis. She phoned en route expecting a rebuff, but they promised to meet her. And when her bus pulled in, there they were, unmistakeable somehow, and beaming a warm welcome.

They were middle-aged, short and smart. They could be identical twins. Mr Leffman took her rucksack and Mrs Leffman took her arm.

'This is very kind of you,' said Eva.

'We only have one child,' said Mrs Leffman. 'Having you here makes us feel closer to him.'

Eva didn't say anything. She knew Gary Leffman was in Vietnam.

They drove through the wide, sunny suburban streets. They climbed a steep slope towards the garage of a long bungalow. Mr Leffman fingered a gadget in the car, and the garage door opened.

Inside the house, Mrs Leffman lifted a thin leather thong with a small copper fob on it from a hook by the front door and hung it round her neck. The fob bore the words: 'War is not healthy for children and other living things.'

'My wife's an agitator,' said Mr Leffman.

'But not a very brave one,' said Mrs Leffman sadly. 'Now, I expect you'd like to take a shower, and then would you prefer a late breakfast or an early lunch? Here's a bag for your clothes.'

Eva realised that Mrs Leffman was offering to wash them.

'I don't want you to go to any trouble,' she said.

'It's no trouble.'

The guest suite had a king-sized bed, a terrace with venetian blinds, a well-stocked drinks cabinet and a private bathroom. She stripped and stood under the shower, gazing up into the faucet so that water poured into her eyes. Afterwards she could hardly open them, and she crept into the huge bed without telling the Leffmans, knowing that they would understand. She listened to the sounds of day-time, drifting luxuriantly on the edges of sleep. She could still feel the vibrations of the bus in her bones but it was easy to return briefly to reality if they disturbed her. It was lovely to hear the phone ring and turn over.

'Wake up, Eva! It's your sister Liz, calling from England!'

It was the sort of thing that ought only to happen in dreams, where it would be amusing and not a threat, like walking on impulse into a strange hotel and finding a message for yourself on the board. Adrenalin charged her brain; somehow her body knew what to do and remained convincingly somnolent.

'Your sister's getting married! Isn't that wonderful?'

'Hmmmnnn.'

'She has to talk to you about your dress.'

'Go away . . .' She considered adding a *please* but decided that a little bit of rudeness, for which she could apologise if told about it later, would add authenticity. She must have been mad to come here. She would be mad to go to any of the addresses supplied to her by her family. They would by now be desperate to find her, but she was not ready to be found.

'Okay, honey. Have your sleep.'

She heard Mrs Leffman return to the phone and say, 'I can't wake her, Liz. She's exhausted. Yes, it must be difficult for you. Don't worry. I'll measure her myself when she wakes up and I'll have her call you right away.'

Hunger gnawed at Eva, but she dared not wake up. Night fell. She tiptoed to the drinks cabinet to see if there might be peanuts or crisps. There were only bottles. Which was more nutritious, coca-cola or beer? She chose coca-cola because it was easier to open quietly. She drank three bottles and returned to her bed. Mrs Leffman came in several times to look at her, accompanied by delicious cooking smells. Eva heard her pick up her dirty clothes and carry them away. She heard the washing machine hum. At last the lights in the house were extinguished and the Leffmans went to bed. She dressed, wrote a profusely apologetic note about a remembered engagement in another state, and left through the french windows, climbing across the railings of the terrace and walking the long dark miles into the centre of town. She remembered too late that she had left the clothes that she had arrived in and which Mrs Leffman had taken to wash. And she realised that the skilled dressmaker that Mrs Leffman doubtless was, would be able to look at those clothes and make an educated guess at her measurements.

*   *   *

She looked at a map of the United States in the bus terminal, imagining her family poring similarly over an atlas at home. *We know she started from Virginia,* they would say, *and we know she went to St Louis. Obiously she's heading for the west coast, to stay with the Jacksons in San Francisco.* Judy Jackson, nee Barford, had been at school with Eva's mother.

She turned south-east, for Florida. People started sitting next to her again on the buses, her See America vouchers having marked her out as an overseas visitor, but she was too busy to talk. She was sorting out her list of addresses. First she discarded all the ones that came from home, but that wasn't enough. She scrutinised girls she'd met at college, trying to remember which ones she had ever mentioned by name in letters home. If there was the slightest chance that she might have, she discarded them too.

After that there weren't many left. But fortunately, one of them lived in Miami.

Her name was Jeannie, and Eva remembered her mainly for the enormous grief she had suffered over her failure, a few months ago to be invited to join a sorority and go and live in a sorority house. A 'straight A' student, she had also been rather irritated by the college authorities' decision to cancel the end-of-semester exams, giving everyone an honorary pass.

Eva called her from a pay-phone at the Miami bus terminal.

'At last!' Jeannie exclaimed.

Eva panicked. Maybe she *had* mentioned Jeannie in a letter home. God, she had, of course she had. She had told the story of the rejection by the sorority . . . 'What do you mean?' she said, preparing to bang the phone down and flee.

'I've been waiting for you,' said Jeannie. 'Where are you?'

'At the Greyhound terminal.'

'Stay right there!'

Eva waited, imagining Jeannie arriving with her mother, a sister or two, ropes and a tape-measure. Actually she came alone, in a taxi which she did not ask to wait. She wore an anorak and her curls were scraped back into a ponytail.

'I've decided to drop out like you,' she said. 'Mom and Dad wanted me to go to summer school to get my grades up but I'm through with the system.'

'What will you do?' said Eva.

'What you're doing,' said Jeannie. 'What do we do?'

'Take the next bus. And see where we end up.'

'The *bus*?' said Jeannie. 'Are you kidding me? I thought we were hitching.'

'Too dangerous,' said Eva. 'I've got one of these. They're good, I can exchange each voucher for a ticket to anywhere.'

'Can I use it too?'

They enquired, but the ticket clerk was strict: See America tickets were not transferable, and could only be issued to holders of non-US passports.

They ended up with tickets to Key West, the furthest distance Jeannie could afford. All the way, past the long orange groves and the white beaches, Jeannie kept saying, 'I can't believe you're travelling by bus!'

Eva became irritated. 'If you want to hitch,' she said, 'hitch.'

At a rest-stop Jeannie went into a supermarket and came out with a loaf of bread and some apples. As the bus moved out she smugly revealed what else she had, hidden in the sleeves of her anorak: cheese, chocolate and cup-cakes.

'Did you steal those?'

'The big corporations,' said Jeannie, 'have been stealing from the people for years.'

'Yes, but –' Eva closed her mouth tight and glared out of the window. How had she acquired this companion? She should never have called her. To call her had been a presumption. Like everyone else, Jeannie, had said, *call me if you're passing my way*, but Eva should have trusted the instinct that told her people only said those things because they seemed like the next thing to say.

Like her mother assuming that she wanted to get married with Liz just because she was engaged.

Getting engaged only meant you were going to get married *one day*, didn't it? It didn't mean it had to be a particular day.

She remembered it happening and wished it hadn't been her idea.

It had been all tied up with going on the pill so that she could sleep with Steve without putting her trip to America at risk. The terror of it had numbed her. Every time she changed her clothes she had imagined they felt different, that she was putting on weight, and not just easily-shiftable fat this time, but hard, permanent muscle from the male hormones in the drug. Every ache or stab became a tumour or a thrombosis. She believed with total conviction that she would die. The thought did not frighten her so much as make her feel guilty: that she was throwing away a life full of potential for reasons of fleshly indulgence. But getting engaged made it different. There was an inevitability to the risk-taking if you were engaged. With the ring on her finger she had accepted the risk, and the fear had abated into exhilaration. She was no different from racing drivers and mountaineers, taking their chances to do what they loved.

Still she wished that it had been Steve who had asked *her*.

He'd been enormously gallant, of course. In her absence he had entered fully into the responsibilities of a fiancé. Someone had sold him a life assurance policy and he had named her as his dependent. 'I know you wouldn't like it,' he had written, 'but that's the word they use.' And his mother had bought her a set of casseroles. It had not been thought worthwhile to post them to her in America, but they awaited her return. They were red with a white floral design. They were non-stick, and oven-proof.

Eva and Jeannie wandered around Key West and went into a bar. Eva guessed that Jeannie would try to leave without paying if she could, and resigned herself to paying for both of them. How had she acquired this companion? Her longing for her own solitary company and freedom to think was like a pang of home-sickness in a child.

'Just two beers, please,' she said firmly to the Cuban waitress. But the waitress brought soup as well, bright red watery soup with floating croutons. 'Do not eat the soup,' said the waitress.

'What?'

The waitress explained that the soup was not soup, merely water coloured with dye. There was no charge for it. Her licence did not allow her to serve alcohol without food. If the police came in they must pretend to be starting a meal.

Jeannie appeared delighted. Eva said, 'But if you'd told us we couldn't have beer, we could have had cokes.' The waitress walked away, smiling with pleasure at having satisfied her customers.

Jeannie kept saying, 'I bet *he's* a plain clothes man.'

Eva was frightened of being caught and deported.

She felt a stab of pain in her leg. A mosquito flew off with a reassuring buzz. She'd been worrying about the pill again. She decided to stop taking it until she went home.

A group of Cuban men gathered round. One of them shared Jeannie's seat with her. They wanted Jeannie and Eva to go to a party with them.

'I love parties,' said Jeannie.

'Go to it, then,' said Eva, gathering up her things.

'How come you're such a coward?' Jeannie demanded furiously. 'I thought you were dropping out.' But she followed Eva onto the street. The Cubans called after them.

'I wasn't stopping you,' said Eva.

'Do you think,' said Jeannie, 'that they'd have wanted us to go to bed with them?'

'How should I know?'

'They probably would. It's good that you stopped me, thanks. Will you lend me the money for my ticket home? I need someone to stop me making a fool of myself. Because there's nothing to stop us, is there? What's to stop us? I mean, guys are always asking for it and there's never as many girls who will as there are guys who want to, are there? So if a girl wants to, she can whenever she wants to, can't she? What's to stop her?'

'Marriage?' said Eva.

Jeannie stared for a long time. 'Of course,' she said slowly. 'I forgot you were engaged. Why didn't you go straight home when school ended?'

'I might as well see America while I'm here,' said Eva irritably.

'Remember that time I found your ring in the washroom? I said, there's a girl who's going to break off her engagement. The other girls said, don't be so sure.'

'Did they?'

'You despised us, didn't you? For thinking so much about it. I thought you were dropping out but you're as scared as I am, about . . . things.'

'Why do you think you can talk to me like this? I didn't ask you to come with me.'

'You did,' said Jeannie, her eyes shrewd with a kind of vicious sadness. 'You were always telling us to join this, join that. I though you had a cheek, you're a visitor –'

'All right, the women who set up the group weren't visitors. And I'll be the same when I go home.'

'What will you do if you don't get married?' Jeannie's voice was soft now, compassionate. 'I often wonder that, it's worse for me. I've never even been pinned. You'll always have that, won't you? Even if you have to give the ring back, you'll always be able to say, somebody wanted to marry me once.'

Eva let these trivial words flow over her. Her one aim was to get rid of Jeannie so that she could return to her own journey.

Jeannie clutched her arm. 'I'm seeing after-images.'

'What?'

'There's two of everything. That's what happens when you start tripping.'

'*What?*'

'They must have put acid in our beer.'

Eva stared: acid? LSD, that sent you mad, had you walking out in front of cars in the belief that you could stop them by force of your will? Illegal drugs, that could get you locked up or deported?

This would not happen of course. They would go straight to the police, before the drug took hold, and explain. They would be looked after, and prevented from harming themselves. She proposed this to Jeannie.

Jeannie said: 'Are you kidding? They'd never believe us.'

Now that she knew what after-images were, Eva was seeing them too.

'What can we do?'

'I don't know,' Jeannie moaned. 'Let's go back to the bar – to the party – those guys will look after us.'

People who had poisoned them would look after them?

Eva dragged Jeannie into a cinema. Jeannie was afraid that the noise and light would bring on drug-induced panic, but Eva felt there would be safety in the darkness.

'I'm all right,' she said desperately. 'So they might not have –'
'It takes different times,' said Jeannie, 'with different people.'

The film was noisy and boring. Eva drew comfort from her boredom. Boredom was the one emotion from which a person who had unwillingly swallowed LSD would not suffer.

Jeannie seemed all right too.

'Shall we go to the party now?' she said when the film was over. 'I definitely saw after-images. I need to know if it was acid, or if I'm –' she gave a broken little laugh '– just going crazy.'

Eva wondered if it had all been a delaying tactic. She said she was not going to any parties.

She bought Jeannie a ticket back to Miami. The Miami bus left after her own, and she wondered if Jeannie would really get on it.

She herself travelled on alone. Six days remained on her ticket: time enough to go to California, and come back again. This way she really would see America. She made a point of sitting next to interesting-looking people. She met a boy who was running away from home because his parents wouldn't let him keep his baby alligator. It died en route and Eva helped him bury it in the desert. Tearfully he left her, to be replaced by a shopping bag lady who said, 'I was born on August 4th 1905 in San Antonio, Texas.' Two hours later her unfaltering account of her life had only reached her thirtieth year. Shaking her off, Eva sat beside a man who said he was a marine going AWOL and who shared his jam sandwiches with her. Their succulent sweetness was an enormous pleasure to her, a new pleasure almost, as if eating were a grown-up pastime that she was just starting to get the hang of.

She reached Berkeley with an afternoon to spare before she must take the bus back east to get her flight home. She looked up an old friend from England who, like her, was out on an exchange. He agreed to let her use his phone for an international call to be paid for when they were both back home.

Steve sounded quite pleased to hear from her. He didn't ask why she hadn't been writing. He hadn't heard about her sister Liz's wedding plans.

'The idea is,' she said, 'for us to do it on the same day.'

'What? Why,'

'To save my father money.'

He laughed.

She said, 'What do you think?'

He said, 'Well, it's a bit sudden, and I'm quite busy right now.'

'We'll wait, then,' she said, knowing that he didn't want to marry her, knowing that she wasn't even going to be allowed to decide this for herself. She was shaking with fear.

She phoned her sister. 'Congratulations,' she said. 'Sorry I didn't get in touch before.'

'Well, the Leffmans phoned and said you were a size ten. Why did you skip off from them like that? They were quite worried –'

Eva was fighting for control of herself. Liz moved on tactfully. 'Are you really a size ten? Thats *tiny*.'

Eva looked down at her body. She had no idea what size she was.

'It is tiny.'

'Well done!'

'Why?'

'Losing so much weight.'

'Thank you.'

'And is it, er, a white dress, or –'

'No.'

'Oh. Okay, right.' Liz would not enquire. 'We'll get cracking on the bridesmaid's dress then. It's a floral print, it'll suit your colouring –'

'Liz.'

'What?'

'I may be bigger when I get back.'

'Well, could you try not to be? It's a bit difficult to make wedding clothes for people when you don't know what size they are.'

'I know,' said Eva. 'I mean, I can imagine.'

Michelene Wandor is a poet, playwright and critic, as well as writing short stories. Between 1971–1982 she was Poetry Editor and theatre critic for *Time Out* magazine. She has written extensively for radio, television and the theatre; her work for radio includes dramatisations of *Persuasion* (Jane Austen), *The Brothers Karamazov* (Dostoyevsky), *Kipps* (H G Wells), and features about writers Antonia White, Dorothy Richardson and Jean Rhys. Her dramatisation of *The Wandering Jew* by Eugene Sue is due to open at the National Theatre in 1987. Her many publications include *Upbeat* and *Gardens of Eden* (poetry); *Guests in the Body* (stories); *Five Plays* (stage plays), and, as editor, four volumes of *Plays by Women* and a collection of essays by contemporary men and women writers, *On Gender and Writing*. Her writing on contemporary theatre includes *Carry On, Understudies* (on theatre and sexual politics) and *Look Back in Gender* (the family and sexuality in post-war British drama).

Michele Roberts was born in 1949 and lives and works in London, Boston and Italy. Her previous novels are *A Piece of the Night* (Womens Press, 1978), *The Visitation* (Womens Press, 1983) and *The Wild Girl* (Methuen, 1984). Her volume of poetry, *The Mirror of the Mother* (Methuen), was published in 1985, and together with Judith Kazantzis and Michelene Wandor, she is the author of the poetry collection *Touch Papers* (Allison and Busby, 1982). She is also co-author of the short story anthology *Tales I Tell My Mother* (Journeyman Press, 1978). She has contributed essays to *Walking On The Water* (Virago, 1984), *Gender And Writing* (Pandora, 1984) and *Fathers: Reflections By Daughters* (Virago, 1984).

Valerie Miner is a grateful veteran of the *Tales* collective and other feminist writing groups. She believes that good fiction is a social act, drawing inspiration and momentum from 'an imaginative collectivity of writers and readers'. Her own work focuses on cross-class and cross-cultural movement among women. She is a first-generation American who grew up in a Scottish-Irish working-class family. Miner's novels include *Winter's Edge, Blood Sisters, Movement, Murder in the English Department* and the forthcoming *All Good Women* (1987). She is co-author of *Tales I Tell My Mother* and *Her Own Woman* as well as co-editor of the forthcoming anthology, *Competition Among Women*. Her work has appeared in *Spare Rib, Conditions, TLS, The NY Times* and many other journals. She teaches mass communications at UC Berkeley.

Since *Tales I Tell My Mother*, **Sara Maitland** has gone on to publish a wide variety of books, including two novels – *Daughter of Jerusalem* (Blond and Briggs) and *Virgin Territory* (Michael Joseph), both now available from Pan; some theology – *A Map of the New Country* (RKP) and with Jo Garcia, as editors, *Walking on the Water* (Virago); some short stories, *Telling Tales* (Journeyman) and, with Aileen La Tourette, *Weddings and Funerals* (Brilliance); and a biographical study of the music hall drag artist *Vesta Tilley* (Virago) which was also the basis for a television play which she scripted, *Following in Vesta's Footsteps* (Central TV). Later this year she will publish another collection of short stories – *A Book of Spells* (Michael Joseph) – and a novel, collectively written with Michelene Wandor, called *Arkytypes* (Methuen).

Zoë Fairbairns was born in 1948 to a mother who did domestic work full time and did not get paid for it and a father who surveyed buildings from Monday to Friday and did. Finding this arrangement rather perplexing, she beame a feminist. Her published novels include *Benefits* (Virago), *Stand We At Last* (Pan), and *Here Today* (Methuen), winner of the 1985 Fawcett Book Prize. She has also written short stories, poetry and plays and worked as a journalist. She has been writer-in-residence at five schools in the London Borough of Bromley, at Deakin University in Australia, and, from 1983 to 1985, Sunderland Polytechnic. She is unmarried and so is the man she lives with. She writes full time and her ambition is to go on doing that for as long as possible. Her next novel, *Closing*, will be published by Methuen in 1987.

Other Journeyman books of interest

Goblin Fruit by Margaret Power

This beautifully-written novel is an evocative story set in Victorian society. In its stifled atmosphere the principal character, vainly repressing her own sensuality, is drawn to an artist, himself a distorted reflection of Victorian patriarchy. His arrogant rejection of her love is only matched by his emotionally-stunted desire for the reworked image of another woman.

Disturbingly menacing, its hint of the pre-Raphaelite verges on the decadent. The highly descriptive language weaves a story of emotional and sexual tension, where resistance and self-assertion finally bear fruit.

0 904526 40 2/144pp/198x130mm/paperback/£4.95

Tales I Tell My Mother by Zoë Fairbairns, Sara Maitland, Valerie Miner, Michele Roberts and Michelene Wandor

The fifteen stories forming this collection were written as a collaborative project, involving critical and political discussion about the issues which concerned the authors as women, writers, feminists and socialists.

The book is divided into three sections: in the first, stories about work, abortion, sexuality and discrimination filter the writers' everyday experiences as feminists. In the second, stories examine the varied politics in the Women's Liberation Movement. And lastly, new perspectives are offered on the everyday lives of women in a society where the roles of both sexes are under close scrutiny.

0 904526 34 8/168pp/216x135mm/paperback/£3.95

The Daughters of Egalia by Gerd Brantenberg

In Egalia wim have the power. Menwim wear pehoes (penis holders), dress their beards and make themselves attractive to please the wim. And of course it is the menwim who take care of the children - after all, they conceived them!

Wim's control of Egalia seem assured until a group of menwim start to discuss their oppression. They start a menwim's group and in spite of public ridicule in the media, are drawn into increasingly daring action. The public peho-burnings are just a beginning...

By a skilful inversion of male language and roles Gerd Brantenberg has created a hilarious satire of male society.

0 904526 74 7/224pp/216x135mm/paperback/£4.95

Telling Tales: short stories by Sara Maitland

This collection of sixteen short stories, mostly about women, takes the reader from Greek mythology to the present, from South America to China, from the Creation to clinical death

The techniques are as varied as the settings, and as satisfying. None of these tales are disappointing. Many are disturbing, most are uplifting, and all are highly stimulating.

Sara Maitland was the recipient of the Somerset Maugham Award for her novel *Daughter of Jerusalem*.

0 904526 86 0/144pp/216x135mm/paperback/£3.95

Upbeat: poems and stories by Michelene Wandor

This is Michelene Wandor's first collection of poems, to which have been added several short stories.

Written between 1971 and 1980, the poems reflect the turbulence in her life and the rapid development of the new wave of feminism during the 1970s.

This collection successfully infuses the poetic statement with the critiques and insights of feminism. These are poems to be read and re-read, each time gaining something new in the recreation of their imagery and multiple meanings.

0 904526 69 0/72pp/210x148mm/paperback/£2.50

Gardens of Eden: poems for Eve and Lilith by Michelene Wandor

Everyone knows the story of Eve, the first woman, who along with Adam, was banished from Eden after eating 'forbidden fruit'. Fewer people know of Lilith, Adam's first wife, who also (as secular myth has it) 'transgressed' by refusing to be a submissive wife.

In this sequence of poems Michelene Wandor gives both women voices: witty, ironic, philosophical and questing. In this re-telling of the Old Testament there is a seriousness and irreverence, a love of language and a contemporary tone.

0 904526 92 5/88pp/210x148mm/paperback/£2.50

Johnny Come Lately: a short history of the condom by Jeannette Parisot

This book is devoted entirely to the humble condom. Fully illustrated, it includes photographs of the oldest condoms yet discovered, Japanese and Swedish condom packaging and much more.

Written by a woman the book argues that men should take on greater responsibility in the use of contraception and that condoms should no longer be treated as objects of derision, especially since the 'discovery' of AIDS.

Little has been overlooked: startling facts are revealed about their history and use, while literary references, statistics, interviews, curiosities and a survey are brought in to provide an indispensible guide to the mysterious, twilight world of the condom.

1 85172 000 6/140pp/illustrated/216x135mm/paperback/ £4.95

Reviewing the Reviews: written and edited by 'Women in Publishing' (WiP)

With the rapid growth of feminist publishing, where is a woman's place on the book review page?

WiP analysed 28 publications - weekly, monthly, specialist, newspapers, general and women's magazines - to answer questions like...

What percentage of authors reviewed are women?
How are books selected for review?
Do women reviewers only review books by women?
To what extent do literary editors promote women's writing?

Interviews with Zoë Fairbairns, Andrea Dworkin, Barbara Burford and Margaret Forster give the author's viewpoint and revealing comments are provided by publishers, booksellers, librarians and literary editors.

1 85172 007 3/112pp/198x130mm/paperback/£4.50